Robin is a retired university professor of Biology who has worked for most of his life abroad. He has published four scientific books, over forty articles and four self-published novels. All of his books are about places he has lived and worked in so the background is always accurate as are the historical details. During his time abroad he has witnessed the corruption and greed so prevalent among leaders and diplomats while seeing the horrors of violence and war. Luckily, he has observed people's ability to find kindness and courage even in the face of certain death.

CODE NAME:
THE PAINTERS

To the Greek people who have suffered from fascism
and who still suffer from exploitation.

Robin H Meakins

CODE NAME: THE PAINTERS

A novel about the Greek Civil War

AUSTIN MACAULEY
PUBLISHERS LTD.

A CIP catalogue record for this title is available from the British Library.

ISBN 978 184963 450 2

www.austinmacauley.com

First Published (2013)
Austin Macauley Publishers Ltd.
25 Canada Square
Canary Wharf
London
E14 5LB

Printed and Bound in Great Britain

Acknowledgments

I wish to thank Victoria for her support and my son Timothy for designing the cover. I hope that I have done justice to the Greek people who still struggle for justice after suffering by poor governments including military rule. Their current economic plight is made worse by the rich avoiding taxes.

Contents

1. An Unusual Funeral

Parting is such sweet sorrow, sadly everyone must die.

The shadow of the Grim Reaper Death stalks all of us from the cradle to the grave. Death is simply the cessation of life, indeed life's last adventure we all must travel alone. The poor, sick and those in wars understand him much better than the pampered rich who think money can keep him away. It cannot because he always collects his dues. Many of us are destined to die alone and unremembered. Some extraordinary people die leaving a hole in our hearts while others we forget in the blink of an eye. Carl was a person who once met you never forgot. Some said he was a pearl among swine that always fought tyranny whatever the cost.

On 14th February 1975, five people flew to attend a funeral on the small Channel Island of Alderney. It was a day when the wise stayed indoors leaving only those who must travel or the foolhardy to risk venturing out into the raging storm. Through threatening dark skies, a small plane fought to stay airborne against the prevailing high winds and freezing rain accompanied by lightning and rolls of thunder. The pilot Maria Hands held the plane on course by flying mainly using instruments, as she could see nothing through the plane's windscreen covered with hailstones and ice. On board, her Britten-Norman Islander, light aircraft was her husband Jim, General Fergus McNeil, his bodyguard Alan Thompson, and the Italian politician Mario Carlini. They remained quiet, deafened by the roar of the two Lycoming engines and the incessant banging of hailstones bombarding the metal fuselage. They were so determined to attend the funeral of Carl van Stoff, their leader in The Painters, otherwise known as

Churchill's Private Army, that they never thought of turning back.

Now Maria had to decide whether to try to find the Alderney airstrip or divert to the larger airport in Guernsey and be late for the funeral. Therefore, Maria radioed the Alderney airport for assistance.

'Gulf Echo Lima Foxtrot calling Alderney Tower. I request permission to land. Over,' she radioed ahead. The radio was silent except for the horrible sound of static caused by the lightning. Then she checked the compass to calculate they were on course, but the visibility was so poor they could easily miss the small airstrip.

'Gulf Echo Lima Foxtrot calling Alderney Tower. Have VIPs on board and urgently request permission to land. Over,' she again radioed. There was no reply until two minutes later there came a faint response that gradually became clearer.

'Lima Foxtrot this is Alderney Tower receiving you loud and clear,' the Traffic controller replied. 'You are cleared to land. Repeat cleared to land. Wind is NNW at 10 knots with light rain, visibility 600 yards but clearing. Make your approach from the north. Over.'

'Roger Alderney Tower will approach from the north. ETA is ten minutes. Thank you. Lima Foxtrot over and out,' Maria replied calmly while straining to locate the airport beacon.

Suddenly, the rain eased allowing the de-icers to clear the frozen hailstones from the windscreen. Now Maria saw directly ahead the airport beacon and the runway lights. With a feeling of relief, she started to make the plane descend. In minutes, the wheels touched the runway, and the aircraft slowed down. They finally parked near the airport building. When the propellers stopped rotating Jim Hands placed the chocks on the wheels to prevent the plane moving. Then the passengers each carrying his luggage disembarked to run to the airport building. Once out of the rain, Jim, Maria and Mario sat down as General Fergus MacNeil accompanied by his bodyguard Alan Thompson talked to a waiting plain-clothes police officer.

'General MacNeil welcome to Alderney. I am Sergeant Andy Moulyneux from Century House sent to arrange the funeral and protect your party. Can I get you something to eat or a drink before we go to the church?' Andy Moulyneux said.

'Thank you Sergeant. Maybe you can show us where we can change into our mourning weeds?' General Fergus MacNeil said shaking his coat like a dog sending water everywhere. Realising he had made everyone wet, he apologised. 'Sorry forgot my manners but I hate standing around in wet clothes.'

'Quite understandable sir, let me show you the changing rooms and the lounge where they serve coffee, tea or something stronger,' Sergeant Molyneux replied.

'That would be grand. Is everything arranged as requested?' Fergus MacNeil asked.

'I hope so. The coffin arrived last night from France and is in the church guarded by six large undertakers. As requested, it will be a private burial with no military formalities or photographs. However, I have allowed the locals to attend the Admiral's funeral. I hope that's OK,' Molyneux stated. It was unusual for a coffin to arrive just before the funeral on a private jet from Cherbourg accompanied by undertakers who looked more like secret service agents. All the documentation was in order and stated that the dead man was Admiral Carl van Stoff who drowned in a fishing accident.

'Well done Sergeant, it is only proper for the local inhabitants be allowed to pay their last respects to Carl. Of course, you know he retired to Alderney to paint and was popular in this small close-knit community,' replied Fergus MacNeil.

'Thank you Sir, I'm told he lived with Mr. and Mrs. Weiss in a bungalow by the sea, and one of his oil paintings hangs in the Town Hall. Was he an artist, or a sailor?'

'I like to think of him as a marvellous artist whose paintings are displayed around the world, an excellent sailor, and a man of many parts who will be greatly missed', said Fergus MacNeil.

Ten minutes later The Painters were sitting in the front pews next to Karl Weiss and his wife Angela. Around them were men in uniform or dark suits and veiled women in black sitting quietly. Standing in front of the congregation was the oak coffin draped in both the Union Flag and the *Reichsmarine* Admiral's ensign and guarded by six pall-bearers. Only a few realised this was an unusual funeral as the pall-bearers and police had Walther PPK pistols. As instructed the vicar used the simplest service for the burial of the dead wondering why everything was so ungraciously rushed. However hard he tried; he could not remember much about the deceased except, he always attended communion wearing a long dark blue overcoat with shiny gold buttons and a naval officer's hat. After the prayers, the vicar invited Klaus Weiss to the lectern to say a few words.

'Ladies and Gentlemen, friends and neighbours, it is my sad privilege to tell you about Carl. He was the best of friends but the worst of enemies. Carl served this nation, never questioning the danger as he tried to destroy fascism wherever it raised its ugly head. One might say he was the best friend Britain ever had. Some of you thought he was Dutch but like me, he was German. In death, I pray that after years of hardship and sorrow, he may rest in peace no longer troubled by his many enemies. God Bless you, my friend,' Klaus said with a lump in his throat. Then he bowed towards the altar and returned to sit by his wife Angela, who held his hand.

General MacNeil walked to the lectern stopping briefly by the coffin to salute his comrade and waited for everyone to be quiet then said. 'Friends we are gathered here today to mourn and celebrate the passing of a colossus, a man of great integrity, quiet and modest. For all the years, I knew Carl he never complained or demanded any recognition for his services to the Crown. The Prime Minister has ordered us to bury Carl under his real name as Admiral Carl Von Graf and not as Admiral Carl Van Stoff. I also have the honour to announce that Her Majesty Queen Elizabeth the Second has made him a member of the Order of Merit for his work for this nation.' He stopped as a gasp of surprise resounded throughout the church at this prestigious award rarely given posthumously.

'Carl was a kind man, loyal to his friends, while destroying all those who he thought evil. He hated fascism and communism, while openly distrusting extreme capitalism that he thought wanted to enslave the world. Throughout his life, he was not free to paint and live as most men a life of peace. Instead, he entered a world of intrigue, betrayal, and violence that few of us can imagine, emerging clean like a medieval knight riding a white horse. He suffered in silence when his wife, Helga was murdered and when hunted by assassins. Carl was a man who knew too much about the terrible atrocities that so-called democratic nations did to become victorious. Even his lifelong friend and fellow painter Winston Churchill said he was a man too dangerous to live but too vital to world peace to die. Indeed, a colossus whose equal I will never see again. Goodbye dear friend, in death may you meet your Helga and be free from your enemies.'

Then they sang a hymn before the vicar led the coffin into the graveyard in the rain as if the skies were shedding tears for him. After a short prayer, they lowered the coffin into the grave. Then the General and Jim Hands shovelled the soil on top of the coffin to honour their fallen comrade. The only noises were the earth hitting the wooden coffin and the church bells ringing in his honour.

Half hidden among the yew trees stood a hooded man in a green anorak watching everything but not saying a word. He remained until the funeral was finished before vanishing into the mist. Many of the mourners went to the Weiss' cottage for a buffet lunch where they talked about the deceased. Afterwards, The Painters flew back to England just as a rainbow appeared in the sky. It was a good omen making them feel they buried the past to have a new beginning. They knew somewhere ahead was a plane carrying Carl to the safety and seclusion of Fergus' Scottish estate to begin another life as Carl MacNeil. The body in Carl's grave was that of an unknown man drowned at sea. This was to satisfy the assassins and reporters who wanted him dead or to get a story so unbelievable they could become millionaires. Anyway, who would believe a tale of a German Admiral being a friend of Churchill to succeed where others failed?

Back on Alderney Carl's enemies had already taken pictures of the grave and checked with the vicar to confirm his burial. They would have dug up the coffin except for the armed pole bearers who over the next few months guarded the grave. As Fergus, suspected Carl's powerful enemies believing him dead breathed a sigh of relief knowing he could not publish his memoirs or expose them for being fascists. Some called them traitors, ruthless opportunists, bloodsucking parasites that became rich while their compatriots died fighting in wars to keep their nations free. Sadly, the warmongers and profiteers have hearts of stone and make fortunes out of the misery of other people because wars result from national pride, greed, or for territorial gain.

Meanwhile on Alderney the stonemason read the inscription he had to carve in Italian marble for the dead man's headstone.

Here lies the body of a champion of freedom.

Admiral Carl Van Stoff OM, RNR
Aka
Admiral Carl Von Graf OM, Grand Iron Cross
Born 22nd July 1915 died 12th February 1975

RIP

2. Poole 1935, Strange Friendships

Like Antony and Cleopatra, chance meetings make history. Someone you meet today will change your life, if you look at them with your eyes wide open. The hand of fate often for the better influences us, but unfortunately, sometimes it is for the worse.

In 1935, the British ignored the clouds of war engulfing parts of the world to enjoy life to the full. As always, the season and of course, the changeable weather influenced everything. In Poole high above the harbour was an Elizabethan coaching inn converted by Mrs. Evelyn de Broyen into the Sea View Hotel known for its fine cuisine. In the old stable was the artists John de Broyen's Studio from where he painted the sea in all its moods. His work sold locally and in London, going nearly as fast as he could paint them. The most popular were seascapes followed by the portraits of local people and the town. Every autumn, he held a residential oil painting course for up to four people who he chose as those painters wanting to improve their techniques.

On warm sunny days, everyone was out enjoying the weather but when an autumn storm descended upon the port, most stayed indoors while the fishing boats raced to shelter inside the harbour. During one, exceptionally violent storm, dark clouds cloaked the sun making it hard to tell if it was night or day as the wind and rain lashed the town. Inside the Sea View Hotel, only the grandfather clock reminded the three men attending her husband's oil painting course the time. They were the politician Winston Churchill, his friend Fergus MacNeil, *Kapitänleutnant* Carl Von Graf, and of course

Churchill's bodyguard. They were different in age and character but drawn to each other like moths to a light by the serenity found while painting.

Late one afternoon the maroon summoned the lifeboat crew to aid a sinking ship. Within minutes, John de Broyen was steering the lifeboat through huge waves and high winds watched by the crowds gathered on the foreshore. They stood unable to see in the dark and soaked to the skin by the driving rain. Though cold and wet, they stayed as if transfixed to the spot. Occasionally, the light from distress flares together with streaks of lightning revealed the lifeboat alongside the sinking ship taking off the crew one man at a time. Each descended a swaying rope ladder into the wooden lifeboat as it smashed against the metal hull of the stricken vessel. Only when all the ship's crew were safely on board did the lifeboat sail for home. The weight of the ten rescued men made her ride lower in the sea so that each wave sent more water into her open hull. All aboard started bailing out the water and together with the pumps kept the boat afloat. It was a race against time, as in the past in such conditions lifeboats disappeared without trace with no one to rescue them if they sank. Above the sound of the tempest, the passionate singing of the people on the waterfront reverberated across the bay as the priest led this congregation crying out to God to protect all those in peril on the sea.

After what felt like hours, they saw the lifeboat fighting her way back.

'Shore party take your positions,' yelled the butcher in his oilskins to five men in shoulder high waders each with a rope around their waist securing them to the lifeboat slipway.

'Aye, aye, sir,' they replied jumping into the foaming sea so that the water reached above their waists and carrying firing lines. It was dangerous as the strong undertow constantly tried to pull them off the sea bottom and out to sea, but they knew the risks and stood firmly. It was what their ancestors, had done unquestionably for as long as anyone could remember. At times, the lifeboat vanished engulfed by mist and water only to re-emerge a few feet closer. One moment the waves threw her up into the air before sucking her down. Still the small craft battered by the waves slowly drew nearer to shore.

'Dear God she's going to capsize if she takes in any more water,' the butcher yelled out.

'No, she'll make it,' another man replied, looking anxious as everyone prayed he was right.

'Now lads aim carefully,' the butcher ordered as the five men in the water fired their lines into the gusting wind towards the lifeboat. Only one was caught to be slowly pulled aboard followed by the heavy rope that made fast.

'Everyone come over here and help us pull her in,' someone ordered.

'One, two, three...Heave,' the butcher called out as the people pulled the wet rope in.

'Come on Fergus let us help,' Carl challenged.

'They'll need all the men they can get,' Fergus responded as he, Winston, and his bodyguard joined in. It was hard work as cold hands became sore fighting the forces of nature, but they pulled the lifeboat close enough to attach the steel hawser from the lifeboat station. Then they released the rope as the hawser now winched the boat into the lifeboat station.

'Well done, now ladies, please bring the tea,' the butcher shouted as a smile lit up his rugged face.

In minutes, women appeared to serve steaming hot cups of sweet tea and biscuits from the shelter of a nearby hall while ambulances took the rescued sailors to a hospital. Suddenly, the peace disappeared as a joyous riot broke out when girlfriends, wives, children, and parents ran to welcome the life boatmen back to their bosoms. Evelyn de Broyen led the pack running blindly towards her husband followed by their son Charles. She looked frightening with her shiny long hair blowing in the wind, and her mascara washed down her cheeks forming black lines like ancient war paint. However, her loving smile said everything. Minutes later, she was walking home in her man's arms followed by Charles and chatting to Carl, Winston, and Fergus. The three men and the boy did not know it, but they were destined to become close friends.

The first thing Winston noticed about Carl was his incredible drawing skills. He could draw a bird that only stayed still for a minute as if it had posed for an hour. It was as accurate as the best photographer could have produced and as skilled as the old German master Albrecht Dürer. By contrast, the middle-aged Fergus loved using bright colours making his canvas modern, and a copy of what he saw, while Winston painted colourful impressionist landscapes in his own style. After dinner, they sat by the fire to talk over a brandy or two, smoking Havana cigars while Winston's bodyguard quietly paced around the hotel making certain everything was exactly as it should be.

'Carl, I hope you do not mind me asking but where did you learn to draw so well?' Winston asked in a friendly but forthright manner.

'Sadly sir, I never had any tuition so what I know I taught myself. I joined the navy, as a boy and did not go to any university or art school. Drawing has always been a hobby for as long as I can remember. I started drawing our pets and home, people we met and animals in the garden. Later, on the goodwill cruise of the *Kreuzer Koningsburg,* I spent my off-duty hours sketching pictures while others lost their hard-earned cash playing cards or slept. Purely, by accident, the Admiral saw my sketches and liking them ordered me to draw everything of interest such as harbours, animals, flowers, and people in traditional costumes. After the Admiral saw the first drawings, he asked me to be the expedition's artist, but I declined saying I wanted to be an Admiral like him. He laughed but demanded I drew everything I saw,' Carl explained.

'There's many a good man who never went to university, I for one. However, I write books as well as one. Indeed, a self-taught man is better equipped to live in this world than those who have accumulated the biased thoughts of their often prehistoric teachers. There is nothing more wonderful than the ability to think freely without inhibition. Progress relies on originality that only comes from creativity unbridled by other's prejudices,' Churchill commented.

'Thank you sir, maybe I'll be an Admiral or heaven forbid an artist,' Carl stated with a grin.

'I am a politician, writer, and painter and so can you be if you put your mind to it. Pray tell us why you study oil painting when you're excellent with charcoal and pencil?' asked Winston.

'The walls of my family home are adorned with my ancestors' oil paintings so my father only hangs work in that medium. So I'm here to learn oil painting in the hope that one day he will hang my work next to the others.'

In time, their conversations became controversial as the politician in Churchill surfaced.

'Carl what do you really think about the Treaty of Versailles?'

'Sir, I'll answer your evocative question but remember I'm no politician but please do not take offence at my Germanic bluntness,' Carl replied after some hesitation.

'Carl, call me Winston. I'm not interested in niceties but what you think.'

Fergus was uncomfortable about the turn of events but said nothing. Experience had taught him not to question Winston when he was in one of his embarrassingly inquisitive moods.

'The Treaty of Versailles let the victors rape Germany forcing us to grovel in poverty. Ruthlessly the victors stripped our factories of their machinery, stole our valuable art, and looted precious objects from museums and homes. Meanwhile, they treated us like slaves to starve or freeze to death. It was a pointless humiliation we will never forget.'

'I appreciate your honesty for what you say is echoed by many free thinking historians. As a Scotsman, I understand how you must feel because the English did the same to us. However, in time we became strong enough to rebuild our nation,' Fergus encouragingly added.

'Thank you Fergus, as you know, Germany is being reborn. Now we fear communism which spreads through the masses like an uncontrollable plague, especially as Russia is too close to our borders to ignore. I need not remind you how quickly Trotsky defeated the Tsar's forces before turning against the aristocracy and middle classes. I believe that the world must unite against the corrupting forces of Marxism and Capitalism. Only then can a democracy exist where the rich and poor reap their just rewards for work well done,' Carl passionately warned his friends.

Winston was puzzled. 'I agree communism is a threat stopped by fascists like Hitler. However, as a dedicated capitalist I believe that all those who fund industry deserve their just rewards.'

'Luckily I'm no politician, but Hitler's National Socialist Party is rebuilding our nation and creating jobs. Now we can look forward to a prosperous future as we regain our place among the major industrial nations. What more can we want?'

'You're right but I pray we will not see another European war,' Winston asked.

'I don't understand the British with armies around the world. Your so-called volunteers fought in Spain with the communists against the armies of General Franco. Surely, you knew that if the communists won they would attack France and Britain?'

'We don't consider the Spanish Civil War as a conflict between communism and fascism, but as a monarchy against the generals,' Winston replied wondering where the conversation would end. To be honest he was beginning to think his questions were to say the least unfortunate.

'We don't want war but will fight to regain our lost lands and prevent Russia establishing a foothold in Europe. I believe what the Red Army currently lacks in sophistication it makes up for in numbers and will develop modern military equipment to threaten all free people. Remember Stalin promises to export communism around the world even if it takes a hundred years! I think he may succeed. Then only God can save us! Can you imagine being ruled by atheists who suppress all opposition and freedom of expression while pretending everyone is equal?'

Winston was silent as he digested some disagreeable truths stated by an honest young man.

'You must admit Carl has a valid point. What do we do about communism? The only winner of the Great War was America as we lost a fortune and too many good men. Surely, the days of Empire are over!' Fergus said trying to end the discussion.

'Carl I apologise if I have been offensive, it was not meant. Some say I am tactless and even like a bull in a china shop. I appreciate your honesty. Let me just add Fergus has never spoken such a lot of poppycock. The British Empire will last for a thousand years as a trading partnership of self-governing states. Capitalism must survive to allow investors to benefit from funding the employment of the workers. Now it is bedtime. Goodnight gentlemen and thank you for an enjoyable and educational evening.'

Fergus respected Carl as he understood how it felt to be defeated being a direct descendant of the House of Stuart whose Jacobite army of highland Scots was destroyed by the forces of King George II at Culloden in 1746. Afterwards, the English hunted and executed those survivors they caught, while some sought refuge in France. His clan hid in remote islands like Barra taking the name MacNeil. Systematically, the pro-Stuart highland clans lost their tartans and claymores until 1822, when King George IV wore a tartan kilt in Scotland. Etiquette demanded that all who attend the royal functions must wear their kilts. So people rushed around to take out of hiding their old tartan kilts and sashes or have new ones made. From that day, forth the tartan kilt and Scottish attire became their national dress.

One day when Winston was in London, the others visited Brownsea Island situated near Poole. It was where Baden Powell held the first Boy Scouts camp and famous for its natural beauty. Therefore, Fergus, Carl, and Charles explored the island looking for anything to draw. First, they came across red squirrels rushing around gathering nuts to store for the coming winter. In seconds, Carl captured the scene on paper to show one squirrel climbing a tree with a mouth full of nuts while on the ground, others gathered more food for their stores. Next, they saw a Great Green Woodpecker noisily drilling with his bill into a rotten tree for insects, watched by a pair of yellow-breasted Blue Tits and a lone red-breasted cock Robin. After a few minutes, they left to continue walking on the leaves falling from the trees while overhead flocks of geese and swallows flew south for winter. Too soon, the sun started to set just as they found a pair of Black and White Woodpeckers tapping away at another tree while somewhere a wise old owl hooted. As darkness descended, the trio sailed to Poole tired but happy. That night Carl started to paint six miniatures, the animals and birds they had seen. Later, he gave Charles the Great Green Woodpecker and Fergus the pair of squirrels. When the course was over Carl gave John de Broyen the Blue Tit, Winston the Robin, Churchill's bodyguard the Wren and kept the Black and White woodpeckers. Charles took his painting wherever he went to remind him of the tall Carl with spectacularly bright blue eyes and happy times.

When the course ended, Carl and Winston agreed to write to each other about important matters without betraying their nations. Both believed talking was much better than fighting any war and negotiation the only way to stop the global spread of communism. So they wrote to each other every month via the Red Cross office in Geneva, Winston as Mr. Constable and Carl as Herr Jung. This correspondence continued throughout the war.

3. Berlin: War Changes Everything

All that is necessary for the triumph of evil is the good men to do nothing.

An old saying often erroneously quoted as said by Edward Burke.

In 1939, The Third Republic more commonly known as the *Deutsches Reich* invaded Poland forcing the badly prepared Britain and France to declare war. Within months, the Allies were overwhelmed by the Germans fast Panzer tanks, Stuka dive-bombers and well trained infantry until by May 1940, when the remnants retreated to the sea at Dunkirk. As the Germans stopped, an armada of little ships evacuated the Allied forces to England. Then the smaller RAF defeated the mighty *Luftwaffe* in the skies over Britain. This made Hitler abandon the invasion of Britain. Surprisingly, Deputy *Führer* Rudolph Hess flew to Scotland landing near Glasgow to meet the Duke of Hamilton with an offer of peace. Hess broke his ankle on landing and was subsequently captured. After being interrogated, it was decided that Hess was mentally unstable and unreliable. Therefore, no one took the peace overtures seriously and the war went on.

On 22nd June 1941, in Operation Barbarossa, three German armies attacked Russia. One went to Leningrad, one to Moscow and the third, east through the Ukraine. Within weeks, they captured six hundred thousand Russian soldiers and were outside Leningrad and 250 miles from Moscow. Then the freezing Russian winter halted the invasion. The Germans were not equipped to fight in the extreme cold where oil froze in engines and people froze to death. Their forces were so far away that the *Luftwaffe* could not supply them. Everywhere broken buildings and burned fields from the Russian's scorched-earth policy deprived them of shelter and food. Therefore, the invaders went hungry.

Many Germans distrusted the National Socialist (Nazi) Party while pleased with the prosperity they brought. Gradually, they feared the *Geheime Staatspolizea* state secret police or *Gestapothat* eradicated all opposition. For every person they killed, whole families were alienated who often formed resistance groups. When they destroyed one group, another took its place. At first, these groups tried to get assistance from friends and relatives in neutral USA, but only a few took them seriously and some told the Nazis. This resulted in more deaths with the survivors fleeing the country or hiding with the powerful traditional Prussians.

During the war, Carl Von Graf lived in his ancestral home outside Berlin with his beautiful blonde blue-eyed wife Helga, who he knew since childhood. From the very first time they played together, they knew they were always happy and safe whenever the other was around. When Carl was away at sea, travelling, or learning to paint in England Helga wrote twice a week. Letters usually took a long time sometimes arriving four at a time with strange stamps from distant lands that she kept tied together with a pink ribbon. What made their separation bearable was that he said how much he missed her, so whenever they met the sun seemed to shine, and the birds sang even in the depths of winter. Both were intoxicated with each other and inevitably married, but though they tried, sadly, they never had children. He blamed himself, but Helga never complained and was always there for him. When he was sick, she nursed him. When he was tired or worried, she comforted him. Every night she made him feel loved in the special way only a woman can. When Carl felt they were in Hell, she reminded him that where there was life, there was hope, and in death, God would receive them. As the war progressed, they felt that all around roamed the dogs of war ripping apart the essence of life. They comforted each other knowing that in the end things had to get better, they could hardly get any worse.

Luckily, they did not know what lay ahead so were happy being loved and loving. While Carl worked, Helga helped organise a First Aid unit often ending up consoling young mothers whose men had died or returned seriously injured. Her smile and soft voice were welcome in many a household bringing comfort to the hurt and disillusioned. Whenever Carl was free, they would go out to listen to music, dance, or stay at home while Carl played Tchaikovsky on the grand piano or well-known tunes that she would sing.

Carl never saw combat or used his pistol in anger because his planning skills and accuracy found him in command of planning long-range naval operations. This was mostly the supplying of pocket battleships and modified U-boats in the Atlantic attacking enemy shipping. At first, it went well until the Royal Navy severely damaged the pocket battleship *Admiral Graf Spee* in the River Platte and scuttled her. In 1941, Carl transferred to the *Abwer* under the command of Admiral Wilhelm Canaris. Here the *Gestapo* watched everybody, so he was not going to betray his country unless it was important. His first letter to Mr. Constable told Winston that Germany would not invade Britain but instead attack Russia. It took only a week to reach Churchill who was not convinced until after it happened. In the next letters, Carl sent lists of Americans who supplied Germany with money and essential materials, but Winston still did nothing. Perhaps he was annoyed at Carl's insistence that those Americans who hated Jews and even their non-white citizens supported the Nazis. He stubbornly refused to believe America harboured fascists who made their fortunes by exploitation because he often failed to see things as others did. Indeed, he never understood President Roosevelt's New Deal that helped end the Depression by creating jobs and modernising the country. Things changed when Hitler declared war on America in support of Japan after their attack on the American Navy at Pearl Harbour. He thought the Axis powers were so strong that they would control the world or most of it. It was an ambitious plan with one major flaw, now the Axis was at war with the vast Russian army, the British Empire and the industrially powerful America, in fact, half the world.

Life in Berlin became increasingly dangerous as the *Gestapo* looked for both real and imagined enemies. First, they rounded up and eliminated the communists, then the Jews and so-called 'undesirables'. Inevitably, *Gestapo Oberführer* (Brigadier-General) Hans Kruger and *Sturmbannführer* (Major) Franz Leitz investigated the *Abwer*. It should have been the normal routine check on the staff looking for enemy agents, but it was not. *Oberführer* Kruger was convinced the *Abwer* contained anti-Nazis who could attempt to destroy the newly formed *Grobdeutschein Reich.* On finding nothing against Admirals Canaris and Von Graf, Kruger turned his attentions to their families. It was risky but Kruger wanted to show the arrogant *Abwer* the power of the *Gestapo*. Therefore, he waited until Carl was inspecting a U-boat base in Brest before acting. He lured Helga von Graf to a non-existent meeting where he made her unconscious using a chloroform soaked cloth, taken to an interrogation room, stripped naked, and tied up sitting in a chair. When conscious she realised, she was a captive but did not know where or why. Even the man watching and leering at her nakedness said nothing. In fact, Kruger enjoyed seeing her beautiful body knowing he could do anything he wanted. He was tempted to take her but decided not to as he preferred young men and did not want to waste time. Helga stared defiantly knowing she had done nothing wrong and thinking no one would dare to harm the wife of an admiral.

'Frau Von Graf if you cooperate and answer my questions you have nothing to fear,' Kruger whispered into her ear, but she did not reply.

'Just tell me about your husband's friends.'

Still she was silent, so he hit her face and body but she just weakly smiled back. She did not utter a word even when severely whipped until inevitably she became unconscious. Everything was taking too long, and he was learning nothing. This made the impatient Kruger angry. Therefore, he suspended her from a metal frame with electrodes attached to her damaged body, allowed her to regain consciousness before sending enough electricity through her body to cause horrific pain, but not death. Previously, torturing women proved effective as afterwards some proved cooperative and worked for him as informers. Everyone answered his questions, but Helga was different. He watched her body convulse as every muscle unwillingly contracted until with one last shake her weak heart stopped. This complicated matters even though Kruger had to kill her to prevent Carl knowing what he had done. That night, he secretly placed the body in her car before setting it on fire during an air raid so little remained when the fire-fighters investigated the accident. A week later *Oberführer* Kruger attended Helga's funeral to watch the devastated Carl as he buried the love of his life in the family vault. He was glad to have inflicted pain on the arrogant admiral but decided, for the time being, to leave the *Abwer* alone.

From that day onwards, Carl was a changed man becoming more serious and rarely smiling. Gone was his charm as life no longer had any meaning to be lived in a round of routine gestures. He was a mere shadow of his former self struggling to understand why Helga was in her car when it was bombed and not safe in their air-raid shelter! He had lost his only love, and from that day kept her picture next to his broken heart. He never loved anyone again as he could not get Helga out of his head. She was everything he wanted. She had kept him sane and was always there for him. Indeed, a gap he would never fill. He consoled himself with the knowledge that when he died, they would meet in a far, far, and better place. Often an invisible little bird annoyingly whispered into his ear that his enemies murdered Helga but as hard as he tried to stop her saying such things, she did not.

'You know Carl we lost the war when we attacked Russia,' Canaris remarked. 'It was a mistake to fight a prolonged and costly war when we could have got all we wanted by negotiating a peace with Britain.'

'Maybe, but we have won most battles,' Carl weakly added.

'True, but we've exhausted our supplies of aluminium and steel. It makes building more aircraft and tanks increasingly difficult. Do you know how often we have to stop building them due to the lack of silly little things like ball bearings?'

'Too often, but it is no longer a problem since we received supplies from Sweden. Perhaps you're right though the Luftwaffe didn't have enough long range aircraft to support our beleaguered armies on the eastern front,' Carl replied wondering where this dangerous conversation was leading.

'Whatever the reason we are suffering a devastating defeat that could cost us the war, unless we make peace with at least one of our enemies. We have made the same mistake as Napoleon by invading Russia in winter,' Canaris thought looking very pensive. As always, he lit another cigarette to blow small smoke rings that he watched slowly rise upwards.

'I agree but who will negotiate with us?'

'It must be the Americans as they have not lost much in the war,' Canaris responded.

'Indeed we still have many friends living there who would support our request and make sure our nation survives with at least some dignity.'

'But will the *Führer* ever agree to such an action?'

'Probably not, but then we will have to make him see reality using whatever persuasion we can muster,' Canaris commented wondering how to do it. 'Whatever happens this must be our secret, if anyone found out we would be punished for having defeatist thoughts. I do not think we want to be guests of the *Gestapo*. What made our magnificent nation descend to such depths that mad men and murderers walk the corridors of power?'

'Bad luck or poor judgement,' Carl answered. 'We were so busy fighting wars; we failed to see the growing terror of the *Gestapo* and the power of the Party.'

Canaris nodded. There was nothing to say, as both knew they had helped create the monster who, if allowed to go unchecked, would destroy millions, like an evil dragon. But who would be the dragon slayer?

Before Canaris could approach the Americans, the Red Army decimated the German army besieging Stalingrad. After running out of food and ammunition on 31st June 1943 *Generalfeld Marschall* Paulus surrendered ninety-one thousand men of the sixth Army and fourth Panzers while another ten thousand continued fighting until eliminated. The news of fierce battles where Russian T34 tanks defeated the 'invincible' Panzers worried the Generals, sending shock waves throughout Germany. No longer was the victory a certainty, so they looked around for someone to blame.

On the 20th July 1944, an attempt to assassinate Hitler in his heavily guarded Wolf's Lair command centre, failed. Not surprisingly, the wounded *Führer* demanded his men hunt down all those involved who purged the army of all senior army officers involved or suspected of being disloyal. Within days, they eliminated many experienced officers and replaced them with less able party members. It was during this time that Carl overheard an informer on the phone to the *Gestapo* denouncing Canaris's engineer and pilot Klaus Weiss as a Jew. Therefore, Carl purchased a first class return train ticket to Barcelona, withdrew 100 marks from his bank, and ordered Klaus to see him immediately.

'Klaus don't say anything but listen very carefully.'

The startled Klaus wondered what he had done wrong starting to fear for the worse.

'Don't worry dear friend, just do exactly what I tell you and don't look back. Take the tickets and this money to go to Spain as the *Gestapo* are coming for you. In Spain go to Gibraltar and then on to Britain,' Carl ordered. 'May God bless you and keep you safe.'

Klaus arrived in Barcelona just as the *Gestapo* came looking for him in the *Abwer*. Now the *Gestapo* and their informers walked the corridors looking into every nook and cranny with a newfound arrogance and powers to arrest anyone. No one from Admiral to sweeper was safe and could disappear without trace, be tortured or made to do anything the *Gestapo* wanted. Many a pretty girl and boy ended up as playthings of the black leather coated men, whether they liked it or not. No one dared refuse, however young and innocent, fearing reprisals against their families. Very few dared reprimand them or check to confirm their victims were guilty. The *Gestapo* watched everyone, including priests and nuns as their power grew everywhere the Germans occupied.

One day Admiral Wilhelm Canaris stood with Carl on the office balcony overlooking Berlin while as usual, smoking a Turkish cigarette.

'Carl there are dangerous times ahead,' said Canaris very quietly.

'Thanks for the warning, but surely we're safe?' Carl replied.

'I'm afraid all of us are in danger since *Oberst* Claus von Stauffenberg tried to kill Hitler in the Wolf's Lair. Unfortunately, a wooden table saved the Führer. Afterwards, he demanded the elimination of all involved and Claus von Stauffenberg arrested and shot. Next, they arrested *Generalfeld Marshall* von Witzleben and *Generalobserst* Ludwig Beck, though brutally tortured both said nothing before they died. Now we must trust no one but ourselves,' Canaris added smoking another cigarette.

'We may doubt the *Führer's* methods but are loyal to our country,' Carl added.

Admiral Canaris did not reply but gave Carl a penetrating look questioning his statement. Carl knew Canaris disliked Hitler wanting to negotiate peace but only now realised how deep that hatred was. The man they called the good Nazi was much more complicated than Carl had thought. He had a brilliant mind with the ability to understand people within seconds of meeting them. Indeed, he was irritatingly someone who was nearly always right. Now people disappeared and were summarily executed. Often whole families died including grandparents, wives, and children. A knock on the door, especially after dark often meant death. They even arrested Hitler's priest Pastor Dietrich Bonheoffer, but they did not investigate Canaris or Carl. The Gestapo placed all the blame for the plot among the ranks of the senior army officers.

Then everything turned upside down.

'We have little time left my friend. They will arrest me for belonging to the anti-Hitler group that tried to kill him and his nest of vipers. I don't know when, but soon,' Canaris said.

'I don't believe it,' Carl uttered surprised that Canaris had tried to destroy Hitler, sadly with no success.

'It's true we failed to cleanse Germany and now must save our friends. You must contact your Mr. Constable and flee to Britain. It's your only hope of survival,' the Admiral ordered.

Carl was stunned Canaris knew about Mr. Constable and allowed the correspondence to continue.

'Who did you say,' Carl stammered very frightened.

'I'm your friend, so don't deny your correspondence as this is not the time for childish games. Now take these orders and leave as quickly as you can, if you're to survive to forge a better Germany when peace comes,' Canaris quietly added. They firmly shook hands knowing they would never meet again and parted without uttering another word.

On the day, they arrested Admiral Canaris; Carl was inspecting the E-boat base on Alderney with SS officer *Oberst* Hans Strauss as his guide. Carl selected Strauss because he was the same height and build but physically unfit due to lack of exercise and too much good living. Indeed, he was the ideal *dopplegänger*. Then every night after dinner, Carl would walk with *Oberst* Strauss along the dark, empty seashore to look out across the Channel towards England. When it was time to leave Alderney, Carl found a deserted place to smother *Oberst* Strauss with his overcoat. Then he dressed Strauss in Carl's Admiral's uniform and burned the face to disfigure him. It was a nasty business but necessary if Strauss was to be identified as Carl.

Nauseated by what he had done Carl placed the corpse into a boat before rowing out to sea. Carl left everything behind except for the picture of Helga next to his heart putting his identity papers into Strauss' overcoat. He checked his watch to find out that he had a few hours before anyone missed them, as they often did not return until after midnight. He carefully took his bearings from a pocket compass, set the timer on his watch to calculate the time since leaving land, and started rowing as hard as he could into the fog to find a patrol boat. He stopped once when a German E-boat raced and waited until he could no longer hear her engines. Carl knew there was no turning back and with luck, the Royal Navy ship was somewhere ahead waiting for him.

With no moon to guide him, Carl navigated exactly to the pick-up point taking into account the strong sea currents. He looked at his watch to note he was two minutes late, a serious crime for an Admiral when at sea, but he hoped not fatal. Therefore, he waited hidden by the fog until he heard the distinctive purring sound of the British Perkins diesel engines before signalling with his torch to the boat that he was there.

4. A SBS Patrol Boat Vanishes

Sing me a song of a lad that is gone,
Say could that lad be I?
Merry of soul he sailed on a day
Over the sea to Skye.

Robert Louis Stevenson (1896); *Songs of Travel.*

Leading Seaman Charles de Broyen was the lookout aboard
the Special Boat Service (SBS) motorised yacht waiting off
Alderney. The engines slowly turned over making a quiet
purring noise while keeping the ship on station while rolling in
the waves. The ship's low profile with sails and mast lowered
made her nearly undetectable. Even so, the crew were at action
stations as her commander Lt. Jan Van Gross scanned the
darkness for the boat they came to meet. Things were deadly
quiet in a thick mist except when a German E-boat passed by a
little too close for comfort but luckily turned south. Then
exactly on time, they saw the signal they were waiting for - a
long flash followed by two rapid ones. Charles as ordered
replied with two long flashes. Then three minutes later, they
heard the sound of oars breaking the water as a rowing boat
appeared out of the fog carrying two men, one in German
Naval uniform and the other in a black pullover. As it drew
silently alongside the SBS boat, a voice broke the silence.

'Ahoy Midday, this is Leopold. May I come aboard?'

'Leopold you have permission to come aboard,' Lt. Jan
Van Gross stated. 'No, wait for a moment we were to collect
only one man.'

'The other gentleman is unfortunately dead. With any luck, he will be discovered carrying my papers and identified as me,' Carl said.

'Welcome Admiral it's an honour to meet you,' the Lieutenant said.

'You are mistaken Captain, sadly the Admiral is dead,' Carl firmly stated. 'I'm Fred Jones the absent-minded bird watcher you found adrift in a sinking boat.'

Charles thought it strange a German would surrender from a rowing boat in the middle of the night, but in those days he thought all the good people were British and the bad ones German. He had just time to notice that the tall Admiral, or Fred Jones, had remarkably entrancing blue eyes before he disappeared below deck. Then Charles released the rowing boat to drift in the strong current towards the rocky coast. The newcomer's unusual bright blue eyes made him wonder where he had seen them before as the engines roared to life to speed them towards the Atlantic Ocean.

One day the Admiral, Mr. Jones, came on deck to speak to Charles.

'Leading Seaman may I ask if you're related to the de Broyen's of Sea View Hotel in Poole?' he asked.

'Yes sir, they were my parents,' Charles replied.

'I thought they might be. You won't remember me, but we met in 1935 while I was on a painting course at your parent's hotel,' the Admiral stated.

'Sir, you must be the painter Carl Von Graf. I have your painting with me to remember the good days,' Charles replied with a large smile as he thought of past, happier times.

'Indeed I am, it's good to see a face I recognise after all these years and pleased you still like the little painting,' the Admiral replied as he shook Charles firmly by the hand. 'I hope your family is well.'

'Sadly they died when their hotel was bombed,' Charles added.

'I'm very sorry to hear that. They were good folk. I know war can be cruel as my wife Helga died in a bombing raid. It is sad that both of us have lost our loved ones. All I can say from experience that in time we learn to live with our loss but never forget the faces of our dearest,' Carl said looking old with tears forming in his eyes before disappearing below deck.

The voyage took them around the tip of Cornwall and north to the West Coast of Scotland. At first, they expected a German aircraft searching for their missing man, it did not happen. Maybe they found the disfigured body and fell for the dead body trick. The only aircraft they saw was a Coastal Command Sunderland looking for U-boats. Eventually, they took Mr. Jones to the Isle of Barra where Fergus MacNeil met him. He left with a look back and a wave as the SBS boat sailed to Skye.

'Leading Seaman de Broyen,' the Lieutenant called out.

'Aye, aye, sir,' he replied.

'Take her out to sea and sink her or hide her. As far as I am concerned, you died at sea. So do not let me see or hear from you for many moons. Is that clear?' The Lieutenant ordered.

'Aye, aye, sir,' Charles replied grateful for the chance to mourn his WREN fiancée Wendy and his parents who recently died when their hotel was bombed. Anyhow, no one would miss him while the rest of the crew had families awaiting their return.

At Skye, the crew landed on a deserted beach and found a few days later as survivors from the SBS boat they claimed had sunk. Now alone Charles sailed north searching for an island, any island, to hide the boat among the many sparsely populated Western Isles. The communities on the larger islands received weekly ferryboats while the smaller ones only visited by boats bringing supplies and the occasional visitor. Most islands had one or more houses while others were too small to hide anything bigger than a bicycle. After a week, Jim found a deserted island with a mooring navigable at high tide with only a flock of long abandoned unshorn sheep, rabbits, chickens and a stream alive with trout. After hiding the boat under camouflage netting, he explored the island. He could not have found a better place to vanish as it had an old abandoned farmhouse with an adjacent large stone barn. Both had strong slate roofs and solid stone floors but there was no glass in the windows or doors to keep out the weather. In the yard was an old hand pump that only needed oiling to supply the farmhouse with water. Inside there was a large fireplace in the sitting room and a kitchen with a peat fired oven for cooking and heating the house in winter. Upstairs he found a number of empty rooms where dust had gathered but everything was dry and the wooden floors intact. It was all that Charles could have hoped for and a good place to live in.

Now Charles concealed the identity of the SBS boat by converting her into a civilian yacht. It was not too difficult as a yacht builder on the Isle of Wight made her to be sleek, have an easily lowered mast with an adjustable keel. She was ideal for Special Operations off hostile coasts, having two Perkins diesel engines for speed and a single 20mm Oerlikon gun for defence. As no civilian craft had such a gun, he removed the barrel from its stand then started to undo the four bolts fastening the gun stand to the deck metal mounting plate. They proved hard to undo except by using a hammer. It took Charles two days before all four bolts were undone and the stand hidden in the barn. Charles changed the ship's profile by raising the sides with running boards and extending the wheelhouse aft. When this was complete, he hauled her at high tide out of the water onto a nearby muddy. Then when the tide was down, he removed the navy grey paint before repainting her white with a blue stripe under the deck line. Finally, he painted her new name Snow Goose II on the bow and across the stern with Poole as the place of registration. Only when all the paint was dry did Jim lower her into the water. He left the radar and radio equipment intact as many motorised yachts had them but checked they worked and tuned the radio to the BBC. Then he reorganised everything first hanging the painting of the Great Green Woodpecker on the cabin wall as a reminder of home and happier days. The memories made him feel sad and alone knowing he would never see his parents or Wendy. He sat with tears in his eyes as he remembered his Wendy, her smile, the touch of her hands, and the feeling of making love to her. She was his first and only love, warm and exciting, tender yet sexy, and above all someone he could tell anything to - even his fears for the future. He could still see her naked on his bed smiling as he kissed her. It was beautiful but sadly, only a dream he swore he would never forget. After a while, he got up to find in the flag locker a Red Ensign to fly as a civilian yacht to replace the navy White Ensign. Next, he placed the Admiralty sea charts and requisition forms in the drawer under the chart table and the tinned food and cooking supplies in the lockers near the cooker and the two gas cylinders. He put the Very signal pistol in the wheelhouse and hid all the munitions, and guns wrapped in oily cloth in the forward sail locker under the spare ropes.

While doing the housework, he found a letter from Lt. Jan Van Gross that somehow he had missed. It said:

Dear Leading Seaman Charles de Broyen,

If we are to hide Mr. Jones, successfully we need time, so it is essential our ship disappears or reappears under a new name flying a red ensign. I chose you to hide her as I thought you needed time to recover from the recent tragic death of your fiancée and your parents. To help you remain hidden there is a parcel for you at the Aringour Post Office on the Isle of Coll. It contains ration books, money, and warrants for the supply of diesel for your ship under the name James Hands retired RN wounded working for SOE. If you get everything, please confirm by sending a message to 'Old Alderney' at SBS, Poole.

It would be best if you stay hidden for at least a year so Mr. Jones is part of the local fishing community.

May God bless you and keep you safe.

Signed

Lt. Jan Van Gross RN, SOE.

It was like Christmas Eve with the promise of presents to come. In the letter were five hundred pounds and a naval ID card under the name of James Hands. Immediately, an excited Charles plotted a course to Arinagour to collect his papers. They were the answer to his prayers as with these documents, he could disappear for years with little risk of discovery. The SOE thought of nearly everything so Carl the Admiral, aka Mr.

Jones, could do their bidding hidden somewhere in Scotland. The fact one of their boats was missing was understandable as was the idea of a motorised yacht being the home of man convalescing in private from the wounds of war.

During the voyage, a soft breeze filled the sails to carry the boat gently to Coll. After mooring at Arinagour, he went straight to the village shop that acted as the Post Office to collect his parcel. Then using the ID card of James Hands, he purchased some supplies and filled the boat's tanks with diesel. The local shopkeepers were helpful, promising to send a letter to the SBS as fast as they could. It took a week to arrive, which was not bad under war conditions. Though he often checked for mail, there was never a reply. Then he started to rebuild his life in the peace of the island. He quite liked being Jim Hands and decided to use the name to have a clean start by wiping out the shadows of his unhappy past.

Back on the island, he settled down to fish and to live as a man of leisure. He decided he should find out who owned the island and buy or rent it. Jim discovered while in Arinagour that his island was Black Island named for its large peat bogs and deserted after the death of the owner. Eventually, Jim met the present owner who quoted a fair price for the island that without any argument, he paid for in cash. The sale was sealed with a signed deed and a glass of twenty-year old single malt whisky with handshakes all round.

While tidying the boat, he found another cache of three hundred pounds hidden in a small box at the back of the chart locker that was more than enough to fund his meagre expenses for years. Jim felt it was a matter of 'finder's keepers' and there was no one around to prove otherwise. Now Jim repaired his house. Luckily, the thick slate roof was intact and the solid walls were in good condition, but there were no windows or doors. Therefore, he sailed to Coll to buy a table and two chairs, four thick oak doors and window frames with glass in them. When fitted they kept the wind and rain out from the kitchen where he ate and slept. When everything was finished, he spent his time reminiscing about the past often waking up at night thinking Wendy was there to keep him warm. On his own, he realised the full extent of his loss to wonder what it would have been like to have her with him. The thought made him smile so that when feeling alone he would talk to her as if she was still alive. Maybe he was slowly going mad, but he knew he was not. When the weather was fine, he went to the bogs to dig peat for fuel passing the ancient prehistoric sites known as crannings or loch dwellings. These hillocks had a central depression in which people lived, worshiped, or kept their sheep. They made him feel part of history by carrying on the traditions of the crofters who lived there in past times. Slowly, he felt reborn. His mind turned to the future to think that maybe if God was kind he would live long enough to find another lover or just be glad to be alive. For the first time in his life, he was free to do what he wanted without a care in the world but must remain in hiding.

Life changed when over the radio, he heard the war in Europe was over. Therefore, he left Black Island to sail down to the Essex marshes where he moored Snow Goose II among other craft. Then he went by train to SBS Poole, to come out of hiding and collect his back pay. In July 1945, the SBS base had changed with less staff, and the beach littered with redundant ex-Naval craft awaiting the breaker's yard. As it turned out no one knew anything about either a Leading Seaman Charles de Broyen or James Hands. After explaining he was an ex-SBS man come to be demobbed, he was greeted with vacant smiles, and a handshake then sent from room to room. Eventually, he met a WREN who explained a bombing raid destroyed many of the records. After asking Jim a few questions she issued a year's back pay, his demob allowance and of course, a civilian suit. Then Jim completed all the formalities before spending the rest of the day wandering around the town and putting flowers on the graves of his parents and Wendy. On the way back to the train station he paused to look up on the hill to see the bombed ruins of the family hotel and left with mixed feelings wondering what the future held a man with no family. In Essex, he opened a bank account under the name of James Hands while keeping some cash for expenses. At last, he was free to settle down to watch the flocks of birds feeding in the salt marshes and in the evening walk to the pub to play darts or enjoy the traditional English fare. Usually he had a pint of ale and the dish of the day that varied from a tasty steak and kidney pudding to jugged hare. He decided to enjoy life to the full until when he bored he would sail to Spain or even Italy looking for adventure, employment or at least a change.

Strangely, in rural Essex no one asked any questions but eagerly showed him around. It was a time when everyone had stories to tell, but most strangers to these remote parts came to hide or grieve. One was Stefen an ex-RAF Polish fighter pilot living in an old MTB whose scarred face showed the extent of his burns. Jim enjoyed Stefen's company, especially his sense of humour. Stefen avoided scaring anyone, so he only went out after dark to sit in a corner in the pub. In time, Jim and Stefen became friends talking about everything but nothing of any importance. Jim lived on Snow Goose II moored among numerous ex-RN M.T.Bs and smaller vessels that would regularly go away for days at a time to return during the night. It was rumoured they smuggled brandy or displaced people into Britain but Jim never commented. Whatever they did was none of his business, anyway who was he to criticise? Most people wanted to enjoy a few luxuries unavailable in the shops. Anyway, the trade brought money and goods into this poor, remote region. Here most people living in the marshlands wore military surplus overcoats and boots because they were readily available and very cheap.

5. A Mediterranean Charter

L'homme est né libre, et partout il est dans les fers.
(Man was born free, and everywhere he is in chains.)

Jean-Jacques Rousseau (1792): *Du Contract social.*

Life was easy, perhaps too easy. Some days Jim fished from the boat while on others, he lay back to observe the flocks of colourful waterfowl flying low across the marshes. Occasionally, a vessel would overtake the Snow Goose II causing her to roll as her captain waved cheerfully from the wheelhouse. This life of luxury of getting up at sunrise and sleeping when tired was not to last. For without warning it abruptly ended. Jim couldn't remember exactly when it was only, that he was half-asleep in his hammock and more relaxed than he had been for years. For as any seamen will tell you there are few better remedies for tiredness than lying in a hammock gently swinging in the breeze as the sunshine warms one's body. Jim woke in his hammock when approached by a bearded man wearing a sailing cap. His upper-class English accent with the slight hint of his native Dutch tongue made his voice unmistakable.

'Hello old chap. Sorry to disturb you when you're so comfortable. Silly of me to forget your name, is it Charles de Broyen or maybe James Hands?' the man whispered with a grin.

Jim recognised his old commander Lt. Jan Van Gross that he last saw on a beach on Skye.

'Welcome aboard sir and thanks for the papers. Nowadays, I am Jim Hands. If people knew I was Charles de Broyen, they'll search for the ship and ask about the Admiral,' he uttered, concerned Jan had come to reclaim Snow Goose II.

'That is true, Jim. It is good to find you looking so well. You need not worry about anything, as no one wants you discovered by a nosey journalist to decide the Admiral is not dead. I have unofficially come to ask you to sail your ship around the Med this summer. As far as the Navy is concerned, she is yours, and I am sure they have no interest in your island estate. It is now, and will always be, a matter of what they do not know will not hurt them. Anyway, the government does not want to accumulate any more unwanted military equipment they must sell or scrap. So your secret is safe,' Jan watched Jim's eyes to note his relief.

'However, I do think it's time you stopped moping and made the best of what life has to offer. I've a proposal that will make you rich and keep you busy,' Jan arrogantly continued before asking. 'Did you know you can make a lot of money sailing around the Mediterranean islands?'

'I don't feel like taking the rich on their holidays, so no thank you. If there was a charter to somewhere new or a chance for excitement, I'd be interested,' Jim replied. Then wanting to reply to Jan's insult he said. 'Anyway it's none of your bloody business as I'm not moping about anything, just enjoying a rest.'

'Sorry to upset you. Maybe you're not the tough likeable man I relied on during the war,' Jan apologised making Jim feel as if he was only six inches tall.

'I would jump at a chance for adventure, but there's no need for my expertise. You know I enlisted in the navy before I finished school and so know little except what I learnt from the service. Still I'm open to all suggestions if they pay well, are legal and exciting.'

For the first time Jan smiled. 'If you're willing, you could join SOE that is now known as MI 6. Then you can transport me and my lads from our naval base in Gibraltar to Greece.'

Jan noticed the suspicion in Jim's face and so added. 'We urgently need to get my lads and supplies to our friends in Greece. There is a major problem because after the Germans left there is a political vacuum even though we have troops there trying to prevent a civil war. My work is to transport arms and munitions to unofficial Greek government supporters. It is just like the old cloak and dagger days, except for one small difference. Officially, our government does not support these activities while paying us to do them. Welcome to the crazy world of post war Europe where no one knows who is friend or foe? Our wartime allies the Greek communists are now our enemies, and we fight for the Nationalist Government.'

'I suppose you have all the documentation to legalise the charter and a cheque for my services for maybe four or five months?' Jim commented while concerned he was not caught as a gunrunner. For all their historical importance, the modern Greeks had a reputation for knife fighting. There were tales of unspeakable brutality during the war against Germany that one ignored at one's peril.

'My men will move the cargo on and off your boat. So all you have to do is sail us around the islands stopping wherever we say to spend your spare time swimming, eating, and drinking in the local *tavernas*.'

'If it's so simple why choose me?'

'Anyone who can conceal an RN patrol boat for a year and sail her single-handed around the western islands must be ideal for the job. You used to be calm under pressure, a good navigator, and know how to keep your mouth shut when necessary. You'll remember Mr. Jones, the German Admiral we collected off Alderney, well now he works for us in Greece trying to stop a civil war or making sure the communists lose.'

'He's an extraordinary man.'

'He's unique,' Jan continued.

'It seemed only yesterday the communists were our best friends, and today they're our enemy,' Jim muttered in amazement. 'Now the poor sods are really in for it!'

'Jim it's hard to understand. Everything is upside down as both the Americans and Russians are prepared to fight to stop the other taking over Europe. On our part, we're doing all we can without sending more soldiers to Greece or being more politically involved.'

'And where do we fit in? It looks like we are just the small tail of the American dog?'

'Strictly, off the record, the bloody Americans are making us repay the loans they gave us during the war. Now Britain is so bankrupt she has little choice but to do exactly what they want. Indeed, the idea of a special relationship and being the best of friends has vanished overnight. Whitehall calls it the Cold War, but I see it as a dangerous affair. Mr. Jones thinks the two superpowers wish to make us all subservient as they fight like packs of hungry wolves to be the top dog. By the way, Mr. Jones is now known as Carl Van Stoff. You know he was an Admiral in German Naval Intelligence who passed information to Britain. Strangely, he refuses to work with the Americans because he thinks they are economic colonialists, and he is disgusted by the fact that so many brilliant but ruthless Nazis now work for them. Some make Hitler's long-range rockets and jet aircraft while others do the same in Russia. He fears the world will divide into pro-Russian and pro-Americans groups. I find it hard to believe, but Carl sees things; we don't.'

They talked happily for a few hours during which time Jan handed Jim a cheque for the enormous sum of three hundred pounds together with two hundred pounds in cash and one hundred US dollars in ten-dollar notes. With it came new Ship's Papers and Log Book for a Snow Goose II registered in Poole as a private yacht as well as Jim's Ship Master's certificate required to sail her in foreign waters. Of course, this included the latest official requisition order forms required to obtain supplies from all British military establishments worldwide without payment or a ration book. Then, there was a brand new passport with a photograph showing his new full beard and long hair. It must have taken weeks, if not months, for someone to collect everything. This confirmed that Jan's visit was not a casual event but part of a carefully calculated plot. It was just like during the war, little cloak and too many daggers. The papers stated he was Sub Lieutenant Jim Hands in the Special Operations Executive (SOE) of MI 6. What a jump from a Leading Seaman to Sub-Lieutenant! It made Jim realise the work must be dangerous if His Majesty's government paid so well when money was hard to come by. Still he signed the papers Jan had brought from MI 6 promising to keep secret all he did and saw until he died. Jan witnessed his signature before placing the papers inside a large brown envelope marked OHMS. Then Jan left as quietly as he had come.

'Sorry to leave so soon,' Jan said waving goodbye. 'I'll be in touch if anything changes, if not see you in Gibraltar at the end of the month. Don't be late as time is not on our side.'

'Don't worry I'll be there after I've refitted Snow Goose II at Chatham docks so we can cross the Med with no problems,' Jim commented feeling elated at the prospect of sun, open seas and excitement that lay ahead. Now he had three weeks to refit his boat and sail to the Rock.

Early next morning Jim deposited the cheque in his account. The bank clerk looked up at him with a degree of respect not given to sailors like Jim, as he was now one of their richest customers. He kept back most of the cash for expenses, though he would restock with goods and fuel using the requisition books. Then he had a last beer in the pub telling everyone he was going to take rich Americans around the Mediterranean. He was certain they thought he was going to smuggle displaced people, alcohol, or even drugs, but he did not care. Next morning, he sailed down to Chatham dockyard to have Snow Goose II cleaned of barnacles, fitted with long-range fuel tanks, obtain a spare set of sails as well as having the radio and radar upgraded. He needed the extra sails in case a storm damaged the main ones. When the work was complete, he filled the fuel tanks and took on all the provisions allowed using the requisition book. He signed for the work and thanking the Officer of the Day sailed through the English Channel into the Bay of Biscay. Eventually, he rounded Cape Trafalgar through the mythical Pillars of Hercules marked by the Rock of Gibraltar to moor among other small boats. Jim received a pass allowing access to the civilian and naval areas after the Harbour Master had inspected Snow Goose II.

Now it was the time for housekeeping. Jim found a laundry where he left his dirty clothes to be properly washed and ironed, then went to a cheap café to eat a breakfast of eggs, bacon, tomatoes and toast with marmalade. Feeling relaxed and well fed he looked in the shop windows eventually purchasing a local newspaper to see what was going on in this small country. Later, he refuelled Snow Goose II and replenished the water used for drinking and for salt free washing. The fresh water was necessary not only for drinking but also for washing. The combination of salt water and a strong sun quickly fades one's clothes. The secret is to rinse the clothes in freshwater before hanging them out to dry in the hot sun. In addition, a freshwater shower after a swim washes away both the dirt and salt. Next, he greased the pulleys and checked the rigging so it was tight, secure and the sails easily raised and lowered smoothly. He checked the engine and washed down the decks, so she looked as good as new and ready for anything. He had just finished his chores when four tough looking men approached his ship.

'Sorry to bother you sir but am I addressing Captain James Hands of Snow Goose II?' A rather large German asked.

'Yes I am he. Who are you?' Jim replied not expecting anyone else but Jan. Then he remembered Jan said he was to collect him and some others before sailing to Greece.

'I'm Klaus Weiss. Jan Van Gross told us to meet him on your yacht. If that's alright may we come aboard and stow our gear?'

'You all better come aboard. You will bunk aft and stow your gear in the lockers or in the stern,' Jim said pleased they were well mannered. At first glance, they looked a motley bunch consisting of the huge German Klaus, a thin Italian cook, and two sullen Greeks. However, they became good company playing cards and joking while they waited for Jan.

Gibraltar was little more than a huge rock emerging from the sea, separated from fascist Spain by a strongly guarded border. It had its history written for all to see such as the large

Napoleonic War cannons and the naval base with a hidden network of passages. It was rumoured that inside the Rock were stored the entire Navy's requirements for a year ranging from ropes to radar units, heavy guns to light ammunition, and underground bunkers to house staff and communications. Likewise, there were vast stores of food and water to replenish the visiting ships and keep the Rock safe even when threatened by Spain.

Jan arrived in an Admiralty launch looking like a weekend sailor with everything, including the finest VSOP French brandy and freshly baked bread. The others greeted Jan, as though they had worked with him before or knew him by reputation. It was clear he was their leader, and Jim was merely the paid hand to transport them and not to fight in someone else's war.

'Jim let me introduce our team. The thin talented cook is the Italian Mario Carlini; the German engineer is Klaus Weiss, while the larger of the Greeks is Christos with his boss Janus.' Then Jan continued looking at Jim. 'Captain Jim Hands a good sailor and cool under fire. I recommend you treat him with respect as he handles this ship better than any man does. In addition, he served with me in the navy. I am sure we'll all get on well and succeed in our mission.'

During the next few days Jan's men collected some crates which they stored decks. Meanwhile, Jim explored the Rock going up the spiral road to look down over the colony and beyond to Franco's Spain. Everywhere the famous Gibraltar Barbary Apes proved a nuisance. No one will remove them because an old tradition said that when the Apes leave the Rock, then Britain would follow. In Gibraltar, everyone spoke English and supplied all the usual British food as well as some Spanish ones. It was like Britain but with the Union Flag flying from the shops and offices. The best thing was there was no rationing so the market was full of fresh fruit from Africa and Spain. The choice of wines and spirits was enormous so Jim purchased two large bottles of VSOP Napoleon Brandy and three boxes of Havana cigars to help pass the time while on watch or while he was alone at the helm.

From Gibraltar, they entered the Mediterranean, what the Navy calls the milk pond because it does not have the violent storms common in the Eastern Atlantic. Therefore, with the sails set, the wind blew them towards Malta. It took a few days for everyone to gain their sea legs. The larger Greek Christos suffered from seasickness initially spending most of the time lurched over the side. The others proved good sailors until they had to help below deck, especially in the engine room. The best sailor was Mario the cook who in all weathers served an excellent meal, mostly fresh fish, and rice with tomato, olive, and cheese on lettuce. Klaus volunteered to be the ship's engineer, as he knew his way around the Perkins diesel engines. When it was not raining or too hot, they ate on deck finding the cool sea breeze refreshing. However, some of the crew developed severe sunburn after wearing only shorts in the hot sun. Klaus was the worst affected and appreciative when Jim applied dollops of cooling calamine lotion on his bright red body. Afterwards, they copied Jim by wearing hats, long-sleeve shirts and using sun cream on their face and legs.

This was a delightful period. Everyone behaved himself, even when going for a swim. There was a bit of splashing and jokes about man-eating sharks, but otherwise everyone enjoyed the swim followed by a freshwater shower. Often Mario and Janus trailed a line behind the boat to catch fish for their meals, sometimes attracting a curious shark that took one look before vanishing beneath the waves. They argued for days, whether it was a shark or just a friendly dolphin swimming around the ship. As the trip continued, Mario named his dolphins, though Jim doubted he could tell one from the other. Still the commentary on whether Graca or Madelina had returned and which one was fastest kept them busy so no one worried what lay ahead. Mario said Graca had a cross like scar on her dorsal fluke making her holy, but no one else saw it. Still to the religious Mario, who made the sign of the cross whenever worried, Graca was an angel sent to keep them safe. Soon everyone welcomed Graca as a sign of beauty and hopefully of an uneventful voyage. To both Greeks and Italians, dolphins are lucky as legend tells of dolphins who died protecting people from sharks. One said that a dolphin found a drowning boy and carried him on her back to a beach. She returned for the next few days until his people took the boy away before she went out to sea never return.

At last, they sailed into Malta's Valetta Harbour under the great stone Crusader Castle built by the Knights of St. John, to moor in the RN Yacht Club. Jan went ashore leaving Jim to refuel the boat returning an hour later to send his men off to collect supplies. Then he scrutinised the charts of the Greek islands and the eastern Mediterranean coast to plot a course.

'Doesn't our course take us too near Turkey?' Jim asked.

'Don't look so worried. I know what I am doing, even if we sail a bit close to the wind to avoid hostile shipping. Carl reported the loss of many boats sailing from Italy to Greece and recommended they sail in the Greek waters via the north-eastern islands to the island of Skiathos whose people are pro-nationalist. Thankfully, the Greek Orthodox Church loves us British declaring communism is a heresy. Let us hope Carl is right, and we will be welcome. First stop Cyprus and then Skiathos,' Jan said.

'It should be easy,' Jim replied.

'In Cyprus we'll refuel and have a concealed Oerlikon installed?' Jan said looking for the first time concerned about the venture.

After looking over the charts, Jim replied. 'If we use the sails, we'll conserve fuel and attract less attention. Do we have enough time to sail or must we use our motors?'

'If we sail tomorrow we'll be there in time to rendezvous with our friend. He will be delighted to see you, but do not play cards with him. He always wins, and I suspect cheats,' Jan commented.

They laughed as they drank a fresh mug of coffee.

'Cheat or no cheat, he is a man in a million. Remember the way he found us at night through a thick fog in a rowing boat at exactly the right time. He's a bloody genius!'

'Genius or not, let us hope Carl has worked his unique magic over the nationalists, so they wait for us with open arms,' Jan added while nervously stroking his beard.

6. Janus and Christos

Throughout life it is the people you meet who make things interesting. They often introduce us to new thoughts and different cultures

After leaving Malta their mission became clearer when over a cup of coffee, the Greeks told Jim as much as they thought he should know. 'It's time you know why we take arms to a militia in a country needing peace. We sail to the island of Skiathos to arm the local nationalist militia,' Janus said.

'Well Jim, let Janus explain the situation and our part in it. He's a Captain in the Hellenic Army working with the irregular Democratic National Army known as EDES,' Jan stated.

'Just call me Janus, it's safer. We're trying to form a national government to represent all Greeks.' He stopped as if contemplating a campaign, to light a cigarette and inhale the nicotine. After a few minutes, Janus continued. 'During the war all Greeks were united in fighting Germany but now there is a political vacuum which the communists wish to fill. Since the British troops arrived in Greece it is more peaceful and even the civil war has died down.'

He stopped making sure they understood his Greek accent before continuing. 'For months the communists have received large consignments of arms from Albania, Bulgaria, and Yugoslavia to help them take over Greece. They are well-trained soldiers with bases in Yugoslavia who ruthlessly purge their ranks of anyone not utterly loyal. Maybe we should emulate their example, especially after some recent atrocities committed by our side. Things changed at the end of 1944, when what we call the December event or Dekemvriana occurred. It was when the terrorists mindlessly shot and massacred civilians in remote villages and in the cities. It was so bad that even the battle-hardened British soldiers were shocked at what they saw, but somehow they managed to maintain some kind of normality. The worse was in villages where EDES or gangs fighting in our name, massacred men, women, and even children during surprise attacks on what they said were communist bases. To cut a long story short whoever carried out these atrocities have driven many Greeks to fight with or be more sympathetic to the communists. Now there is an uncomfortable lull as both sides await the results of the general elections while privately preparing for war. I fear that if we win, the communists will resume the civil war. There is no need for you to worry as the Skiathos people are nationalists who want to fight communism, but have only the arms the Germans left behind. I hope the arrival of our cargo will rectify this unfortunate situation,' Janus stopped to inhale the last precious drops of nicotine from a dying cigarette stub.

'Even during the uneasy peace both sides continue to rape and murder. In places, mobs have become uncontrollable unless trained or kept at bay by the National Army,' Jan added angrier than Jim had ever seen him. 'If we fail in our mission, Greece will become a boiling cauldron that when it erupts will engulf the whole region in war. At present, Stalinists run Albania while Marshall Tito makes Yugoslavia a communist puppet state. Only Greece, Italy, and Turkey remain free to keep the communists out of the Mediterranean Sea.'

'Greece is a nation divided by politics while used like pawns in the great game of chess played by the American and Russian Presidents. Your people have helped but cannot afford to stay much longer while the communists have many more combatants than we can muster. Most are from the anti-Nazi resistance group ELAS short for *Ethinikos Laikos Apeleftherotikos Stratos* meaning the Greek National Liberation Army. Our mission is simply to arm the nationalists and wherever possible stop ELAS supplies coming in from Yugoslavia. We keep our work a secret by only working with proven friends like Carl van Stoff. Sadly, recent experience suggests there are communists in your Foreign Office who helped ELAS intercept the equipment sent to us. I hope I am wrong, but my gut says I am right. Unfortunately, we must sail near Turkey whose navy keeps the Yugoslavians out of their waters while not liking us Greeks. Strangely, we both fear a strong Soviet presence throughout the region. Hopefully, your yacht flying the Red Ensign will be welcomed.' Janus stopped to go to sit with Christos on the stern looking out to sea.

'We know things will be difficult but with Janus and Carl on our side, not impossible. Let us hope Janus is wrong about the communists in the Foreign Office but after losing so many men in Albania, it is rumoured that they are pro-Russian. Did you know my father worked for Naval Intelligence that is now part of MI 6?' Jan commented.

'No I didn't. I know I signed on with MI 6 but wonder if they are our paymasters? Who has enough power and money to run such a clandestine operation?' Jim replied.

'It's unwise to ask too many questions. You know all about what lays ahead. I doubt if anyone other than Churchill's men know about us. We're so secret that we are probably known as Churchill's Secret Army,' Jan suggested.

They laughed. It sounded too outrageous to be real, but was it?

In Cyprus, they refuelled and had a 20mm Oerlikon fitted on the foredeck hidden beneath a wooden cover. Then they sailed north as everyone prepared for war. Mario, when not cooking sharpened a vicious looking sharp, long, and thin knife called a stiletto. Klaus checked and lubricated all the weapons before placing them into boxes as well as maintaining the engines. The others prepared the Oerlikon, pistols and rifles so that each weapon was fully loaded ready to fire. Before Crete, they hid everything so that only a professional customs officer could find them. Then he would find the Very pistol for firing distress flares, and an old rifle used for killing sharks! Unfortunately, they sailed in shark-infested waters inhabited by some fifty species but luckily most were harmless. The dangerous ones were Mako (*Isurus oxyrinchus*) and Hammerhead (*Alopias vulpinus*) sharks. It was unwise to be in the sea if bleeding, as blood and splashing attract sharks from miles away!

Three days north of Crete their luck changed when they sailed into a storm whose high winds, large waves, rain, and lightning drove the yacht blindly eastwards. It raged for days so all they could do was lower the sails to ride out the storm while sheltering below deck. Every hour, they took turns at trying to steer the boat to prevent her capsizing, until seventy-two hours later, the storm slowly departed leaving behind high winds and intense rain with poor visibility. For the first time, they did not know where they were, as the sun hid behind black clouds, and the radar ceased working. Therefore, Jim calculated the yacht's velocity and the strength and direction of the wind to plot as accurately as possible their position. He showed Jan, who agreed they were sailing much too close to the Turkish coast for comfort. This was the last thing they needed. So they rapidly motored westwards with motors running at full revs while Jim went on deck to find the radar cable and to reconnect it. Then as he completed the repairs, Jim heard a voice from the bridge of a large Turkish Navy destroyer that suddenly appeared out of the mist. Jan did the only sensible thing and stopped the engines to come alongside the warship.

'Ahoy down there! Are you in difficulties?' asked a Turkish officer in immaculate English.

'Hello,' Jim answered looking up at the destroyer's bridge looming high above him. 'Sorry to be a nuisance but the storm blew us off course. Are we in Greek waters and free to continue our voyage to Istanbul?'

'Yes Captain, you're just in Greek waters. Though I advise you, it may be safer to sail into our waters to avoid the Yugoslav gunboats that roam these waters at night,' the Turkish officer answered.

There was a pause as Jim thought how to convince the destroyer's commander to let them continue sailing in Greek waters, however, great the risk. He was worried if they went into a Turkish port the authorities would discover their cargo and arrest them as gunrunners.

'To tell you the truth we plan to stop in Skiathos for fuel and to visit a friend for a few weeks before going to Istanbul. That is of course if you let us. Please thank your Captain for his good wishes. Maybe we will visit Turkey on our return,' Jan shouted back.

'I'm told Skiathos is a beautiful island that is nationalist and pro-British, so you should have no problems once you reach there,' the Turkish officer wisely suggested. 'However, I must warn you about the communists who use many fishing boats, so replace your Red Ensign with the Greek flag.'

'Thanks for the advice,' Jim answered. 'Are we free to leave?'

'Of course you can; we're not pirates. Go in peace and try not to let your precious cargo get into the hands of the communist pigs,' the officer stated as his vessel sailed away.

As the destroyer vanished over the horizon, they wondered whether the Turks knew about their mission. Maybe the officer's comments were just a lucky guess or intelligence gained from spies in Cyprus. The colonial administrators employed many Turkish Cypriots for their loyalty and hard work. Luckily, most disliked the communists more than they distrusted the British or the Greeks.

'I expect the destroyer commander assumed we're smugglers. Few yachts would risk life and limb to visit Istanbul when the Aegean is talking of war,' Jan commented trying to stop everyone worrying. 'The Turks thought it important to warn us of the Yugoslavian gunboats operating in the north. So we'll use the motors during the day and sails at night.'

From then onwards they constantly scanned the waters for any vessels that could endanger the mission. Even with the firepower of the Oerlikon, they were vulnerable to attack especially from well-armed gunboats. As they pondered their next move, the last remains of the storm dispersed leaving calmer seas with clear skies, so they could see right up to the horizon. As the warm sun reappeared to dry the wet sails, they felt things were beginning to improve. Now even when Jim was trying to sleep, they woke him to identify something on their radar. The Snow Goose II was sailing in a busy shipping lane full of cargo vessels passing from the USSR into the Mediterranean and fishing boats of every size and shape. They avoided the larger ships while passing between the smaller ones. Occasionally, a fishing boat came so close that Christos asked about the fishing, the weather, and the nearest port. Jim did not know what they said as he spoke no Greek, though the tone of their voices and laughter suggested everyone was happy, and the fishermen showed no fear or distrust.

Near Skiathos, they passed heavily laden boats taking their night's catch to the town or to the mainland indicating there were few patrol boats around. No fisherman risked losing expensive nets in storms or other dangerous situations. Their reaction to trouble was to pull in their nets before sailing into the nearest harbour or sheltered bay. On board, everyone was cheerful as Christos sang Greek songs joined by Klaus with a marvellous baritone voice more appropriate to an opera singer than to a soldier of fortune. Jan encouraged this as it added to their cover of being mad tourists venturing into the lands of Ancient Greece. With the boat blown gently in the wind, they reached Skiathos. Soon the first part of the job was over and the rest up to Jan, Janus, and the crew. At that time, Jim genuinely thought he was just the skipper of the transport and not a combatant in an unreported conflict in a strange land. Unfortunately, he did not have Jan's advantage of having learnt Greek at an exclusive private school.

7. Skiathos

The isles of Greece, the isles of Greece!
Where burning Sappho loved and sung,
Where grew the arts of war and peace,
Where Delos rose, and Phoebus sprung!
Eternal summer gilds them yet,
But all, except their sun, is set!

Lord George Gordon Byron (1821): *Don Juan canto 3.*
Murray, London.

The first thing Jim noticed about Skiathos was that in many places olive groves covered the slopes reaching down to the white sandy beaches. The island's coast changed depending on the prevailing currents and wave action. In the sheltered coves were large expanses of beautiful white sand on gently sloping beaches. Elsewhere, the waves formed high cliffs with caves. It was a fabulous place to spend time just swimming and sun bathing with a nice woman or good friends. Everywhere were a myriad of brightly-coloured fishing boats plying their ancient craft with little signs of hostility. Many had nets cast over the side; others were resetting lobster pots while some used long lines to catch the larger fish.

'Well the fishermen appear friendly enough,' Jim commented.

'Maybe but they could have guns hidden under their nets. So keep your eyes open and moor your boat at the jetty, so we can make a rapid exit,' Jan retorted worried about what lay ahead.

Janus came to stand by Jim at the wheel to survey the town square with the steps leading up to the old church. The town had white and blue painted houses with narrow streets and steps covering the hill appearing as if created by an artist's palette to blend with the red-tiled roofs. In the foreground was a large area running from the houses to the harbour wall filled with people carrying baskets full of fish and other produce.

'There is nothing to worry about Jim. I know everything is normal when I see men, women, and children walking around while others eat and drink at the taverna!' Janus insisted.

'Maybe, but we must be careful. The enemy uses hostages and kill without mercy,' Jan commented before asking Janus. 'Can you recognise any of your people?'

'No one I know,' Janus calmly commented. 'Christos, go ashore to find who's in command.'

In seconds, Christos was walking towards the taverna where he met a young man, and together they disappeared indoors. Ten minutes later, he reappeared walking with two large bottles of wine and a pretty, round-faced woman wearing a scarf and carrying a basket.

'Jim, watch the woman and make sure she doesn't take a gun out from the basket. It is better safe than dead,' Jan advised.

Janus burst into laughter slapping his hands while shouting out to the woman. 'Maria you look more beautiful each time I see you and a welcome sign of peace. You're an angel sent to give hope and joy to bad old men like me.'

'How dare you call me an angel? You are an ungodly little man! I'm maybe good, but I'm not holy,' she yelled angrily before asking. 'Have you brought the presents you promised?'

'Maybe I have!' Janus answered jovially. 'Have you brought the transport?'

She laughed pointing to behind the church steps where some old men and five donkeys stood waiting against the wall.

'You're late. What excuse do you have for your inefficiency?' Maria retorted telling everyone she was in command.

'Sorry dear Maria. We encountered a bad storm and ran into the Turkish Navy. Luckily, we passed both safely,' Janus answered then he asked. 'Are there any messages for us?'

'Yes, Carl wants the cargo distributed by Christos while you wait here for him.'

'Will he be long?'

'I don't think so, but take care as the communists travel around the islands in two black Yugoslav gunboats,' Maria informed them.

The news of enemy gunboats was a sharp reminder that they were in the middle of a nasty civil war. Jim thought it sad that it was not the time or place to appreciate the beautiful woman standing in front of him. Indeed, she was probably not quite as nice as she appeared to be and obviously in command of the local militia.

When Maria was satisfied everything was as it should be, she signalled for the old men with the donkeys to come to Snow Goose II. On arriving, they loaded the cargo on rather sad looking donkeys before slowly climbing a wooded hill with Christos carrying a Sten light machine gun ready for trouble, but there were none. Now all aboard Snow Goose II took turns on watch or eating at the seafront taverna. The food was the usual Greek fare of fresh lettuce, olives, tomatoes, and feta cheese covered with an olive oil served with lamb kebabs. Enough carafes of cool white wine accompanied this. Now and again, Maria came to talk to them making it clear that she was the town's leader as well as Janus' representative. Jim was pleased to discover that she spoke excellent English and talking to her reminded Jim of the joy of being with a beautiful woman. Perhaps, though he did not realise it, Jim was lonely. However, there was no room for romance as even when talking to Maria, he was listening for any noise that could herald danger. It was a habit formed from living all his brief adult life fighting a war or hiding on a remote island.

At dusk, Jim returned to his boat to sit by the wheel, watching a bearded Greek Orthodox priest speaking to Janus while sharing a glass of wine and laughing as they discussed the latest news. When Jim arrived, they politely started to talk in English. The priest confirmed that all around Skiathos the Civil War was still smouldering with a few communists hidden among a predominantly nationalist population. Usually, the enemy stayed on the outer islands rarely venturing to Skiathos town or onto the island. He went on to say that in such small communities, they remembered every move and event as if it was yesterday. The German massacres of Greeks, and a few brave British soldiers defending the town remained vivid memories, as was a recent attack by communists in a Yugoslavian gunboat. Like all priests, he accepted death as the natural end of all life whose time and place lay only in the hands of a loving God. Eventually, the priest left when summoned by the church bell to the evening service. On leaving, he stopped to bless Snow Goose II with the sign of the cross.

Less than an hour after Christos returned everyone suddenly rushed around on deck as if making ready to sail. No one had told Jim what was happening on his boat, so he angrily asked Maria. 'What in hell is going on?'

'We must leave at once to shelter in a cave on the rocky side of the island,' Maria responded as if giving the orders.

'I will not risk my boat finding a cave at night in unknown waters.'

'I'm sorry Jim, but the Yugoslav gunboats are coming. Therefore, I have sent the villagers into hiding while setting up defences to punish them if they dare land. Please let me show you where you can hide your ship,' Maria pleaded with that unique look mother's reserve for naughty children.

Jim decided he had no choice but to steer Snow Goose II in the dark through unfamiliar waters. Luckily, Maria knew the coast like the back of her hand so within fifteen minutes they were safely inside a large cave where to Jim's horror, there were two boats moored to a jetty. Reluctantly, he sailed the Snow Goose II to come next to the smaller boat with one hand on the wheel and the other on the throttle for a quick escape should it proved necessary.

'Ahoy Captain Jim Hands. Welcome to my magical world of subterfuge and daring do,' a voice quietly announced; as out of the shadows and approaching them was a tall man a familiar bearing.

As the man drew closer Jim recognised the sparkling blue-eyed Admiral now called Carl van Stoff.

'Is it really you sir?' Jim responded with a degree of trepidation for he had not seen the Admiral since leaving him on Barra.

'I think so, but I'm no good at remembering names. Are you Jim Hands and do we have some mutual friends?' he asked.

'Yes, there was a Leading Seaman Charles de Broyen and his unusual friend the Admiral or was he Mr. Jones?' Jim answered.

'I remember them well as if it was only yesterday though so much has happened since those days. Indeed, I have forgotten what they looked like. It must be old age. Sometimes it's better to let certain memories be lost in the mists of time.'

'I totally agree to leave the past buried so now only the future matters. Many unpleasant memories cloud one's judgement.'

'That is exactly my opinion! Jim, I think your beard suits you,' Carl commented with a warm, cheeky smile.

Standing next to Carl were four men dressed as fishermen, but wearing ammunition bandoliers across their chests with long knives in their belts. These were either his bodyguards or members of a local militia. Jim hoped they were on their side. Soon they sat in Snow Goose II drinking French VSOP brandy that Carl had liberated during his travels. He looked different with his hair in long curly locks reaching down to his neck instead of his former closely cropped hair. Still he possessed those startling deep-blue eyes that smiled at everyone while concealing his innermost feelings. The Admiral, sorry, Carl looked much younger maybe because he no longer lived in fear of torture and death by the Gestapo. Now life in Greece was marginally better.

'We were coming to Skiathos when we heard an enemy gunboat was seen going the same way. So I radioed Maria to bring you here,' Carl explained.

'It's lucky we're in your territory.'

'Much luckier than you can imagine Jim. We had just set up our machine guns when we heard the noise of diesel motors getting closer. On hearing the distinctive purr of the Perkins engines I remembered from that night in the Channel, I told my men to relax. They did, especially when they saw the white-painted Snow Goose II appear like a phantom sailing in from the darkness.'

'What happens now?' Jan asked Carl.

'At daybreak we sail north to a nearby island to attack an ELAS gunboat base,' Carl stated as if they all accepted to be part of his command.

'When you arrived in Skiathos we initiated Operation Gunboat. Now as we speak our men are infiltrating the enemy's defences ready for our dawn attack on the gunboat base,' Maria added.

Jim was shocked to find that such a beautiful woman was so warlike – indeed quite Amazonian. He knew in civil wars both men and women fought side by side to save their country. However, hard he tried; he could never understand women who at one moment were so soft and gentle, and the next became as fierce as any man. In fact, he knew very little about Maria Makropoulos except that what he saw he liked.

'What are you going to do about the gunboats? I do not think they will not fight. Please don't forget Snow Goose's Oerlikon is no match against four or more Russian heavy machine guns,' Jim informed all present. He did not mind dying for a good cause but preferred to live to fight another day. Anyway, he was just the driver.

'Before the attack our men will eliminate the sentries, so they can fire down on the gunboats,' Carl informed them before asking. 'Is there anything else you would do?'

'If I was in command, I would sail an hour before dawn to swim to the gunboats and attach a limpet mine to each to explode before your men attack. Then there would be fewer casualties and victory more likely,' Jim announced not fully aware what he was getting himself into.

'I would agree but do you have any limpet mines?'

'I have some on board left over from the war. They are still in their waterproof wrappings and only need to be primed and set.'

'Can you swim underwater to fix the mines?' Carl asked knowing it was not easy.

'Yes I've done it before, but I'm a bit out of practise,' Jim stated with an air of confidence that concealed his own doubts. Indeed, he now wished he had not said anything.

'Bloody good show Jim, now I know why I chose you for the mission,' Jan said.

'Then Snow Goose II will leave an hour earlier with Maria as your guide while I follow with the other boats. Tomorrow we will teach those heathens a lesson they will never forget. They will not be prepared for an underwater attack from a trained naval frogman,' Carl commented looking forward to the dawning of a new day.

That night Jim found the hidden limpet mines and the frogman suit with all the necessary tools. Everything was in order as long as the air in the cylinders lasted, and the mines worked. Afterwards, he had a big glass of brandy before trying to sleep, as he knew he must conserve all his energy if he was going to survive the morning's adventure.

8. A Lonely Swim into Wars

Let the quiet and darkness of the night be my shield.

Before sunrise, they were at sea, with Maria at the helm while Jim put on the frogman equipment, and Jan primed two limpet mines. Jim knew what to do as he had sabotaged German coastal vessels during the war. The main difference was in the SBS they dived in pairs with a backup crew, but now he dived alone. Therefore, he carefully checked the air levels in the cylinder, regulator, and mouthpiece before tying an equipment bag to his lead belt and putting on the fins.

'Jim, the harbour is hidden behind those false rocks to your right. Please stay alive and don't take too long, we'll miss you,' Maria said with an irresistible smile that would keep him warm for the next hour.

'Hide the bubbles from the breathing apparatus,' Jan unhelpfully advised. This was always a problem as he could leave a trail of bubbles on the surface visible to an alert sentry.

Jim slipped into the water to swim over to, and under the false rocks into the harbour. He swam as close to the bottom as possible until he reached the wooden jetty where a gunboat was moored. Then he surfaced beneath the jetty to breathe fresh air and reconnoitre the area to see the harbour was eighty feet wide but less than fifteen feet deep. This made the work more dangerous as anyone looking down through the clear water to the sandy bottom would see him. Feeling very exposed, he prepared for his next dive noticing hundreds of small colourful fish peacefully swimming around. This added a touch of tranquillity to an otherwise violent situation as their beauty and gracefulness calmed him while he contemplated his next move. Timing was critical for him to place the mines correctly. The sound of footsteps broke the morning quietness as a sailor walked on the gunboat's deck to get some fresh air, or light up a cigarette that Jim hoped would be his last. Jim hoped the man did not look down to see him. As he looked apprehensively upwards, Jim noticed there was a lot of litter floating on the surface of the water consisting of potato peel, old cabbage, and other kitchen waste. This behaviour did not happen in Poole where they believed dirty water indicated undisciplined minds. He hoped it was true as he checked that his bag held two limpet mines and a chisel. The latter may be necessary on older ships to cut away layers of barnacles from the hulls to expose the metal on which to fix the mines.

As he surfaced to take, one last look around, he saw above the harbour an ELAS guards's throat cut and an EDES fighter replace him. Then the soldiers of EDES eliminated their ELAS enemies before swarming down like ants taking up positions around the base ready to attack when ordered. Suddenly, Jim realised he had to move fast before Carl's men arrived or someone saw him. Therefore, he swam under the boat to fit a limpet mine on her clean metal hull and set the timer for thirty-five minutes. Full of confidence he swam over to the second ship that was older with a barnacle-encrusted hull. It took Jim five minutes to chisel away and expose the bare metal on which to attach the mine. The sharp barnacles cut his hands causing them to bleed, but he had no time to worry about the pain. Then he set the limpet mine's timer for twenty-five minutes before swimming as fast as he could out of the harbour. As he swam, he expected to feel a bullet hit him, but luckily, it never happened. Soon he climbed back aboard Snow Goose II feeling both elated and exhausted. It was clear that he was not as fit as he used to be. Maybe it was age or more likely lack of exercise. On seeing the blood on Jim's hands, Maria washed them with iodine and bandaged them making him feel special, a wounded hero.

Exactly, on time, the limpet mines exploded sending the gunboats and their crews into the next world. Even before the noise died down Carl's men stormed the ELAS camp to eliminate their enemies before removing everything of any value such as documents and weapons. Then they planted demolition charges in the buildings and under the jetty before quickly retreating. A grinning Carl came aboard Snow Goose II holding armfuls of documents.

'Let's get out of here,' Carl suggested.

Jim immediately steered the Snow Goose II as fast as she would go to Skiathos and EDES.

Carl slapped Jim on the back, remarking. 'Thanks Jim, your limpet mines did the trick.'

'I told you Jim was one of the best. He has few vices and is totally reliable,' Jan remarked knowing he was adding to Jim's embarrassment. Sadly, Jim was noticing for the first time the bullying reptilian side of Jan's nature.

Things took an unexpected turn for the better when Maria gave Jim a kiss making him feel like a king! They say it is bad luck to have a woman aboard ship, what a load of nonsense. Maria was the brightest star who made them glad to be alive.

'The news of today's work will be celebrated by EDES throughout Greece. We have eliminated one target, but they will soon get new gunboats. However, we have more ammunition and cash to fund our activities,' Carl announced passing out what he called medicinal brandy.

'Jim, you'll be surprised to hear that nearly all the munitions we captured are British. Probably, from Tito when he was fighting the Germans. It looks like all the major players in this grim game wish to hide their involvement,' Jan stated.

Then the normally quiet Klaus joined in the conversation. 'Jim, you know the Germans left behind caches of arms and money, some of it useless. All sides in guerrilla wars use any weapon they can obtain and even make others. A Russian rifle kills communists as well as a British or German one. The only difference is they do not use the same size ammunition, but it does not bother the fighters that know which bullets fit each gun. It doesn't matter who made the bullet that kills you; you're still dead,' Klaus observed before adding. 'Dear lady and gentlemen let's toast our gallant frogman Captain and his motley crew.'

'To Jim the Frog and his motley crew,' said everyone while downing a brandy followed by a hearty cheer. They celebrated an unrecorded victory over a gunboat base the Yugoslavs said never existed. For as everyone knows the first casualty of war, especially secret wars, is always truth.

When they docked in Skiathos they were met by the people celebrating the victory with singing and dancing. Within minutes, they were among the crowd singing and attempting a few complex Greek traditional dances. Jim liked the rhythmic music and the skilful dancing as the men stamped their feet while moving up and down. Soon Maria who everyone knew and liked was the life and soul of the party. She even taught the shy Jim to dance a few of the simpler steps. Throughout that day and well into the night wine flowed like water as Carl, Mario and Klaus danced or sang old Greek ballads. Surprisingly, they sounded like professionals. Indeed all three had before the war been amateur musicians and singers taught by some of the world's finest teachers. Jim was concerned that such revelry was premature when the enemy seeking revenge could arrive at any minute. He thought it was dangerous to make so much noise and drink until confused when everyone should be ready for the enemy. Then he looked up at the church to see a man with a rifle across his lap standing on guard and further away others with machine guns carefully hidden by the harbour wall. So Maria had thought of everything, including their safety! He was beginning to wonder just how powerful this charming woman was who quietly commanded her people. Even the careful and untrusting Carl placed his faith in her or had a soft spot for her beauty. Maybe it was both!

A very tired Jim was the first to retire to Snow Goose II but still awake when the others noisily returned to sleep. Next morning he laughed at his friends with colossal hangovers that even many cups of sweet hot Greek coffee and gallons of water could not cure.

9. Ordered to Albania

One does not know one's true friends until you need them.
Then a wrong choice can prove very costly, even fatal.

Jan unexpectedly received a message that read:

MOST SECRET
TO JAN VAN GROSS

TRAVEL AT FULL SPEED TO PIRAEUS TO CONTACT MR. MARSHALL AT THE EMBASSY FOR FUNDS AND SEALED ORDERS FOR MISSION TO ALBANIA.
AUTHORISED BY MI 6 AT THE REQUEST OF FOREIGN OFFICE. ACKNOWLEDGE AND THEN DESTROY THIS MESSAGE.

Nobody on Sea Goose II was pleased to find out that his operational area now included Albania. However, like so many things the British did, there were no limits as to where MI 6 operatives like Jan and Jim worked. To make matters worse Carl absolutely refused to have anything to do with the Foreign Office. He said he worked to help EDES defeat the communists in Greece and nowhere else. Then Carl, Janus, and Jan had an enormous row. Therefore, Jim felt it best not to get involved so he took Maria to the taverna to dine on lamb kebabs and salad followed by cake and ice cream.

'I'm in no hurry to return to the ship until they all calm down.'

'I feel the same. Jan knows Carl will never work with anyone from the British Foreign Office because he does not trust them and feels betrayed,' Maria explained with a smile.

'I know how he feels. This was meant to be a secret MI 6 operation with no diplomatic involvement,' Jim remarked before angrily adding. 'Bloody British - you can't trust them.'

'Relax Jim and do not judge all the British by a few bad ones. Remember the ancient Trojan saying about never trusting Greeks when they bring gifts,' Maria said pausing to offer Jim a cigarette. 'Even when I offer you a cigarette, it could be poisoned!'

'Thanks, I'll take the risk. You are no murderer. Anyhow, we do not have a wooden horse.'

'I hope not but maybe the enemy does.'

They both laughed nervously dreading what the future held and whether they would see each other again.

Jim was beginning to like the Turkish cigarettes with their black wrapping that Carl and Maria smoked. Strangely, they were Sobraine Black Russian cigarettes made in England. He suspected they came from an uncovered secret cache or had gone missing from an Admiral's table.

'Sometimes fate sends people in opposite directions even when their hearts say to stay together. I feel now is such a time, and yet I hardly know you,' Maria said sadly regretting his pending departure while at the same time sensing disaster.

'Carl and I don't want anyone looking at our past to come to the wrong conclusions. It is too full of death and despair. You see all my relations are dead. My parents and girlfriend died when our hotel was bombed during an attack on Poole harbour. It was when my uncle died fighting for SOE in Yugoslavia. A month later my last living relative, my deceased uncle's wife suddenly died, some say from a broken heart. Though there were rumours of traitors in the FO, no one investigated Uncle's death. I know there are pro-Russians in high places as well as thousands of Mosley Blackshirt fascists who never changed their beliefs; they just said they did.'

'I'm sorry, Carl said he was a German Admiral, who worked with the British before you and Jan rescued him. I know I have never met a more intelligent, trustworthy or lonely man. Everything that Carl does works and what he refuses often fails. He is someone who always cares for everyone and yet when you look deeply into his eyes, sometimes I see such sadness making me want to cry or just hug him.'

'Carl is very reliable unlike Jan. Jan does exactly as ordered, even when it holds unacceptable risks. He chooses what he considers to be in the national interest over survival.'

'So you don't fully trust Jan?'

'Let me just say he always accepted very dangerous missions that most others would wisely decline. He is either brave or blindly obedient like a trained dog - it is hard to work out which.'

'So what do you do now?'

'Dear Maria I must stay with Jan through fire and brimstone, but first must return before Klaus smokes himself to death,' Jim joked.

Back on Snow Goose II, things were abnormally quiet as Carl packed his clothes into a small case while Jan looked on helplessly.

'Sorry to leave so suddenly,' Carl said to Jim before adding. 'Jan has his orders and expects you to stay with him while I remain here to help defeat the communists. Therefore, Janus, Christos, Maria, and I will leave to continue the long fight. We will miss you and ask you not to take too many risks. The only advice I can give is never trust anyone except each other as I fear nothing is what it appears to be. But then I'm always suspicious of anything I can't control.'

'I am sad to see you go but will stay with Jan whatever disaster befalls us,' Jim heroically added having no clue what he was talking about.

Snow Goose II left Skiathos in an ungodly hurry as a strong breeze blew them towards Piraeus. The voyage took them into a major shipping lane full of vessels transporting people and goods to and from the Mediterranean. They varied from large oil tankers to small coastal steamers. Some registered in Britain, France, Italy, and Greece while others came from Russia, Turkey, and Panama. It was a time when every nation traded with each other, including their enemies. It was clear that whoever held Greece controlled the eastern Mediterranean!

The town and port of Piraeus were full of people repairing and replacing buildings damaged by war. On approaching the harbour, Snow Goose II had to navigate between half-submerged wrecks to follow a narrow channel marked by buoys. The yacht harbour was well away from the main harbour where cargo ships and tankers unloaded their goods. It was an unfriendly place. Jim found the Greeks were reluctant to refuel Snow Goose II remembering how the British bombed the port to hasten the German departure. It took all of Klaus' Greek to get the fuel, though they were still overcharged. Meanwhile, Jan went to the Embassy to collect his orders and returned with five men in peasants' clothes carrying heavy rucksacks.

'We're to take our guests to Albania to join the anti-communist forces fighting for King Zog. Klaus, and Mario need not come, but I would be happy if they stayed,' Jan informed them.

Both agreed to go to Albania before they sailed.

'We sail north through the Strait of Otranto to Albania where Jim will go ashore with the men until they meet their allies. It shouldn't take more than a day, so I will return for him on the second night.'

'I don't see why I should go. I'm a sailor not a fighter like you?'

'I know the sea around Albania better than you do,' Jan angrily replied never liking anyone questioning his authority.

'Are you really being honest with me? I was recruited to provide transport for your work and not risk my life on any hair brained venture you should be doing.'

'I'm sorry you feel like this, but you know orders are orders. Therefore, I stay on the ship, and you land with the others. Remember I am the boss so everyone does what I order. You will go ashore whether you like it or not. Is that clear?'

Just as Jim was about to mutiny, the new men entered the cabin led by a stocky middle-aged Englishman with a short moustache. 'Jim let me introduce us. I am Major Don Fox, and the others are Alexis, Andreas, Apollon, Demokritos, and Tomas, they fought with me during the war in Albania. Now we return to join the fight against the communists.'

'But I still don't see what use I'll be, once you're safely ashore?'

'You're our messenger and escape route if things go wrong. Do not worry as I would never take risks unless necessary. We are going by sea because all our agents who parachuted into the country disappeared, probably betrayed or captured. Sadly, some were friends, so I hope they died quickly or escaped to join our people in the hills,' Fox added.

The penny dropped; they were the instrument of last resort, and typically, Jan accepted the mission from an Embassy man he did not know from Adam!

During the journey north, Jim became acquainted with the newcomers. They were a varied bunch. There was Apollon a tough character who liked flexing his muscles at everyone except Klaus and spoke of bringing King Zog back to rule his people. Then the likeable Demokritos who was the intelligent, quiet type that explained his name meant 'Judge of the People' and Apollon was 'The Destroyer'. Demokritos said his father was Greek and mother Albanian, so he spoke both languages fluently to be accepted as a shepherd. As a child and during the war, he wandered the hills where his group would now go and knew nearly every cave and gorge.

'Jim, once we're in Albania and across the first few hills, we'll be safe as no one will find us, unless I want them to. Then you will return to your ship,' promised Demokritos.

'There's absolutely nothing to fear. Our men will be waiting to take us to their base to carry on the good fight. All you have to do is stay until we meet the others and leave,' added Apollon, the Destroyer, with a cheerful grin. Jim thought he was like The Cheshire Cat in Alice's Adventures in Wonderland whose grin could conceal anything – both good and evil.

The team packed their equipment in rucksacks for the journey but kept a long knife and a rifle at hand. This would deter a few opponents, but little use against well-armed soldiers. Then in the middle of the night, they reached the Albanian coast to paddle ashore in a rubber dinghy.

'I'm assured by Horace Marshall of the FO this is a maximum-security operation organised by Kim Phiby, the Head of the Balkans Office. Therefore, I foresee no difficulty. At the first sign of trouble, or when you want to return, go to the beach and radio for us to pick you up.'

As Jim said goodbye, Jan avoided looking into his eyes. This would be the last time they met.

After landing, they hid the rubber dingy and radio in a nearby cave before walking to hills and hopefully safety. Throughout that night, all they saw were a few stray goats feeding on the grass until at sunrise, they entered a gorge where Demokritos planned to meet his men. Finding no one there, he signalled for the group to go on to the next wooded valley. There they found fifteen armed men who greeted Demokritos with hugs before they sat down to eat while Demokritos discussed their plans.

'Thanks Jim, now it's time you went back to Snow Goose II. Good luck,' Demokritos said.

'Demokritos let me take Jim to the beach as it is a long way, and we don't want him to get lost or caught,' Apollon kindly offered.

Therefore, without much discussion, Apollon took Jim to the beach to hide in the cave until midnight. He was charming company making Jim laugh while totally winning his trust. If Jim were as wise as Carl was, he would have refused the white wine and dried salted goat meat Apollon lavishly supplied. The more Jim ate the thirstier he became making him take another to become relaxed. Indeed, he was slowly becoming very drunk.

Before midnight, Jim radioed Jan.

'Calling Mother Goose. Calling Mother Goose this is Gosling. Over,' Jim said and repeated the message three times before getting a reply.

'Gosling, Mother Goose receiving you loud and clear. ETA in ten minutes. Glad everything has gone as planned.

Over and out,' Jan replied sounding cheerful to dispel any doubts Jim felt about him.

Then all he heard was static as though the radio was being jammed. He tuned it to Snow Goose II's frequency praying for Jan's voice to answer his repeated calls.

When the signal came, it was one final faint message.

'Gosling, get the hell out of there! Mother Goose is under attack. Repeat we are under attack. Klaus is wounded and Mario is operating the Oerlikon. Goose holed, but I think we can make Corfu.'

Then, there was an ugly silence as Jim realised he was abandoned wondering what else could go wrong. He did not have to wait long to find out! Without warning Apollon knocked him to the ground then tied his hands behind his back.

'Capturing you was as simple as feeding a baby,' Apollon laughed hitting Jim a second time.

Jim was horrified to find Apollon the Destroyer was also Apollon the Traitor. The thought made him sick at how easily this slimy creature betrayed him and probably the others. Now his brief visit to Albania was looking like a short stay and a quick, though he expected, very painful death. Sadly, he knew no one would appeal for his release as the mission was not official and anyway, he did not exist having died during the war. It was all too convenient. Now he was in deep trouble in an unfair game of chance where the result was always the same – heads you lose, tails you still lose. It was sod's bloody law!

10. In Adversity Jim Meets his Confessor

My God hath sent his angel, and hath shut the lions' mouths, that they have not hurt me: forasmuch as before him innocency was found in me; and also before thee, O king, I have done no hurt.

The Bible, Daniel, Chapter 7: 22.

After walking all night along narrow goat tracks, they reached a road. There Apollon threw Jim unceremoniously into the back of a black van that drove off at dangerously high speed over bumpy roads. While being thrown around in the van Jim struggled to get free, but his ropes were too tight, so he only managed to make his wrists sore. Now he was very angry at ignoring Carl's warning about not trusting anyone, especially Apollon, who had misled him. Exhausted he wondered how many people Apollon had betrayed and what happened to those he left in the hills? He hoped they were free to fight these tyrants. He became more afraid the longer he was alone, realising he was a prisoner of the Albanian communists who would treat him, if lucky, as a foreign combatant or more likely execute him as a spy.

Eventually, the van stopped outside a large stone building so that Apollon could take Jim inside into an ancient prison cell. It was a small dark room with no windows or beds, containing only a jug of water and a bucket. The good thing was his wrists were untied before being stripped naked, pushed onto the cold stone floor and left to sleep. Jim knew from his survival training with the SBS how important it was to get as much sleep as possible and keep drinking water. This would prepare him for the ordeals ahead and dilute the alcohol still in his body and drying his throat. Therefore, he slept. Luckily, Jim could sleep anywhere and dreamt of swimming in a warm clear blue sea surrounded by brightly coloured fish. He awoke with a hangover and feeling very cold, to the noise of boots marching on stone floors and the clanging of metal doors. He looked around trying to observe everything, hoping to find a way of escaping or tolerating the horrors ahead. He remembered people saying that no one would risk their lives to rescue lowly erks like him. He knew it was true, but what was an erk?

When his eyes were used to the darkness, he could distinguish the metal door and the cold walls with water running under them. Maybe the cell was underground, perhaps near a stream. If he was lucky, the walls were old and crumbling so, he could make a hole to escape, unfortunately they were made of solid, immovable rock. Then his mind returned to Jan, who would not save him or even bother to think about it. Was Jan a friend or had he used Jim because he was dispensable? For an ex-leading seaman, the ways of officers were difficult to understand because they always left the dirty work to the ratings. They could not help it as at Dartmouth, they learnt to be an elitist with their personal batmen to clean their shoes and make their beds. This, he felt, made them lazy bastards. Of course, they dined like princes in the Officers' Mess while the ratings were in the canteen eating spotted dick and boiled cabbage. Jim felt that this destroyed any sense of equality and any idea of a land of the free!

As Jim searched the dark cell, he stumbled upon a bundle of blankets huddled in the corners that moved and murmured when he touched it. When he lifted the blanket, he was shocked to see the bloodied face of an Orthodox priest wearing the remains of his robes with his beard encrusted with blood. The priest suffered at the hands of his tormentors making Jim realise he could soon be on the receiving end of such punishment.

'Sorry to disturb you, father,' Jim apologised. 'Is there anything I can do to help you?'

'Water my son. Please give me water,' the priest pleaded in English with a strong Greek accent pointing to the water jug; he was too weak to reach.

During the next few hours, Jim carefully cradled the priest's head in his arms to get the old man to sip water and gently washed his face. The priest never complained even though he hurt when being washed, instead his shining eyes-only expressed gratitude. Slowly, the priest started to smile and talk in Greek that Jim did not understand.

'I'm English,' Jim uttered desperate for company hoping the old man understood.

'It is indeed a sad day when an Englishman ends up in an Albanian cell. The communists hate you even more than the Holy Church and us priests. May God protect you and his angels keep you safe.'

'Thank you Father,' Jim uttered wondering if he was in hell. Nothing more was said as both men rested, glad to have each other.

About two hours later the metal door opened as a guard placed two bowls of soup with two chunks of hard black bread on the floor. Of course, there were no eating utensils, so they had to use their hands. The guard said nothing before noisily closing the door to leave them alone. Jim passed a bowl to the priest who grabbed it and rapidly ate all the food as if he had not eaten for a week. Therefore, Jim followed his example by dipping the hard bread into the soup to soften it before slowly chewing every morsel. With every precious mouthful, he swallowed; the void in his stomach filled making him feel stronger. Jim hoped it was breakfast but knew it could well be lunch and dinner as well. Indeed, it could be the only meal for days or even weeks!

Later, the priest said his name was Mathias and told Jim about what was happening in Albania. It was a very old-fashioned rural country where people worked on the land. The arrogant aristocracy that supported the unorthodox King Zog and a small middle-class of merchants previously ran the nation. It had two major ethnic groups, the Ghegs in the north and the Tosks to the south. Historically, it was part of the

Turkish Empire until in 1912 when a revolution led by Gjergj Skanderberg threw them out. Even today, his symbol of a black two-headed eagle was on the national flag. During the war, the Germans occupied the country resulting in many Albanians joining the Resistance armed and supplied by communists in Yugoslavia. After the German withdrawal, the communist resistance fighters took over the country except where pockets of King Zog's men kept them at bay. The Ghegs in the north opposed the communist regime being mostly Christians and Muslims, while elsewhere the Marxists ran a ruthless peoples' state. The Minister of Internal Affairs, Koçi Xoxe, presided over the trial and execution of all opposition, clan chiefs, and members of the former administrations who he accused of being traitors and war criminals. Xoxe established work camps where men and women drained the marshlands using only the most basic materials and their bare hands. They shot all who refused to work. At first, they ignored the priests who fought against the Germans until Koçi Xoxe's thugs attacked the monasteries. Some priests were shot, tortured, or forced to renounce God. Mathias refused to cooperate preferring to rely on God's Angels to preserve him, while praying for God to send someone to keep him company and stop him going mad.

After another bowl of soup and black bread, Jim found himself dragged out into the light and down a flight of well-trod stone steps to a darkened room to confront his interrogators. Jim sat in a chair facing a table on which were his knife and radio next to a typed statement in English and one in another language, presumably Albanian. Jim could see nothing except for a powerful lamp shining into his face concealing the interrogators. The intensity of the light and its heat burned into Jim's eyes, so he tried to look away. It was to no avail as firm hands forced his face into the light to await the inquisitor's questions. With sheer determination and bloody mindedness, he decided not to be humiliated as he felt no shame at being naked. Therefore, he behaved like a male model posing for some famous artist while answering silly questions and smiling like the village idiot.

The interrogation started exactly as he had rehearsed years before at SBS.

'Comrade I must warn you to answer all questions clearly and truthfully or you will be severely punished,' someone asked. 'What is your name?'

'Sir, I am Jim Hands.'

'Well Jim Hands, explain why you brought saboteurs to our peaceful nation?'

'Sir, I'm just an unfortunate sailor who managed to swim ashore in a strange land. I never meant anyone any harm. Honestly, I didn't,' Jim tried to appear the victim of circumstances.

'You could be telling the truth as you look too young and idiotic to be a man of importance. You are not the former German officer we expected, who could tell us about western intelligence. That is unfortunate, but be warned we have captured all the spies and supplies you British sent to Albania. Every one of them died alone and disillusioned to be buried in an unmarked grave abandoned by his masters.'

'I know what you say is true, and I'm sorry I'm not the man you seek. I am just a sailor who was too ignorant and trusted the wrong people. You know I gain nothing by lying to you and will tell you all you need to know, if indeed, I know anything important,' Jim slyly replied hoping to gain the upper hand or gain time to think more clearly. They obviously wanted Carl but ended up with him. Therefore, he was not there by accident but after a carefully designed plot to capture Carl and destroy Major Fox.

'Don't listen to him Comrade Commissar. He is a liar. I sailed with him, and his bandit friends aboard a small ship called Snow Goose II bringing money and guns to the exiled tyrant Zog's men,' bellowed his betrayer, Apollon the Destroyer.

Instinctively, Jim turned towards the treacherous voice, and before he could control his emotions stupidly tried to react. Using every muscle in his body, he rose to hit the vile snake Apollon. It was a wasted effort rewarded with hits on the chest with wooden sticks. For the next few minutes, he heard nothing as he tried unsuccessfully to protect his body and conserve his energy for when he would need it. With each breath, the pain from his bruised chest was a reminder of where he was. He wanted to hate but knew it was a foolish gesture, especially when there was nothing he could do about it.

'Captain Hands try to be sensible as resistance is pointless. Whether you like it or not you are our prisoner abandoned by your people with only your own actions and the mercy of this court to save you from a slow and painful death. You can save yourself a great deal of pain if you sign the confession that is on the table in front of you,' another advised Jim in a soft fatherly tone. The inquisitor was telling the truth, but Jim felt he had to do something. Therefore, he started to read the confession, but told to stop reading.

'Fascist reactionary scum you need not read the confession, just sign it,' Apollon ordered as he pushed a pen into Jim's hand. Jim wanted to drive it hard into Apollon's hand, but did not as it would evoke more punishment. Apollon had won, and Jim knew he could do nothing about it except refuse to listen.

'Let the bourgeoisie pirate read his confession to know what to do next time we meet after he has been vigorously interrogated,' an older voice stated. There followed an intense argument until everyone agreed with the man's proposal.

'Captain Hands you may read your confession as slowly as you like. We have all the time in the world, but the longer you make us wait the more impatient we will become. See it is exactly what you would have told us. Why be so belligerent and try to protect the people who abandoned you? They have already forgotten you exist. To those in the ruling class, you are just a replaceable servant. So be a good chap and sign the document,' the old man advised in a very persuasive voice.

Therefore, Jim read the confession that simply said:

I, Jim Hands, an officer in His Majesty's Imperial British Royal Navy, hereby declare the following statement to be true and written freely in my own words without

guidance or under undue duress. Since coming to Albania, my captors have treated me well according to the rules of all international conventions.

I hereby freely confess to be a fascist working for the British and the evil exiled Zog formerly King of Albania. I am the sole survivor of an unprovoked attack on the victorious navy of the Democratic Republic of Albania by the British Imperialist Navy. I understand under International Law such incidents are considered to be as acts of terrorism punishable by death or life imprisonment.

I am indeed deeply sorry, apologise for my actions against the good people of the People's Republic of Albania, and throw myself upon the just mercy of the People's Court to decide my fate.

Signed

Captain Jim Hands RN.

Jim nearly laughed at the childish statement noting he was suddenly promoted to be a Captain in the Royal Navy, quite a jump for an acting Sub Lieutenant and ex-Leading Seaman. He noticed there was no mention of Major Fox and his men. Maybe he was the sacrificial lamb whose trial would conceal the activities of Major Fox. Was it possible Major Fox was a party to this venture, or was he also captured and fighting for his life? It was all very confusing. Therefore, after refusing to sign the document, they beat him until unconscious before throwing him back in the cell.

Then Father Mathias nursed and prayed over him. 'My son you must be strong in the knowledge that our Lord, and the Holy Mary protects all who believe and are truly repentant of their sins. What we are going through is the path of a martyr. The Angels of the Lord will help us with the promise of life eternal to teach us the spirit of forgiveness. Do not hate your torturers, but smile, as they hate cheerful defiance. Hatred is the Devil's game; Our Lord taught us the importance of forgiveness. Understand we cannot win, however; your soul can defeat them. For after being tortured, you will sign a confession saying you are an enemy of the state. Then all they can do is to kill you so you are received into the loving arms of Our Lord.'

'Thank you Father for your kind words; I only wish I had half your faith to understand my frailties,' Jim replied as Mathias made the sign of the cross.

'Remember my son we are held behind stone walls with little light, while guarded by more people than we can ever hope to overwhelm. Only by showing compliance with their wishes can we live to fight another day. Anyway is death so terrible?'

'Father I'm much too young to die.'

'Then may God listen to your prayers and guide you to safety.'

The next morning everything changed as gentle questioning stopped and crude torture started. Again, Jim descended a long flight of stairs to an underground room where three men stood around a metal table. Here he was spreadeagled face down across the table with hands and legs tied tightly to stretch his naked body making breathing difficult. None of his torturers spoke while they beat his back with canes until they gradually cut deep into his skin. It was excruciatingly painful and as much as he tried not to, he cried out as his body trembled with every stroke. After about fifty strokes, for he was not counting, Jim lost consciousness. Then he was revived with a bucket of cold water and violent slaps in the face. As he slowly became conscious, he heard his torturers talking and laughing while his precious warm blood ran down his back. When they saw that he was awake they rubbed salt into his wounds making them burn while his body uncontrollably shook as each nerve screamed out.

'Stop you bastards. In the name of God, please stop.'

'Of course we will stop when you decide to cooperate. Just sign your confession and the pain will cease,' an inquisitor said softly.

'I prefer to die rather than give in to you swine.'

'That is such a pity. Nobody can survive torture when carefully and scientifically applied to cause as much pain as possible without killing the subject. What you decide to do is your choice, so if you want to be a hero, you will die. I can promise you the pain will continue until you give in or wish you had. Every man has a breaking point and in the end always does exactly as I want. Remember I am a very patient man, and you unfortunately have nowhere to go. Your life, soul, and body are mine to do with as I please. For your information, I have only just started to use my skills on you and know many ways to make even the bravest man beg for mercy.'

Then they rubbed concentrated iodine on his open wounds as the inquisitor commented, 'It may hurt, but iodine stops the cuts festering and getting infected by gangrene. It is important you do not die too soon to deprive us of the pleasure of hurting you again tomorrow.'

Jim thought of all the grime around letting gangrene enter his body that could infect his body. The thought made him shudder, as his bonds were undone before returning to the cell. Again, Father Mathias washed Jim's face before gently feeding him like a baby, with soup and bread. If Father Mathias had not been there, Jim would have curled up and died. The priest's beliefs helped Jim endure the pain a bit longer and maybe things would get better.

The second day was like the first with more caning and salt pressed into the ever-deepening wounds. This time the torture only lasted less than an hour before the pain was so intense it made Jim unconscious.

On the third day, Jim was physically and mentally exhausted. The torturers continued saying nothing while they set about destroying what was left of Jim's body. Now they changed tactics by grabbing his hair to immerse his head into a deep metal bath of icy cold water. He struggled to hold his breath as strong hands held him under while punching his chest. They laughed, as they pulled him out half dead and no longer resisting but gasping for air. The second time around they held his head under water for over four minutes, so when pulled out his lungs felt like exploding as he struggled for air. After a third immersion, he screamed with pain too weak to resist. Nothing made sense other than getting some sleep and not getting hurt. Why should he die for nothing in a place where nobody knew who he was or cared about him?

Then the Chief Inquisitor seductively advised. 'Captain Hands, please stop making us hurt you. We are not animals but only serve our nation. Please be sensible and sign the confession then I promise you there will be no more pain.'

Jim nodded not wanting to fight anymore. Therefore, he was dried and dressed in clean clothes before they gave him a pen to sign the confession. Without hesitation, he signed the damn document, no longer caring whether he lived or died. In fact, death was preferable to life in this hellhole. Maybe Father Mathias was correct and God would deliver them like Daniel from this lion's den.

The Inquisitor smiled at seeing Jim's signature before ordering the guards to take him away. He went to a newer cell, had a shower, and received medical attention. Afterwards, he had a substantial meal and a bad haircut. In the following days, he regained his strength to show few signs of his ordeal. Alone, he prayed for his spiritual mentor Father Mathias. Then the games started at a different, more sinister level. They took him to a courtroom where in one corner stood four badly beaten men looking very afraid - they were Major Fox, Alexis, Andreas, and Tomas, but no sign of either Demokritos or Apollon.

'Captain Hands has confessed to his part in the British Naval actions in Albanian waters to await sentence. He has been very cooperative telling us everything we needed to know,' a uniformed man stated before reading Jim's confession.

The four captives watched in horror with eyes wide open full of contempt. Maybe they thought Jim had betrayed them.

'Now all you have to do Captain Hands is to identify these men as the British agents you brought to attack our Republic,' the man continued in a manner suggesting Jim would do just that.

'I am very sorry Commissar, but I have never seen them before. As you know, from the confession you made me sign; I'm just a sailor who survived a battle off your shores,' Jim said loudly for all to hear. Before he said any more, the guards beat him until his wounds reopened letting his blood seep through his shirt for his friends to see. Then they knew Jim was also a prisoner.

'I must ask you again to consider your fate before answering my reasonable question. Captain Hands, do you recognise these men as the agents you brought to Albania to commit acts of war against this peace-loving nation?'

'I am sad to say honourable Commissar; I don't recognise any of them. They are all too short, dirty, unshaven, and swarthy like Greeks and Albanians. It is true as God is my witness,' Jim blasphemed hoping to help his friends.

He knew he was undone when out from the darkness appeared Apollon, who was not only the traitor, but also the main witness for the prosecution.

'Commissar General, Captain Hands knows them. They work for British intelligence to reinforce the fascist terrorists in the southern part of our great nation. The People demand that they all die,' stated Apollon the traitor.

'This court recognises Apollon Hoxha the nephew of our beloved leader Enver Hoxha. We will consider his comments when we do our duty for the State and the People. Now the court is dismissed, and the prisoners will be returned to the care of their interrogators,' the Commissar General stated while rising from his chair to leave the room.

All Jim could do was to pray for his friends who faced a future of pain and suffering.

Next day Jim received clean clothing, his back bandaged by a doctor and given a decent meal of ham, tomatoes, and an egg together with a cup of sweet tea. Then he was paraded before a room full of international newspaper men who were carefully selected for their socialistic sympathies. He stood, half blinded by the flash bulbs exploding near his face while photographed him alongside his confession that was projected onto the nearby white wall. The reporters asked their questions in Albanian, which the Commissar General answered. The only words Jim understood were those said in English such as 'British Gangster' and 'Enemy of the People'. Maybe someone would see his photograph, but he knew Jan would do nothing either because ordered to stay silent, or because he did not care! What a slime ball. Well, he was just an uneducated rating of no importance to anybody, especially to an officer and a gentleman, like Jan.

After this propaganda stunt, they placed Jim in a new cell with Father Mathias, who had wisely denounced his Church. When the guards left and the iron door closed, the two hugged each other glad to be alive, knowing that God had not abandoned them. As Father Mathias said, 'God acted in unusual ways through any manner of people, so they should always love and forgive everyone whether friend or foe.' He added with a beautiful smile on his scarred face that, even in Albania many knew in their heart that God lives to save the true believer. Jim did not know why, but he believed Mathias' good words.

11. Carl to the Rescue

Sweetly above the sunny wold
The bells of churches rang;
The sheep-bells clinked within the fold,
And the larks went up and sang;
Sang for the setting free of men
From devils that destroyed;
The lark, the robin, and the wren,
They joyed and over-joyed.

The Hounds of Hell in *The Collected Poems of John Masefield* (1923): Heinemann, London.

After the Snow Goose II crawled into Corfu, Mario took Klaus to a hospital while Jan ordered the shipyard to repair the ship before sailing to Malta. When Jan asked the Foreign Office to help Jim, they replied he should stop being childish and accept that Jim was another casualty of war, an expendable pawn in the great game. He, of course, did exactly as he told.

It took two days to cover the holes in the hull to make her watertight and repair the damaged wheelhouse. Someone desperate to hide what happened in Albania sent British sailors to make sure Jan carried out his orders. This was necessary because Klaus was ill and Mario stayed by his side while refusing to abandon Jim without some gesture of support. It was the end of a friendship. An angry Mario told Jan that Snow Goose II was Jim's ship and registered as such. Therefore, if he sailed her from Corfu, he was a pirate and should rename her The Ship that died of Shame. This comment haunted Jan so much that on arriving in Malta, he resigned from MI 6. Some said he started drinking heavily and joined the French Foreign Legion to die fighting at a place called Diem Biem Phu in French Indo-China.

Unknown to Jan, Klaus when recovering in the hospital contacted Carl to tell him what had happened. Klaus was a man who said little but was always reliable, gave good advice and above all was trustworthy whilst expecting loyalty in return. The message took two days to reach Carl, who was in the mountains of northern Greece hunting communists and only twenty miles from the Albanian border. On hearing of Jim's betrayal, he hit a table with anger vowing that his enemies would never win, while remembering how he felt something was wrong with the Albania mission. Without thinking about what he was getting into, Carl asked Janus if Christos would go with him to Albania to try to rescue Jim. Janus was unhappy with the risks involved, warning Carl it would be nearly impossible, but he would help in any way he could. Within hours, Christos supplied Carl with the names of Albanians, who could prove helpful. Therefore, two days later, Carl had assembled a small army while waiting to hear from his many contacts where they imprisoned Jim before deciding how to free him.

This turned out to be quite simple when Ente, an old friend, sent him a newspaper containing a picture of Jim. Carl knew Ente, who fought for Germany, until changing sides at the end of the war to become a Commissar in the Albanian State Police while remaining pro-western. The commissar Ente promised that he would move Jim to a less secure prison at Korça from where the rescue would be easier. As he had always been, he was as good as his word. Therefore, without warning, the Albanian authorities moved Jim and Father Mathias after Commissar Ente circulated a rumour of an imminent attack by British Commandos on Memaliaj to release Jim. When they arrived at the prison in Korça, they ate a good meal served with warm thick Turkish coffee. Even more unexpectedly, they found themselves in a pleasant room with a large barred window overlooking out some fields and to a lake. That night they slept soundly, grateful for some peace and quiet in the surprisingly good surroundings.

Carl planned to cross the border east of Korça with ten men wearing some quickly obtained Albanian soldiers' uniforms. Every detail was correct down to the latest documentation; new Yugoslav made weapons together with maps of the area and the town. His plan depended on surprise and on not meeting any real Albanian soldiers. The problem was only two of his men spoke Albanian-Tosk and a third Albanian-Greek, so any long conversation could expose them as impostors. Before departing, Carl made Janus swear not to let anyone, especially the British, know anything about his mission. If they persisted in knowing more Janus should tell them, he was in the mountains fighting for his life with a serious case of pneumonia and not expected to live. Janus shook his head angrily saying such comments were too close to the mark to be a joke. Carl laughed then slapped his friend on the back before leaving for a strange country to save a friend.

The journey was not difficult as there was little difference between the harsh landscape of northern Greece and southern Albania. Even the people wore similar peasant clothes, and during the day worked in the fields or tended their flocks. The lucky few stayed indoors baking bread, working as blacksmiths or selling supplies. At the border, they all changed into Albanian military uniforms before Christos guided them down a small narrow path and through an unmarked minefield to Albania. This was the dangerous part. Carefully, they placed each foot on the ground where the grass was flat suggesting the path was safe. One mistake would not only blow the unfortunate man to pieces, but the noise of the explosion could compromise the whole operation. Therefore, they crossed the minefields one at a time, keeping ten feet apart. Once safe in Albania they moved fast, only pausing while Carl made certain no one had seen or followed them. After two hours, they sat down at the side of the road to Korça to rest, drink water, and brush the dust off their boots. Then just as Commissar Ente had promised Carl, they found an abandoned, dark-green lorry with the keys gently swinging in the ignition, a tank full of petrol and a note saying in English – Good Luck Old Friend.

Carl needed time to collect his thoughts so he lit a cigarette to enjoy the taste of nicotine and helping him concentrate on the task ahead before noticing a map on the passenger seat. It was a reminder, that there was little time to waste so he ordered everyone onto the lorry while he read the map. On the map, marked in red ink were the back roads into Korça as well as the prison holding Jim and the numbers 2. 22. 25. This puzzled Carl until he remembered an old German soldier's code where two was the second event to occur at 22 hours or 10.25 pm. It was the time when the guard changed. This suggested that the best time to attack was just before 10. Trusting his Albanian friend, he decided to attack at that time.

They waited by the side of the road until 9.15 pm, before slowly driving into Korça. On entering the town, they found it cloaked in darkness that was only broken by the occasional light from a window or an ancient street lamp. It was very quiet with a few people walking about carrying goods and old men passing the evening in street cafes drinking and smoking as they had always done. Now and then, they passed women dressed in black and a few police officers casually walking around with their hands in their pockets. Korça was a town where everyone went to sleep at sunset to rest after a hard day's work, as was the way villagers have lived since time immemorial. The difference was that in Albania, everyone worked on state collective farms under the supervision of the political officers. These officials severely punished anyone who arrived late for work, so the wise slept early to be up with the sun.

Before 10 pm, Commissar Ente entered Jim's cell to give them the following information: 'If you want to live you must listen carefully and trust me. Your friend Carl is coming tonight to rescue you. So you must do exactly as I say.'

'Thank you, but what next? Jim replied very confused.

'Don't ask questions and be very quiet. If we succeed, you will be free. If we fail, you have lost nothing, and I will be dead,' Ente warned the duo.

'Please tell us what do we do?'

'Five minutes after I leave you must walk down the corridor to the front door and go outside where you will be met. Remember, you must give me time to remove any obstacles,' the Commissar ordered.

Jim thought that if things went wrong Ente had the most to lose, unless the Commissar was leading them into a trap. He looked at Father Mathias, who smiled and crossed himself saying. 'Let's see what happens. Maybe he's an angel sent by God to lead us out of this hell.'

 Let's hope so.'

They did not care if he was the Devil himself as any chance of escape was one more than they had a few moments ago. Five minutes later, Jim gathered up the courage to open the metal door and look out. The corridor was completely empty, indeed as quiet as a graveyard, and equally as spooky. Then they crept forward along the narrow corridor aware of the slightest noise as even their footsteps sounded frighteningly loud. As they reached the end of the corridor, Jim saw twenty feet ahead Commissar Ente shoot a guard in the back of the head before dragging the body away. He then went to the front door to ask another guard for a cigarette. While the guard was getting his cigarettes out of his tunic, Ente stabbed him in the throat before signalling the duo to follow. Very bewildered, they opened the door to leave the prison as fast as possible. Once outside, the soldiers pushed them into a lorry while Commissar Ente set a time bomb by the door before joining them.

'We have ten minutes before the building explodes and maybe an hour before they start searching for you. So leave me tied up and unconscious by the road,' Ente said in excellent English. He was going to remain to continue his one-man war against the communists. A police officer found Ente tied up so the commissar was eventually awarded a medal for his role in fighting the invading fascist forces!

The lorry raced down empty streets and along a dirt road in the direction of the border. A familiar voice whispered, 'Relax knowing you are safe.' Jim at once recognised Carl's distinctive voice. After an hour, they abandoned the lorry to walk as fast as they could through miles of narrow, winding paths. They stopped only once to hide among shrubs when a spotter aircraft flew low overhead and failing to see them, continued eastwards towards the sea. Then Jim noticed Carl resplendent in his new uniform smiling at him.

'Jim it is good to see you again, but you're so terribly forgetful. I warned you never to trust everyone all the time and not any of the bad ones.'

'Yes, you did Carl. The only problem was finding out just who was good and who was bad,' Jim replied with tears in his eyes.

'That is a very common problem that does not get any better with experience. Are you seriously hurt, or can you walk a few more miles without being carried?'

'We'll walk any distance far away from what we are leaving behind us.'

'Good man. It may be painful, but we must travel as fast as we can. I expect the Albanians will come looking for us.'

Carl laughed as they walked like old friends on the way to freedom following the intrepid Christos. Everything should have remained simple, but like in the old saying, even the best-made plans of mice and men sometimes fail. Not far from the border, three Albanian guards suddenly appeared with rifles at the ready yelling for them stop. They did while the guards asked what they were doing so near the border, especially during a general alert ordering everyone to find and destroy some rebels escaping from Korça.

Carl's Albanian speakers said they were escorting two agents across the border to report on the enemy inside Greece. Everything was going well with laughter until a border guard noticed Father Mathias was bleeding from his bandages. So raising his rifle, he demanded to know why they were not taking the injured man to the nearby First Aid Post. In seconds, they killed the guards leaving the bodies in a ditch covered with leaves. It was not a very good camouflage but would be effective from the air until a stray dog found them. Now they had to move fast before someone found the bodies or a team came to see why the border guards had not returned. Knowing this they raced onwards with Jim carrying Father Mathias on his back.

Fifteen minutes later, they crossed into Greece closely pursued by twenty Albanian troops that suddenly appeared from nowhere and who were gaining on them. About half a mile inside Greece, a steep rock wall with steps blocked the way. It was so narrow that, they climbed the rock face in single file, while the others anxiously waited for their turn with rifles at the ready. Jim went first carrying Father Mathias over his shoulder closely followed by Carl. Before the last man reached the top, the enemies were so close Jim could see the whites of their eyes. He wondered why Carl had stopped. It was so unlike him to take any uncalculated risk when retreat was the safest option. Therefore, Jim sat Father Mathias safely behind some rocks before aiming his rifle at the head of the nearest Albanian soldier.

When he was about to fire, he heard a voice say, 'Do nothing my friend, just wait, and see.' Jim turned his head to see Demokritos, Tomas, and the others had set up an ambush for the pursuers to walk into. When he dropped his hand, a devastating hail of bullets rained down to cut the enemy to pieces. Suddenly, the firing stopped; so the Greeks checked that all the Albanians were dead, removed their guns and boots before throwing the bodies onto the mines to be blown to smithereens. It was not pleasant, but war never is, and the explosions removed all the evidence of a battle.

That night they camped with Demokritos who explained how his men tried to save Major Fox's team from execution in a hidden valley used on such occasions. Alas, when they arrived, they found the prisoners lined up with hands tied behind their backs in front of a deep ditch. Before they could act, the executioner shot Major Fox in the back of the neck and pushed his body into the ditch. Filled with anger, they attacked killing all the Albanians but sadly only rescuing Andreas and Tomas as Alexis died next to Major Fox. Knowing time that was against them, they drove as fast as they could to the border before crossing on foot. They stopped above the rocky steps to rest and looking around saw Christos and Carl chased by Albanians. Then they set the trap.

Jim explained how Apollon captured him on the beach. Demokritos smiled adding Apollon led the Albanians to their hideaway but during the fighting, he escaped. Meanwhile, Tomas took Father Mathias to a hospital where he fully recovered and later rejoined his church. That night they sat around a fire to drink to departed friends and discuss who other than Apollon was behind the Albanian fiasco. They decided the Albanians expected Major Fox's group to arrive and used them to identify and locate local resistance groups. Therefore, the British Foreign Office was to blame, especially the office of Kim Philby, while Jan was only guilty of being untrustworthy when it mattered. However, they agreed no one wanted to work with Jan again, and that they would not inform the British Embassy in Athens or the Foreign Office about what happened. A traitor in high places was someone it was wise to fear. Carl explained to Jim how he sent messages to Churchill during the war. It was a strange way of operating, but it worked. When the Third Reich was collapsing, Carl asked Churchill to help him escape from Alderney. The rest, he said with a smile, Jim already knew.

12. To Save a Crown

Most crowns represent the rule of law and are protected from misuse by the greedy, the arrogant and tyrants.

It took two weeks for Jim's wounds to heal though they left two white large scars on his back. Feeling better Jim travelled south while Carl collected Klaus and Mario from Corfu to meet at a British base before flying to Malta. In Valetta harbour, they collected Snow Goose II while Carl visited the naval commander to get money and equipment. Jim was pleased to find Snow Goose II immaculately repaired and looking as good as new. He found out this was because some naval hotshot wanted her for his private yacht. Fortunately, someone ordered the Commander RN Malta to return her to Jim as well as to replenish her supplies. The orders were marked Most Secret so no questions asked or reasons given. The orders came from a politician who stated Jim was working under his orders. This was a surprise as the newly installed Labour Government wanted nothing to do with Greece. Jim saw that the signature on the orders was one word – Winston. Jim smiled knowing Carl's friend Winston Churchill remained loyal even when no longer Prime Minister.

Now Jim lived aboard Snow Goose II with Klaus and Mario. They went on long walks, and Jim had daily physiotherapy. The athletic Mario spent hours in church, sitting on the sea wall meditating or teaching Klaus to catch and cook fish. Sometimes on Sunday, Jim went with Mario to Mass to take the Sacrament; he even went to confession probably giving the confessor nightmares. The good priest said nothing other than giving Jim absolution. It has been so long since Jim's last confession that afterwards he felt like a big load was lifted off his shoulders making him clean. Mario said it was because Malta was the holy island where the shipwrecked St Peter stayed making it ideal to regain one's soul. He likened their problems to carrying the Cross for Jesus, or early Christians fighting against the heathen hordes in the Holy Lands.

After two weeks of idleness, Jim became restless thinking life was passing him by for no reason other than apathy. Therefore, he persuaded Klaus and Mario to sail around the island telling Carl they would be gone for a few weeks. They visited some of the beautiful bays on the coast of Malta and the island of Gozo where they visited the prehistoric Ggantija temples built around 3500 BC. Each day they sailed for an hour before anchoring then swimming ashore totally ignoring man-eating sharks or other dangers. Jim just needed to feel alive and wash away all the mental slime the Albanian experience left. All three were happy in each others' company laughing and dining like landed gentry. Well, Klaus was an aristocrat with a classical education, and Mario was upper class or Mafioso. Both had a fine palate, so they dined at the best restaurants serving every kind of food varying from Greek, Italian and Spanish food to British fish and chips. When they returned to Valetta, they visited the Tarxien temples discovered by a farmer in 1914 when ploughing a field. They are simple stone structures built around 3000 BC that revealed how great the ancient Maltese civilisation had been. No one knows who built the temples, but they probably were the people who built the Phoenician City of Carthage in North Africa. Some say Maltese originates from Carthaginian or an older forgotten language. The temple guide said it was a special site indeed miraculous because when Valetta was bombed, no monument was damaged!

Carl returned with three Greek sailors Dorus, Georgias, and Jonas, who had finished their training as frogmen. Carl informed them that they would sail to Piraeus to meet Christos, Janus, and Maria for the next job. At last, their holiday was over as they happily left Valetta with the sails down and the motors running at the maximum speed. A herd of wild horses could not have held Jim back as he longed to hear Maria's lovely voice and for a short time feel alive in her company. He knew there was no time for romance, but it did not matter. Friendship was what he thought he needed, just a smile and the occasional hug would be enough.

'Gentlemen we have been informed that some of the missing Greek Crown jewels are to be auctioned in Piraeus. All such sales are advertised in so-called art magazines, and we believe a rich American oil magnet is sending his man to purchase the stolen goods. As you know, some Crown jewels went with the exiled Royal family to Cairo, while the Germans captured the rest. Rumour has it that during their retreat, they were hidden in northern Greece or broken up for their gold and jewels. Our mission is to recover the items and capture the seller to discover what he knows about the whereabouts of the rest of the treasure,' Carl informed them. Jim smiled at the thought of going to an auction of antiques where they would use brute force instead of money.

After docking in the yacht harbour in Piraeus, they met Janus and Christos with the delectable Maria. For the first ten minutes, everyone greeted each other with the usual hugs and kisses before settling down to business. Now they were getting a bit crowded but happy to be reunited. It soon became obvious that Maria Makropoulos was again back in the game, as she pointed to a map of western Piraeus and explained her plans.

'I've marked on the map the warehouse outside the docks where local boats trade without going through customs. My informant says this is where Mr. Kristopolous stores his stolen artefacts to sell to the highest bidder. Officially, he is an exporter of Modern Greek art and copies of ancient masterpieces that unfortunately are too often actual treasures stolen from our historical buildings. He advertises the items for auction worldwide through the usual channels for buyers who were happy to operate in this illicit trade. Two days from now, he will auction the Ancient items. There are some gold statues and a copy of a Greek Crown studded with rubies and diamonds. The latter is what we are after, though it is not ancient, it represents the Monarchy and will support the King in the eyes of our people. If we can't obtain it, the crown must be destroyed and not allowed to fall into the hands of the communists or their supporters,' Maria firmly informed them. Then she added 'Mr. Kristopolous is a powerful criminal with contacts in Italy, USA, and the Far East whose armed thugs guard the warehouse and the surrounding area. There is a narrow channel to the sea through which certain people can travel undetected, it connects the pre-war warehouse to the sea. Indeed, it is ideal for running a business that relies on secrecy. All payments are in cash, usually US dollars, diamonds, or gold under the terms of what the British call buyer beware. That is, if you bid for an item and win, you must pay up immediately and accept it in the condition you find it. No criticism is accepted and failure to pay up can have fatal consequences. This warehouse is where the biggest criminals trade in contraband varying from antiques, opium, penicillin, stolen goods and even people. So do not feel any one of them deserves mercy, they do not.'

'I have suggested to Maria that we should try a three-pronged approach, Maria will attend the auction as an international art buyer accompanied by Christos carrying a substantial amount of US dollars. She has already contacted Mr. Kristopolous to obtain the required invitation using the name of Mrs. Ignosis and companion staying at the nearby Grand Hotel. She will bid for some items while trying to identify the American buyer or his representatives. It will not be easy as the warehouse is poorly lit with only the items on sale illuminated,' Carl interrupted.

The Grand Hotel in post-war Piraeus was a well-run, cheap establishment where no one asked any questions. The old but pleasant looking building overlooking the harbour was where the wise guest slept with the door firmly bolted and a loaded revolver under the pillow.

'Jim and I will silently remove the men guarding the seaward side of the warehouse so that Dorus, Georgias, and Jonas can swim underwater to enter the building. When everyone is in place, Klaus, and Mario will sail Snow Goose II to the warehouse so as not to raise the alarm. Now comes the tricky part, we must wait unnoticed until the Crown appears for auction before we make a move. Remember if we cannot steal the Crown, we must destroy it, as maybe it is not too much of an exaggeration to say the future of Greek democracy is at stake. The signal for action will be when Maria bids a hundred thousand dollars to distract everybody, so they will not see us move into position. After the auctioneer restarts the bidding, the lights will go out, and we attack. Beware my friends this could be a bloody business, so we must make sure to kill only those who resist. Wherever possible, attack the guards from behind to render them unconscious by using pressure on their necks. Remember if you press too hard, they will die. Once we eliminate a guard, remove his gun then check if there are any more around and deal with them. To succeed we must leave the warehouse with the crown in less than ten minutes hopefully without casualties. If one of us is injured, we will carry him or her back to Snow Goose II so leaving no trace of our visit,' Carl ordered, knowing they would obey without question.

At 8 pm, Maria and Christos in smart black suits arrived at the warehouse, showed their invitation card, and searched before they were allowed to enter. Inside they saw rows of chairs facing an elevated dais with a lectern, and a felt covered table. On the walls were displayed the objects for sale, numbered as in the auctioneer's catalogue where descriptions were inaccurate. For example, in the catalogue a marble carving of a Greek warrior with a crown of laurel leaves became a copy of an ancient work when, in fact, it was the real thing stolen only days before from the temple at Delphi. Between the genuine pieces were many copies to test the buyers' expertise. Maria joined the others walking around the room to examine the goods for sale, closely followed by Christos carrying the bag of money. Everyone looked like a well-dressed Mafioso with bulging jackets that barely hid their pistols. After a while, Maria located the short obese Mr. Kristopolous standing with some of his men prepared for trouble as they watched their guests. She was delighted to note they were too busy screening the people to look down at the water-filled channel dividing the warehouse into two.

Meanwhile, Carl and Jim crept towards the two guards on the seaward of the warehouse closely watching girls in minuscule bikinis aboard a sailing boat to notice anything. Carl rendered them unconscious before dragging them into the bushes. On cue, the frogmen swam into the warehouse via the channel as Jim followed Carl through a door. By then the auction was in full swing with a lot of chatter and rapid bidding. When they sold an item, the next item took its place on the dais. Many of the poorer fakes had no bids so soon item 246 arrived to be announced as a copy of a Greek Crown and placed on the table for all to see. The auction opened with just one bid of the large sum of fifty thousand dollars from a small man wearing thick glasses with a strong Italian-American accent. No one else bid as though this was the agreed price and the transaction complete. Just before the auctioneer could raise his gavel to accept the bid, Maria yelled out. 'I bid one hundred thousand dollars for the so-called Crown. It will look pretty on my head, and I want it.'

Suddenly, the room became silent as everyone looked at the smartly dressed Maria.

'Madam, do you have the cash with you?' asked the auctioneer nervously.

'Yes I do and much more, in crisp new US dollars. If you do not believe me, come and look for yourself. I am too busy to waste my time lying as business women like me never play games when time is money and I really like money,' Maria answered angrily.

'I don't know what game you're playing Kristopolous but I'm going to buy the Crown whatever the cost. So auctioneer you must get back on your platform to carry on with the auction. Then we will see who has the most cash. I must obtain this crown or our lives will not be worth living,' demanded the short American desperately trying to control his anger.

An air of unexpected drama filled the auditorium as the visibly shaken auctioneer made his way back to his rostrum to restart the bidding. At that moment, all the lights went out plunging everyone into total darkness causing pandemonium as people groped in the dark for something to hold on to while torchlights searched to determine what was going on. The torches helped Carl's men to identify the guards for elimination. Christos kept the front door closed until Kristopolous' guards were unconscious, and their guns removed. Dorus surfaced from under the water-filled channel to pull a surprised guard from the auctioneer's platform down into the water until he passed out. At the same time, Georgias climbed onto the dais to put the Crown in a waterproof bag before disappearing into the water. Nearby, Jonas waited to provide cover in case anyone saw Dorus. He was not. In the confusion, no one heard anything while shouting and trying to escape as the criminals thought it was a police raid.

Then, as suddenly as they went out, the lights came back to reveal there was no sign of the Crown. A loud gasp resounded through the room as the bidders attempted to leave with their purchases being convinced Kristopolous had betrayed them. Then Kristopolous yelled for his men to find and kill the thieves but there was no response. It was total chaos but luckily with no gunfire or killing. Like a coward, Kristopolous tried to escape through the door to the waterfront only to run into Carl. The poor man sweated profusely and fearing for his life promised Carl riches beyond belief. Inside the small American with thick glasses was luckier escaping unharmed but was relieved of his briefcase full of cash by a menacing Christos.

On Snow Goose II, Carl questioned the blindfolded Kristopolous for over an hour only to be told that the Royal artefacts came from the mountains, but no one knew from where. The man was terrified of some rival or one of his enemies killing him. Maria said he knew no more and was only a dirty little dealer in stolen goods. Therefore, they left him in the warehouse tied to a chair with a placard around his neck stating he was a robber of Ancient Art. An hour the police released him in response to an anonymous phone call and discovered many treasures stolen from ancient monuments in Athens and Delphi. To their amazement, some were from the National Museum that had not yet been reported stolen, but they arrived too late to find the attackers. By then Snow Goose II was sailing to Skiathos with the Crown and enough dollars to fund the nationalists for years. Carl kept some for food and diesel fuel that in Greece was expensive, especially on the black market.

What happened to the Crown?

A few days later Janus and Jim dressed as peasants took the Crown to Athens hidden in a linen basket. On arrival, they ate at a street tavern waiting for the night before 'borrowing' two bicycles to go to the palace, climb the wall, and throw the well-wrapped crown directly at a half-asleep guard. They did not wait to see what happened but rapidly cycled away to abandon the borrowed machines near where they found them. Then they joined the queue of early morning passengers boarding the bus to the next car ferry to Skiathos. That morning a Royal Guard felt a heavy bag thrown from over the wall hit him. At first, he suspected it was a bomb and ran back to a safe distance while considering what to do. When the package did not explode, he called in a bomb disposal expert who disarmed the device with a hearty laugh as he took out a solid object carefully wrapped in layers of cloth. Then he lifted the object up to show it was the missing Royal Crown studded with diamonds worth a King's ransom.

In the following days, Athenians and most of Greece celebrated the return of the Crown spending hours discussing how it turned up after having been lost for years. Some said a German officer had returned it as penance, others the royalist resistance sent it, and the best-loved story was that an eagle carried it to the people of Athens as a present from the Ancient Gods who live on Mount Olympus. The one thing they all agreed on was that it was a good omen implying both the King and Democracy would return to rule their nation.

13. A Winter's Rest

It is best when we forget evil old tales and forgive all sins.

After the Snow Goose II returned to anchor in Koukounaries Bay, Carl purchased a large house on the southern peninsular overlooking the bay to be their home. Finding it proved easy, as the former owner, a Greek collaborator, had mysteriously disappeared. No one wanted to live there so the owner was eager to get rid of the house, especially when told the new owners would change its appearance. It was a time when the Civil War was calming down, and no one wanted any foreign presence to upset the apple cart. Therefore, like all good servants, Carl and his team waited quietly in the sun until called into action. There was no shortage of funds as they shared the money taken from the American between their group and a Maltese bank account in the name of Constable. Carl arranged everything in a week returning to tell them they could have a holiday. Klaus decided to return to Germany to see if any of his friends and family were alive. Mario wanted to return to Bari to build a small villa near his family and catch up with the latest developments in Italy. Carl then informed Jim they were going to stay on Jim's Black Island to see if it would make a good base. That was the first Jim knew of the idea, but the more he thought about it the better he liked it.

By now, the water was getting cold so swimming was not pleasant. Still Jim enjoyed walking across the island with Maria to visit churches and places of interest. Maria's grandmother always wore black with a scarf covering her grey hair when welcoming Jim as part of her family. One day when Maria had gone off with Carl to buy supplies, Jim went with Maria's grandmother to a ruined village. The old lady placed flowers by a row of graves, prayed and sat under an olive tree before telling Jim about Maria and her family.

During the German occupation Maria's father, Georgias Makropoulos settled the family in a remote village where he taught at the local school and guided the people. He was a tall man and the island's first graduate teacher. Whether he liked it or not people were always asking for advice on everything from whether they should sell a goat or get married. He considered it his duty to answer honestly, even regarding it as an honour. It made him proud that people respected his opinion and allowed him to stop them doing anything silly. One day the Germans demanded more goat meat from a nearby village that unwisely refused. They preferred to hide their animals in a mountain gorge. The Germans searched until they found the goats, which they killed and left without paying even one drachma. The villagers were so incensed they came to Georgias to ask him to see the German Commandant for compensation for their loss. It was unfair to ask a man from another village to do such a thing, but they did because they were too afraid to visit the Commandant. So unwisely, the good Georgias went to see the German leader in his command post in Skiathos town where after an hour talking about cooperation, the two men agreed that in future the islanders would sell their goats to the Germans at a fair price. Then the Commandant paid Georgias one hundred drachmas for the butchered goats settling the matter with a handshake. When Georgias took the money to the villagers, he was followed by Grivas, a German informer, who told the Commandant about who owned the goats and where Georgias lived. The Commandant was angry, as he did not like being asked to pay for the goats, especially by someone other than their owner and listed Georgias as a potential troublemaker. Therefore, the Commandant placed Georgias' name and house on the Gestapo's list of unwanted people. Even on normally peaceful Skiathos, the Commandant knew guerrilla fighters operated against them from Yugoslavia and northern parts of Greece. During this war, where the enemy wore no uniform, he considered the best way to suppress the guerrillas was to take severe reprisals against the surrounding villages. However, the communists established a base north on the mainland only rarely visiting the island.

On one fateful day, the communists used a captured German patrol boat to attack the German forces in Skiathos harbour. With the element of surprise on their side, fifteen communists captured the harbour killing the six men on duty before attacking the German headquarters. This was to prove more difficult as they had underestimated the German strength and tenacity. For three hours, the Germans fought the guerrillas killing most of them before recapturing the town and patrol boat. However, one communist escaped. Then for the next few days, the Germans searched until they found the man nursed by Maria's mother. She did not know the lad but like the good soul she was, she took care of him as if he was her own son. It was a fatal mistake.

On the day, Maria was visiting her grandmother in Koukounaries; the Germans arrived in the village. The collaborator Grivas led them directly to Georgias' house where they found the wounded man who they arrested and then interrogated. Without any discussion or warning, they systematically killed every living thing, man, woman, child and even their animals before setting fire to the buildings. When Maria returned all she found were burned buildings and the priest burying the villagers' bodies. The only survivors were Maria and two herdsmen that were in the hills with their goats. She was so horrified at what had happened that she could not cry but stood shaking as the rain started to fall. It was as if the heavens opened to wash away the blood and tears of her people, alas not the terrible memories. Even when the priest talked to Maria, she said nothing unaware of what was happening around her. Therefore, he took her to Koukounaries to stay with her grandmother.

Three days later, Maria celebrated her sixteenth birthday when she cried for the first time for her loss, slowly found her voice, and prayed for her family. From then onwards Maria helped alleviate the suffering of others while working to hasten the German withdrawal. She lost her childhood to live with her grief. Luckily, she hid her hatred of all Germans to show only her generosity and calmness that radiated from all she did. In time, the people in Koukounaries and indeed even all over Skiathos came to respect and love Maria Makropoulos.

After the Germans left, there came various political activists. The first to arrive were the communist partisans who took what they had previously failed to capture. The people would have accepted them if they had not foolishly ridiculed the priests and the Orthodox Church. Such tactics may have worked in the cities but never in a religious, hardworking community like Skiathos where life was simple. The people wanted to return to the old ways of a Christian Greece ruled for the good of the nation and not be part of a communist revolution. Finding the people unwilling to accept the importance of the Communist Manifesto, a few communists decided to use force to make them cooperate. They started by breaking down the old church doors, burning the bibles and hymn books before removing the sacred altarpiece. This stupidity so infuriated a normally placid community that they fought back with the only weapons they had, that included ancient shot guns, spades and pickaxes against the communist who desecrated their church. It was the last time the red flag flew over Skiathos and the first day of a new order. No one knew who fought on which side or how many died. However, the next day there were freshly dug graves in the cemetery while the people started to repair their beloved church. Within a week, the church looked like new with a coat of white paint. The sacred icons cleaned, and the cross back on a repaired altar table. It was Skiathos' declaration of their belief in God and their commitment to Mother Church. Then Maria and her friends established a local militia to protect the people and their religion against the ungodly. Within months, they contacted the nationalist forces on the mainland under Janus to ask for guns and guidance.

Against her grandmother's wishes, Maria led the Skiathos militia exchanging her pretty frocks for a khaki shirt and long trousers. However, on Sundays and Holy Days she wore the traditional dress to attend the church services before going with grandmother to lay flowers on the family grave.

Then grandmother said something that Jim would always remember. 'Maria hates everything that is German, their language, music, and behaviour, but she idolises Carl. She knows Carl is German because of his deep-blue eyes even though he pretends to be Dutch. It is good that Maria knows Carl, Klaus, Mario and you, as now she has friends to trust who may make her feel alive again.'

'She is the life and soul of our group. She enjoys life to the full,' Jim unwisely commented.

The old woman gave him a look that would freeze boiling water before saying. 'Maria is only like that when with Carl and you.'

Then she stared into Jim's eyes as if to warn him to treat her well or face her terrible wrath.

Before they left warm Koukounaries, Jim asked Maria if she would like to come with them to his island. He explained he had a bleak house on a remote island with only themselves and sheep for company. Her response was to kiss him firmly on the lips before telling everyone she was going to Scotland for a holiday to live among sheep and peat bogs. Carl remarked that away from this violent place Maria might fall in love with Jim. Jim blushed.

They sailed to Malta to leave the Snow Goose II before flying in an RAF Hastings to London and on to Prestwick Airport north of Glasgow. They arrived in a snowstorm and were forced to stay the night in a Prestwick hotel. Here they spent the evening sitting around a roaring fire to eat fine food and downing excellent whisky. On waking, they found thick snow covering the ground giving it the white appearance that was as enchanting as it was cold. After breakfast, they drove to Oban to board an ex-navy auxiliary motorised fishing boat named Snow Goose III, filled with all the provisions and hard to obtain luxuries they would need for the next few months! The boat was an ex-SOE vessel known as a Shetland Bus used to take miniature submarines and agents from the Shetland Islands to German Occupied Norway. Below decks were two

Perkins diesel engines, the radar screen and a transmitter/receiver radio with six bunks and a well-appointed galley. Though aging, she still sailed between the islands and carried them safely through the rough seas to Black Island.

14. Castle Hands of Black Island

*The consequences of war are destruction,
mutilation of the innocent, and bankruptcy of
all but the arms manufacturers and the looters.*

On arrival at Black Island, Jim was shocked to find two boats
moored at a new jetty beneath his enlarged house. Everywhere,
there were men busy extending the buildings to twice their
previous size to look modern and well maintained. It was
better than his old cold draughty home.

'Carl, do you know who has taken over my island?' Jim
yelled in near panic.

A smiling Carl appeared on deck with Maria in tow and
pointed to the jetty. 'It's a better place for a jetty than before,
and you needed more space,' Carl answered before adding.
'Sorry if I've upset you, but I thought it could be a bit crowded
with at least the three of us, and so I arranged with my friend
Fergus to have your house extended and repaired. Luckily,
he's a chief of the MacNeil Clan known as Fergus MacNeil,
who like Winston is an ardent painter.'

'I agree the house needed modernizing, but you could have
at least asked me first before invading my home,' Jim
commented before adding. 'One good thing is it will be
warmer, and the rain will not come in through the roof. It's a
bit of a shock but thank you for making the house more
comfortable.'

Then Jim noticed waiting on the jetty was a stocky middle-
aged man in a tweed jacket and kilt. He did not wear an
overcoat even though a freezing wind blew across the island
that would chill most men to the bone. Jim knew how hardy
the Scottish people were and how much they liked wearing
their thick woollen tartan kilts. Each clan had their own tartan

to say who they were, rather like a visiting card, but much more colourful.

'Welcome Carl, to the Castle Hands,' the man said with a smile large enough to warm the hearts of most men. 'And you must be Jim Hands. A little bird told me we met once before in Poole, and you are related to my friends the de Broyen family. By the way, I am the Chief of Clan MacNeil, who my friends call Fergus. Many Scotsmen deny our existence as a surviving branch of the once banned Royal House of Stuart. Therefore, we wear either the Royal Stuart or the Hunting Stuart tartan that anyone may wear because we no longer threaten the Crown. My castle is on the mainland north of Oban where I spend most of my time when not in London or travelling. That is enough about me so now let me show you around your new house.'

Fergus showed Jim the changes. Now the house had a huge sitting room looking out over the harbour. Next to this was a new kitchen and a large dining room with a smaller study. Upstairs were four bedrooms; each with their own bathroom fitted out in a manner fit for a king. Each room contained a new double bed with a thick sprung mattress, a large wardrobe and two chests of drawers, one with a mirror.

Later in the sitting room, Jim sat in a chair overcome with emotion wondering, 'Why should anyone do so much for an insignificant person like me'.

'I hope you like it. If so maybe we can use your castle as a base in addition to the one, we are building in Skiathos. Then we'll have somewhere to rest or heal our wounds,' Carl suggested.

'Carl, you know my house will always be your home. During the past year, we have become a close-knit family forged by fire and united in hope. Anyhow, you have made this house so big that if on my own, I might get lost in its vastness,' Jim quietly answered while trying to make light of all the changes.

That evening they were served a magnificent dinner at the large table by the two new caretakers. There was a thick warm Scottish soup, which Fergus called broth, followed by tender roast beef with horseradish sauce and French mustard, roast potatoes with carrots and beans. Afterwards, Fergus took them on a guided tour of the estate. The old outhouse was now a two bedroomed house near two newly built stone buildings. One room housed a diesel-electric generator while the other held a radio transmitter and the radar unit. So now it was a fully operational military headquarters safe away from the eyes of unwanted visitors. Inside the main house, they saw the newly decorated walls displayed large paintings of stags, mountains and glens, and Scottish people, including Bonnie Prince Charlie, and a stuffed stag's head above the fireplace. Thick velvet curtains reached down to the floor covered the windows to keep out any draught and provide an effective blackout. All the table and chairs were of mahogany, and the rest of the furniture consisted of upholstered sitting room sofas and armchairs. Everything was the best, including the cushions, linen, fine porcelain tableware, and cutlery. Jim noticed the dinning service was made by the de Broyen Boy in an Eagle Pottery in Stoke and on the wall was a shield with the de Broyen crest.

'I hope you don't mind Jim, but I thought it nice to remember a friend from the ancient de Broyen. As you know, the shield is that of the Norman knight, Guy de Broyen and the tableware made by his descendants,' Fergus added telling Jim, unofficially, he knew Jim's ancestry.

'Thank you Fergus, it's nice to remember lost friends,' Jim uttered bewildered at how much effort was made to make them feel at home among the things they recognised. Then he realised there were paintings of Skiathos harbour, Bari and a German warship called the *Kreuzer Koningsburg.* The influence of their leader was reflected by an oil painting of a Somerset fields signed simply WS.

After a good night's sleep, Jim awoke to the sound of a low-flying aircraft circling the house, trying to land on the lawn. As he watched it came lower, hovered for a second before the wheels touched the ground, bounced a few times, and stopped. Then the pilot's door opened, and out climbed Klaus in a leather flying jacket and helmet.

'Hello Klaus, did you have a good flight?' Carl yelled out.

Jim was astonished at just how much everything had changed in such a short time. They had everything the landed gentry and very rich dreamt of including a runway on the back lawn and an unusual red painted aircraft.

'It's good to see you. Europe is so mixed up it is nice to be away from the politics and free to speak my mind,' Klaus commented.

'That was a very interesting landing,' Jim joked.

'Jim, she flies like a bird and can land in half the distance on much poorer surfaces. She is strange looking, but reliable military transport developed for the American Air Force. This second-hand Canadian built Noorduym Norseman carries eight people at 150 mph. She's a useful aircraft in which to learn to fly and take us to the mainland quickly when duty calls,' Klaus said with pride.

Jim reflected that all they needed now was a visit from Mario and Mr. Constable to complete the family. It was a holiday with a difference as Klaus taught them to fly the Norseman until they took and passed their Private Pilots Licence (PPL) at Prestwick Airport. This involved navigation, engineering, and a flying test that included stalling the engine and recovering the aircraft before she plummeted into the ground. Maria proved to be a natural pilot, gently moving the aircraft to exactly where she wanted it, while Jim flew with jerking movements alarming even the normally unshakable Klaus. In the evenings, they learnt Greek from Maria while Jim taught radio transmission techniques and the Morse code. Within a month, they knew basic Greek. It was easy pronouncing A or α for Alpha and Ω or ω for Omega, but the others proved difficult. Jim tried but knew he would never master the intricacies of this ancient language.

In their spare time, Jim walked around the island holding Maria's hand while the others went fishing. All they wanted to do was spend the rest of their lives together, but knew they only had a few moments of tender loving to make memories no one could take away. To cut a long story short, they became ardent lovers relishing every moment together, even when walking in the frozen snow or watching the wonderful display of colours known as the Aurora Borealis or Northern Lights. Maria said they were safe, as long as they had their precious love to keep them warm.

Every evening they sat by the fire reading, playing cards, or just talking. They kept in touch with the latest developments by listening to the BBC on the radio or reading the newspapers Klaus brought from Prestwick. This told them that life in post-war Britain was as hard as it was in wartime, as American assistance had nearly stopped and most quality items manufactured in Britain were for export only. To make life more difficult, the winter was long and bitterly cold as even coal was rationed forcing people to search land where bombs had exploded for wood to burn. Now the relations between Britain and USA deteriorated by the latter demanding repayment of the war loans from a bankrupt Britain. They discussed the situation well into the small hours wondering whether President Truman had any idea how much hatred, his country's demands were generating. Many people expressed their anger by joining the minute British Communist Party and writing on walls and other surfaces slogans like 'Go Home Yank' or 'The Only Trouble with Yanks is they're Overpaid, Oversexed, and Over here'. Therefore, as poverty and hardship dug deeper into a starving and ruined Britain, the disillusioned left in their droves to emigrate to Australia, Canada, South Africa, and the USA. For some of the survivors of the war, the latest deprivations were the final straw that broke the camel's back!

The newspapers told of how another country had fallen to the communists or the problems of looking after so large an empire. In public, the British Government called for world peace while promising independence for all her colonies who wanted it. This was not a charitable gesture, but the acceptance that running them was too expensive and the sooner each territory could look after itself, the less it would cost Britain. It was sad that the government learnt little from the negotiations for Indian independence because of the inability of the last Viceroy of India, Lord Mountbatten to get the Muslim and

Hindu leaders to share power. Therefore, the sub-continent was divided along religious lines causing Hindus and Muslims to migrate from their homes to their new nations. Sadly, the authorities did not announce the demarcation lines until after Pakistan and India were independent. It was a recipe for disaster as thousands of frightened men, women, and children died trying to reach safety aboard overcrowded trains, attacked by crowds of bloodthirsty fanatics. The result was that, never again would Britain try to partition a nation on independence. It considered dividing the Sudan into a northern Muslim state and a southern Christian one, but after the chaos in India, decided against doing so. In a wave of rapid decolonization, some people held in prison awaiting trial for war crimes, became leaders of their independent nations. Jim could not believe it when he heard that the once pro-Japanese General Aung San was now head of a new Burma, while Britain abandoned those Burmese tribes that fought for her. The effect was a long civil war that lasted for over sixty years.

Jim summed up their feelings by saying. 'Sadly when the fighting was over, our friends were forgotten, in order to placate our former enemies. I hate to know what would happen to Carl if certain people knew he was alive. Sometimes knowledge can be a dangerous thing and too much can be fatal.'

15. A Painter Visits Black Island

Painting is silent poetry, poetry is eloquent painting

Translated by Bernadotte Perrin (1912) from *Mestrius Plutarchus* (100AD) *Moralia in De Gloria Atheniensum.*

Slowly, the cold of winter gave way to the warmth of spring as they settled into a comfortable routine. Nothing changed from day to day except for the arrival of newspapers telling them how lucky they were to be on the island. Jim had never been happier than now, when walking with Maria through the grassland between the spring flowers making the land full of colour and life. When he summoned up enough courage to ask Maria to marry him, she gently refused his offer by saying people like them involved in war should not start a family. However, they remained lovers and from then onwards slept in the same bed. At first, Jim was needlessly embarrassed at what the others would think, but he should not have been because no one said anything.

After Klaus returned from a trip to Germany, an argument exploded between him and Carl.

'The Russians and the West are bitterly fighting over Berlin,' Klaus told them.

'Demolish all of it and remove all that Hitler and his people built,' Carl responded angrily.

'You must not say that. Berlin is part of our history going back long before the Nazis,' Klaus replied then taking a deep breath added. 'Carl I owe you my life and would gladly die for you. Can I forget the day you gave me a first class railway ticket to Madrid and enough money to reach safety in Britain? Even now, I do not know how you knew my mother was Jewish, and the Gestapo was coming to arrest me. However, I know without your timely intervention; I would have died in a concentration camp. It would not have mattered that I served Germany loyally, worked with you and Admiral Canaris diligently, and I hope with honesty. Carl, we need to build a Germany without racism inside a united Europe. Surely, the time has come to wash our nation clean of the blood of the innocent to build a democratic, free Germany?'

'Dear Klaus you have already said too much, but luckily among friends. What happened during those dark times must never occur again and whatever we think of Berlin, we will always be friends. You and I are carved from the same rock having lost our families and friends, and must create a new world. Unfortunately, still in Germany many influential people can identify me who deny they supported the Nazis. We both know many Germans who became rich and powerful by betraying others to die or survive in hell. If you wanted to remove a rival or take over his business, all you had to do was shout *Juden*, or get someone to do it for you. It is too early to forget the genocide Hitler caused, or that so few Nazis were tried for war crimes. Senior Nazis like Martin Bormann, Dr Josef Mengele, and Adolf Eichmann are at this moment free somewhere in South America building new fascist regimes. If the Russians or USA really wanted to capture them, all they have to do is follow their friends. We do not even know whether Hitler is dead or living with his friends after a few facial changes from a plastic surgeon. However, the war is over, and they survive because people choose to forget justice, thinking those who they tried at Nuremberg were the real causes of the war. We know many of those tried were just puppets left to answer for the sins of their leaders. For as long as any of the original Nazis live, we must survive as shadows of our former selves. Only by being strong and honest can the German people ever hope to have a democracy without fear,' Carl responded.

You could have heard a pin drop as everyone listened to every word in amazement while learning more about their friends. Carl realised they said things no one should know. So he thoughtfully added. 'Please forget what you've heard. Too many people think we died, and if they found out we are alive would try to kill us. We are like phantoms in the night that appear when needed and afterwards disappear without trace. You would be surprised the number of British and Americans who actively supported or worked for the Nazis. Some managed to serve both the Russians and Americans, and I believe many still do. The war was a time when industrialists and bankers made fortunes by supplying both sides. The Swedish sold 40 mm Bofors anti-aircraft guns to anybody with the cash, though mostly to the British. While the American chemical industry supplied Germany with the basic chemicals needed to produce the Zyklon B poison gas that the Nazis used in the gas chambers to murder Jews and too many others. The American Oil tycoon John Paul Getty was a friend and admirer of Hitler, who supplied Germany with over one million barrels of oil via Mexico and Russia. There were so many names listed in Admiral Canaris' secret dossiers, including British public figures such as the Mitford sisters and Sir Oswald Mosley. What shocked me most were the Jewish-run Swiss banks that stored the Nazi gold. I believe these bankers not only fund the Nazis in South America but also those in Germany and Austria. If someone published the files on them, many governments in Western Europe would shake in their shoes and even collapse. Imagine the next time you buy a bracelet that the gold could have come from the teeth of a murdered victim of the Nazis,' Carl remarked in a voice full of emotion.

'You're right Carl. We, who hated Hitler but loved our country, are self-imposed exiles who may never be free to walk down the streets of our youth, in case someone recognises us. It is our fault for not stopping the tyrant before he grew too strong. In the beginning, all I wanted was for Germany to regain her rightful position in the world and retake her lost territories. However, before I realised what was happening, we were fighting the British and French. Therefore, we have no one but ourselves to blame and must accept our punishment like men and not complain like children. Of course, we could do the famous Nazi trick and fake our death.

All we have to do is find a doppelgänger to murder and identified as us. To make it work we must undergo plastic surgery so that even our mothers would not recognise us,' Klaus commented.

'Klaus the more I know you the more interesting you become. For a fugitive, you suggest some very unusual ideas to send an unsuspecting double to a life of hell and certain death. The idea upsets my sensitive stomach as everybody, including the Americans, Russians, and the Nazis would hunt down the doppelgänger. In fact, he would have fewer chances of surviving than a snowball has in the fires of Hell,' Carl joked indicating the end of the discussion.

'Let's toast to all our departed loved ones and to friendship. May God preserve us through all the trials ahead, keep our enemies at bay, and receive our loved ones in Heaven,' Maria suggested.

Taking the hint, Jim rushed around handing out glasses of wine for them to drink the toast.

'To friends, honour, and departed loved ones. May God protect them in heaven and all of us on here on Earth.'

After downing their drinks, Carl and Klaus clicked their heels together before throwing their empty glasses into the fireplace. It was that ancient European ritual performed after a solemn toast, so no one else may ever drink again from the same glass.

It was in March 1946 when the spring crocuses were starting to bloom to cover the land with colour, when Klaus arrived from Prestwick bringing four visitors. First out of the plane was Mario waving, then came Fergus MacNeil in uniform, followed by a tall policeman and finally Mr. Constable in a thick overcoat and fur hat, otherwise known as Winston Churchill.

'Welcome dear friend,' Carl remarked shaking Winston by the hand.

'Glad to see you again Carl, you look younger every day and keeping our belief in freedom alive and kicking. Pity we cannot tell the world what you are doing, but if we did many people would not approve. It isn't exactly playing by the rules, but only fools play cricket against gangsters, cutthroats and tyrants,' Winston stated in his usual forthright manner.

For the rest of the day Carl, Fergus and Winston retired to the study to work in private. The police officer, Winston's bodyguard, said little as he checked inside the house and the surrounding area. He was very impressed with the early-warning radar and outside lights that would deter any but the most resilient assassin. Unfortunately, many existed as such work was highly paid. To make matters worse, Winston had many enemies at home and abroad because of his outspoken attacks on communism and his blind, unreciprocated defence of the USA and all things American. He could not help it because his American mother cared for him when his English father did not. Though he liked the USA, he no longer trusted her Presidents, whether it was the late Franklin Roosevelt or Harry Truman. Both were more concerned with stopping Britain from gaining territory from the war, rather than seeing how Russia had expanded her grip over Europe. In addition, he was concerned about the adverse effect on Britain of having to repay war loans at such a high rate of interest and over so long a time. Surely, you do not bleed your friend to death while your enemies prowl the world wanting revenge. However he felt that the huge US military presence in Europe and especially Germany halted the Soviet troops from moving westwards. Their presence in Berlin had prevented Russia from occupying all of it and stopped communism encroaching. Unfortunately they failed to support the Chinese Nationalist government that was rapidly being defeated by a Soviet supported Chinese Communist regime.

After dinner, Winston told them about his fears for the Free World, as he called it. The USA did not understand that Britain was their truest ally, who they should nurture and not let starve. He surprised everyone by saying if he was still in government, he would experience the same monetary problems as Mr. Attlee and the Labour Government. He added that, no nation could pay off all its debts after such a long war as Britain, and compete with nations using cheaper labour with American financial support. When Jim asked what was their role? Winston replied they were part of MI 6 but in effect, his private army. Their function was to protect his beloved Greece and her Ancient civilization from that scourge of all humankind, Joseph Stalin, and communism. The funding for their work came from special deposits secreted around the world for use when needed, without going through official channels and in any accountant's ledger. If someone discovered the funds, they would disband Carl's group. He believed if Greece was lost to the communists, then Italy would surely follow and maybe France. In both countries, there was enough support for socialism to let the communists gain power. This had to be prevented whatever the cost.

'What good can we do against so many?' Jim asked.

'You bring hope to the Greek people as well as others in the region. It may be a small comfort to you to know even Stalin is not openly supporting the communists; he leaves it up to the Yugoslavs. Stalin is a dangerous, Russian bear who crushes all who oppose him, but is also as crafty as a fox that does not want the world to know the agreement he made for Greece to be under British influence, is not honoured. Therefore, he uses Yugoslavia and Bulgaria to arm the communists throughout the Balkans. I hope we can save a few nations from the heavy Soviet yoke,' Winston commented while sipping his brandy and smoking another cigar.

Next morning the sky was clear making the scenery stunning, so Churchill and Carl sat outside by their easels to paint. Watching them, Jim realised how alike they were, and how much they trusted each other. They hardly uttered a word, lost in the art of catching the scene on canvas in their own manner before it was lost forever. They painted until late in the morning when they came in for brunch cooked by the jovial Mario.

Later, Winston informed them of his plans. 'Alas I must return tomorrow to the House of Commons. I spent last night writing a speech of international importance to warn of the dangers of a divided Europe. Today it is a dangerous place where the armies of the west and east face each other over a new frontier separating East and West Germany. Jim, what do you think of this?' He read from his notes. 'From Stettin in the Baltic to Trieste in the Adriatic, an Iron Curtain has descended across the continent.'

'Sir, except I'm not sure where Stettin is, I think you explain the situation remarkably well. From what I saw in Albania, life under a communist regime is hell. Unless the Americans wake up to the growing evils of communism, we are the only nation prepared to fight for the freedom of others, and we cannot afford to do that for much longer. In my opinion, war doesn't end with the ceasefire, but when everything and everyone can return to live a normal life free from fear.'

'Jim, I appreciate your excellent comments. By the way, Stettin is a port on the River Oder about 75 miles north of Berlin. It marks the beginning of the Soviet controlled region of what I call Occupied Europe. If I succeed in doing anything, I will teach Parliament a bit of geography. Indeed, I hope to encourage the Americans to fund some of our anti-communist projects,' Winston remarked with a grin.

'Do you have work for us or can we return to Greece to build a base in Skiathos?' Carl asked.

'The answer is yes to both, especially in view of the struggle for the port of Trieste between Italy and Yugoslavia that could affect Greece. It is time for you to return to Skiathos, build a base, and monitor the communists in the region. Keep a sharp lookout for any extremist fascists and German activists that may use the situation for their own ends. I sometimes fear the extreme anti-communists more than fear the communists. When can you be ready to return?'

'We'll go next week if that is what you want.'

'I want no more so-called accidents like what happened to Jim in Albania. Good men are difficult to find,' Winston added slapping Jim on the back while giving him a warm, fatherly smile.

'Did you find the traitors in the Foreign Office?' Jim asked.

'I'm told it was a young woman with socialist leanings, but I'm sure she was denounced to cover up for a senior person.

Sadly, I am not convinced of her guilt, as she did not know the details of the Albanian mission, which I think, was to capture Carl. It appears to me some of our older universities have raised a nest of communist vipers. A sad affair and one in which I am not proud. Still we have people working with the Americans to investigate the FO, especially the Albania centre. I do not expect anything, as many of them went to the same school or university as the people they are investigating. It is a typical British recipe for disaster.'

'May we have your personal assurance that all our missions will in the future, be approved by Fergus or yourself and no other?' Carl firmly requested.

'My dear Carl you can rest assured you need not attempt anything you think too risky. You will always get your missions directly from Fergus, who will set up secure offices in the Royal Navy base in Malta to prevent any repetition of Albania. Under different circumstances, Jim would get a medal, but it is impossible, as neither you nor the Admiral, sorry Carl, actually exist. Sadly, it is safer if it remains that way for the foreseeable future,' Winston informed them with a great grin.

'But surely our papers are in order, and we are recorded under our new names,' Jim asked alarmed that maybe he was as good as dead.

'You are both legally recorded as Carl van Stoff and James Hands. What I meant to say was we must avoid anyone looking too deeply into your past to cause difficulties. To make things more secure, you will be known as The Painters that I trust will confuse most people and reflects how Jim, Carl, Fergus and I first met,' the great man answered.

Just after sunrise, Klaus flew their guest back to Prestwick and one assumes on to London. Then the newly formed Painters started to pack for their return to Skiathos via Malta. Everyone was cheerful; they had at last met the great man and delighted Fergus was now their boss while they worked in Greece. Mario commented the Italian government might need their help to deal with a growing problem from some fascists and the communists. The latter had considerable support among the industrial workers and in the rural communities from Trieste through the Po Valley to Bari in the south. Mario explained the situation was similar to Greece where the Italian wartime anti-fascist forces consisted of both communists and democrats fought to run the nation. Sadly, in Greece, the extreme fascists were surfacing in the ranks of the anti-communist forces endangered everything by their violent behaviour.

It took a week to arrange for some of Fergus' men to look after Jim's house. On the last night, Jim walked around his fiefdom and realised how it had changed, and if he would return. As he stood looking up at the stars, Maria held his hand saying, God willing they would be back. Jim did not mind if they never returned as long as they were together in a safe place. For the first time in years, he had someone to love and to live for.

16. Department 6

When wanted War Criminals became respectable citizens simply by working for their former enemies to escape punishment.

Even before the last guns had ceased firing, some of the allies were busy recruiting German scientists and their inventions. They included Wernher Von Braun and colleagues together with their V2 missiles who were secretly sent to the USA along with many of the engines and blue prints. Likewise, under the cover of night, lorries full of documents and gold disappeared. Was this under the orders of a government or just a case of free enterprise? No one knows what happened except some of the Nazi gold that was not in Switzerland or South America, vanished without trace. It was a time when the victors took their unlawful spoils, and looting was more common than publicly acknowledged. If you were wanted for war crimes but useful to another nation, you could make a deal to work for them in exchange for a new identity. Perhaps this is why so many Nazis war criminals vanished to re-emerge in another country under a different name. In many cases, they used their skills in extracting information from the helpless captives of their new masters with maximum efficiency and without mercy. Soon former Nazi torturers worked for the secret police in South America and Europe. There are no accurate records of who took what from Germany, or how many war criminals joined secret organizations to further the cause of their employers. Even Hitler's Deputy Martin Bormann and Auschwitz's Angel of Death Dr Josef Mengele avoided capture to re-emerge under new identities in South America. It is estimated that over ten thousand Germans went to South America, mostly to Argentina through ODESSA or *organisation der ehemaliges SS-Anghorigen* (organization of former SS-members), and other groups. The Americans employed General Reinhard Gehlen and his wartime intelligence group for its extensive knowledge about Russia.

Just as the US troops were entering Germany, the American Office of Strategic Studies (OSS) decided to recruit secret operatives against any post-war threat from Russia or Britain. The logic was simple - who was better at finding a communist or a socialist than the Gestapo. Therefore, OSS Captain Paul Muller was appointed to interview German prisoners to select those inmates who were totally ruthless and desperate enough to avoid their past revealed by any tribunal. It was not a difficult task, especially after finding the first Gestapo *Sturmbannführer* (Major) pretending to be a cook. Sadly, when told to cook a meal he could not. It took Paul three days to break this former man of iron into confessing he never was a cook. This was confirmed when the Major was confronted with a picture of himself in full uniform. There followed the usual waiting game while *Sturmbannführer* Franz Leitz was left alone in the dark with only two meals a day of bread and water. Three weeks later, the former torturer begged to help the Americans locate other war criminals. Choosing his moment carefully, Paul informed Franz Leitz that if he joined a US led anti-communist guerrilla force; he and others of similar rank would receive new identities. Paul made it clear they would be paid mercenaries who could not expect the USA to rescue them if anything went wrong. However, it was their best chance of living, making good money and above all, destroying the hated communists wherever they lived. Then Paul Muller placed Leitz in an internment camp to recruit others for subversive and regime changing secret operations. Within a month, Paul Muller recruited twenty former Nazis for Department 6. He appointed the former Gestapo *Oberführer* (Brigadier-General) Hans Kruger, who he renamed Helmut Kratz, to lead the team operating in Greece and the Italian Giovanni Lucia to work in Italy. Each received a new identity and an American passport. The first priority was to make the Greek forces effective in eliminating all socialists. The OSS knew the communists were a tough breed that would not be easily defeated. Therefore, they supported extremist Greek army officers, some who had worked for Germany in the war, to instigate a reign of terror in central and northern Greece. Helmut Kratz and Albert Mann (formerly Franz Leitz) went to Greece to join an extreme right-wing group led by Captain Petros. They had access to hidden arms caches left behind by the Germans, as well as new supplies and enough money to buy most small nations. With their help, the extreme right-wing elements of EDES successfully fought the communists in the north. Their activity caused rumours to circulate about mutilated bodies found buried in shallow graves after Captain Petros' men left a village. If anyone had bothered to check, he would find the horrific trail of blood and destruction Petros' men left across the mountains. The effects were devastating as many formerly pro-government villagers fled in horror to swell the ranks of the communist forces. Suddenly, the numbers of communists increased and were supported by many Christians. Even some priests started to believe the communists would give the people a better future than the Government forces that rampaged through their lands.

In the American Military Attaché's office near the British Embassy in Athens, Paul Muller was satisfied his men were doing exactly what he wanted. When asked by the British or the Greeks about fascists again operating in Greece, he always laughed to say it was unlikely, since the demise of Germany and Italy. Secretly, he was happy to report to the OSS that they had eliminated three thousand socialists and the right wing, pro-American, elements were gaining the upper hand. He foresaw a time when the fascists would be strong enough to sit in the Greek Government. This was probably his only mistake, as he did not understand the beliefs of his Nazi employees. He was unaware of the growth of the neo-Nazi parties in the USA, South America, and Germany. Washington and the OSS now financed the very fascists whom so many Americans died trying to defeat. Former Nazis joined many South American armies, ran successful manufacturing industries while operating Swiss bank accounts. It was Bormann's plan that, if they lost the war, they would fund an economically powerful Germany that, together with her American capitalist allies would run the world. German factories produced tractors and trucks in remote areas of Paraguay and Argentina to establish new societies away from the public eye.

The devastation of mountain villages and mutilation of anyone with a socialist connection became too common. It would have gone undetected except for Captain Petros' over confidence. For months, they controlled everywhere they went always blaming reports of rape, torture and murder on the communists or moderate government forces led by Janus. Then they made one mistake too many when late one afternoon, they found a camp of Janus' EDES fighters outside a small mountain village. Luckily, Janus was away leaving Andreas in command. Andreas greeted the newcomers as friends to share their food and he discussed how to destroy nearby communist positions. Just before everyone turned in for the night, Helmut started to call Andreas and his men spineless, little cowards. The insults worked making their hosts angry, yelling back insults and drawing their knives. What they did not realise was the newcomers did not want just to argue, but to kill them. As they advanced with knives in hand, a hail of bullets cut them down. Within two minutes, most were dead and the four wounded including Andreas were taken to be interrogated by Helmut and his assistant Albert Mann. In the chaos, Demokritos escaped to make his way south to get help from Janus.

Throughout that night, the wounded screamed as Helmut set about inflicting as much pain on his victims as he could without actually killing them. He had done it so often he never thought about the moral or even the usefulness of his actions. Always, he started by stripping the victim naked, tying them to a chair with steel wire that cut into their wrists, before hitting the subject in the face. This usually caused the subject to cry out or bite his lips so hard he bit through them. Helmut liked the idea of his victim tasting his own blood in the full knowledge it was his life's essence draining from him. Both Helmut and Albert were without doubt hardened sadists living on the edge of insanity. When calm, they appeared quite normal, but when hurting a helpless person, they were depraved monsters.

'Just tell me where I can find Janus, so I can have a little talk with him. It is in your own interest to tell me what you know while you can still walk?' Helmut asked one of the victims.

There was no reply except a deep look of hatred, therefore, Helmut started whipped the victim's back with a steel whip until it bled profusely. Meanwhile, the man next to Andreas had his genitals beaten until screaming he fell unconscious. Helmut looked over at Albert Mann with a look questioning why he had to become violent so quickly. As far as Helmut was concerned a good interrogator, as he liked to call himself, only destroyed the subject's will to resist making him or her compliant to his requests. For he knew that the subject must be conscious subject to supply the information he desperately wanted. As long as Janus ran the largest government militia, he was a danger to Helmut, and Helmut did not like anyone or anything who threatened him. As a senior Gestapo officer, he was used to telling people what to do and never obeyed orders his inferiors. He would tolerate the arrogant Paul Muller until he was no longer useful. Then a little, easily arranged, accident would eliminate Paul Muller so that no one would even bother to investigate his demise. A third man was at first gently interrogated by Albert Mann to respond to his questions.

'Who is Janus? Does he live nearby?' Mann whispered gently in the victim's ear.

'He is the head of EDES in the central district and a Captain or Major,' the terrified man replied.

'Good that did not hurt?' Mann stated with a smile, reassuring his victim. He likened himself to a cobra gently hypnotizing his victims before making the strike to drive his deadly poisonous fangs deep into their flesh.

'No sir,' the man replied.

'Good man, now tell me, where is your supply base?' Mann insisted placing a surgical scalpel against the middle joint of the left little finger of his victim until he felt it.

'I don't know sir. None of us know,' the victim truthfully answered in terror as sweat ran down his forehead.

'Do you like having five fingers? If you want to keep them tell me where the supplies are?'

'As God is my witness, I don't know. I don't know,' he cried out as the blade removed the victim's little finger with surgical precision making him faint from the pain.

Now the tent was quiet as all the victims were unconscious and no longer useful. Therefore, the torturers went outside to get some fresh air, talk and smoke a cigarette or two.

'If we keep them alive for one more day, we will find Janus and his people. So they must spend the night in fearful anticipation of what new terrors the dawn will bring,' Helmut told Albert.

'Yes we can afford to take our time as nobody knows we're here.'

They did not know how wrong they were. Not far away, Demokritos was warning Janus of the attack by Captain Petros and his Germans. An angry Janus took less than an hour to assemble fifty men to attempt to save his men. On arriving, they found the bodies of their dead comrades. Then, in the distance, they heard the enemy snoring and guards casually chatting. Quietly, Janus' men crept forward to eliminate the guards without disturbing the owls hooting in the nearby trees. They then attacked the sleeping enemy from all sides, advancing like a slow killing machine. A few woke up in time to fire back, but in the confusion Captain Petros, Helmut and Albert escaped leaving their men behind to die in their place. They did not want anyone to find out who they were and why they were in Greece, especially the two Germans. Killing people was one thing they enjoyed, but being hurt was a different matter. In one tent, Janus found two men tied to a chair. Andreas was still alive, but the other man was dead. Janus rushed the three survivors to a nearby hospital before ordering a systematic search through the mountains for the enemy. At the abandoned camp, they found very little except for guns, maps and a camera, which they took to have the film developed. It could tell them who the killers were, as they certainly were not communists, and wore EDES uniforms.

The three fugitives travelled rapidly south taking sanctuary in a monastery, explaining they were hiding from the communists. The monks asked no questions, and they accepted them into their holy community. Strangely, during the night, the visitors disappeared as suddenly as they had come. The oldest monk said that, as much as he tried to feel kindness towards them, he could feel the evil flowing through their veins. Therefore, he led the monks in prayers to God and the Holy Mother in thanks for their deliverance from such people. Only then did they purify, with Holy Water and prayers everything their evil visitors touched.

In Athens, Paul learnt from the British Military Attaché how Greek government armies in the northern part of the central district had destroyed a German neo-Nazi group. For the next few days, he wondered what to do and waited to find out what the British knew about Department 6. Therefore, he continued to socialise with the British diplomats as if nothing was wrong while playing a game of deception. He always won at poker because his cheerful countenance and youthful looks hid his emotions. His great grandfather was a professional card sharp that worked the gambling tables on the Mississippi paddle boats, shooting anyone who got in his way or called him cheat. Within a few years working the tables, he accumulated enough money to buy and run his southern plantations where cotton, slaves, and the Ku Klux Klan was part of everyday life. Paul still owned the estates where he grew cotton. However, the slaves were now free though second-class citizens and forced to work on the plantation for a pittance. On the surface, his smooth, slow southern accent was seductive, making him very presentable, especially to some women. Early on in his career, he learnt that after a few drinks, he could get most diplomats or their wives to tell him everything. They willingly told him about the terrible tales of an extreme fascist group that tortured and killed villagers, including Greek government soldiers. The authorities were horrified because the torture used, looked like the work of the

Gestapo. Paul smiled to himself at the thought of how near to the truth they were but did not know it. All he could do was to wait until he found out who was dead, before sending in others from his base in Bari, Italy.

Within days, Paul received a message to go to Bari to visit another of his agents, Giovanni Lucia. He did not want to get involved so he asked who, if any, survived. He was pleasantly surprised to hear Captain Petros and his two Germans were alive and unharmed. Therefore, Paul gave them a month's holiday in Bari before returning to Greece. When he received a written report of what had happened, Paul was apprehensive because, they had taken the war from being against the communists to one that included all moderates and Greek government troops. He asked his controller in Washington for advice only to receive a cryptic message suggesting; the group must be operative within a month. They told him not to worry as both the British and Greek governments would never guess in a month of Sundays the identity of his men. A radio room of the British Embassy in Athens listened to everything Muller sent, so MI 6 intercepted all the messages between the OSS and Paul. They immediately informed Fergus MacNeil of the dangerous development and told him to keep the information under wraps. Fergus already knew about General Gehlen's organization in the OSS and the lack of worthwhile information reaching London.

The war was over and now the victors fought over the remains, with Britain always the loser. When he told Winston of the latest developments, his response was to go into an unusual rage. Now his love for America was diminishing, helped by their refusal to share their nuclear secrets with him. The importance of the nuclear bomb could not be ignored as it had ended the war against Japan after its use at Hiroshima and Nagasaki. It also caused the ambitious Stalin to be cautious when dealing with the USA. As usual, Britain circumvented the US restrictions by giving a job to her citizen, Klaus Fuchs, on the condition he brought with him the details of how to make the atomic bomb he helped build in America. Of course, he did just that. At about this time the USSR obtained the secrets of nuclear fission from other scientists working in the nuclear research facility. Within three years all three nations had built, tested and fitted to rockets and aircraft nuclear bombs. The nuclear arms race had begun.

A week later Brigadier Fergus MacNeil received the photographs from the film Janus found showing two Germans that Andreas identified as his torturers called Helmut and Alfred. Then one of Fergus' secretaries scanned through books full of pictures of former Gestapo officers to find both men in the file of the group who executed Admiral Canaris. The older one was *Oberführer* (Brigadier-General) Hans Kruger and the slightly younger man *Sturmbannführer* Franz Leitz; both were war criminals accused of torture and unlawful execution. Kruger was the more dangerous having personally executed Canaris while knowing the war was ending. It was rumoured Kruger worked for America to subvert communists and socialists in Europe. According to the British Military in Athens, he worked for the OSS under Captain Paul Muller, who was a US Military Attaché and a liaison officer with the Greek armed forces. The files said Muller was a graduate from a little known southern university. On his office wall, he hung the flag of the defeated Confederate States of America and sang Dixie in the shower. Fergus knew that given the opportunity, Captain Paul Muller would be a much easier nut to crack than *Oberführer* Hans Kruger and *Sturmbannführer* Franz Leitz. There remained one important question – should they tell Carl that *Oberführer* Hans Kruger was alive and terrorizing people in Greece. Maybe if Carl knew he would avenge his friend Admiral Canaris' death or hand his enemies over for others to deal with. After careful consideration, Fergus decided it was not time to tell Carl. He thought the Americans would remove the fascists from Greece before Janus found them. Fergus mistakenly thought it unlikely the two Germans, after their narrow escape, would return to Greece knowing Janus' men wanted revenge.

17. A Request from Father Mathias

So nigh is grandeur to our dust,
So near to God is man,
When Duty whispers low, Thou must,
The youth replies, I can.

Ralph Waldo Emerson (1867): *Voluntaries no.3.*

They left the Norseman at Prestwick Airport before joining a regular RAF supply flight to Malta. Inside the RAF Hastings, it was so cold they wrapped up in woollen blankets trying to keep warm as the engines noisily droned away in their ears. The flight stopped in London and Gibraltar to refuel. One of the few good things was the RAF served a simple meal, which the staff reheated in a primitive electric cooker in the aircraft's galley. The meal included hot soup and regular cups of hot, strong, coffee. The landing in Gibraltar proved exciting because the aircraft approached flying just above the waves to land on a short runway below the Rock. The plane arrived at dusk, so they had to stay overnight in a small hotel and were awoken before dawn, to take off, just as the rising sun illuminated the runway. They were all in their seats with the aircraft engines loudly reverberating at full power ready to take off when the main door opened to let in a breathless Fergus. The door closed as the aircraft started to take off, making Fergus hurriedly move to sit next to Carl so completing their little army. In Malta, they collected Snow Goose II resplendent in a fresh coat of paint with new pale yellow sails. Inside, everything was overhauled and the wooden dinghy replaced by a rubber inflatable one. The housing over the Oerlikon looked like a normal aft storage area ready to fire. Otherwise, she felt like she had always been Jim's home from home. The shipwrights replaced all the damaged planks with bullet holes from the Albanian affair. They then removed the barnacles from the ship's bottom and given her a coat of antifouling paint. Fergus MacNeil joined the Painters for the voyage to Skiathos proving to be, unexpectedly, a fine sailor who willingly took his turn on watch and steered her to take the maximum advantage of the prevailing wind.

'You have sailed before. Was it a hobby or were you in the Navy?' Jim asked Fergus.

'Jim it's funny that you should ask. My grandfather taught me to sail in his yacht before I was ten. In those days, all Scotsmen living along the coast had to sail or know someone who did, because it was the only way on and off the islands. It was great fun during the summer spending many happy hours blown with the wind to explore new places. Of course, winter was a different kettle of fish. This was the season when the north wind blew causing the seas to form high waves that one had to enter head on otherwise risking capsizing. Sometimes it was so cold that ice formed on the rigging and in one's beard. It was very frightening when the wind gusted. I believe that we Scots invented whisky to keep body and soul alive through winter's freezing weather. To answer your question, I never was in the actual Navy but served in the marine commandos and SOE,' Fergus replied keeping the sails full, making the yacht cut through the waves much faster.

'Snow Goose II responds well to your handling to go as fast, if not faster than ever before.'

'Aye she's a good ship, especially as she's more of a motor vessel than a sailing boat. I like the way you modified her to keep the sea out and give her a more luxurious appearance. I doubt if anyone can recognise her from pictures of her former self.'

Jim felt flattered at the compliment. He felt privileged that Fergus was his commander. Maybe he would share the role with Carl. It did not matter as both got on well to form a happy team. Since Albania and Jan's strange behaviour, they had all been suspicious of each other. However, since their return to

Black Island, all doubts were gone, as they grew comfortable in each other's company.

'We'll anchor at Koukounaries near your villa. Then we must convert the villa into a base and safe sanctuary just in case you get unwanted visitors. Only when the structures are sound and solidly fortified, will it be worth placing suitable defensive systems. Carl chose the house well as it looks out over the sea with a good panoramic view from both the front and the back. The last thing we need are any blind spots,' Fergus announced rather like giving his SOE officers a lesson on base building.

Soon after arriving back, they started renovating the building using local builders and labourers as well as purchasing most of the materials nearby. This made them very popular as they were well paid when work was hard to find, and the local merchants were delighted to supply all they wanted in what was until then a fragile economy. First, they extended the building towards the sea to give unrestricted views of the area before building a small jetty for Snow Goose II. Then they reinforced the walls with rock and cement, and the cellar converted into five bedrooms. The work lasted three weeks before the workers started fitting heavy metal shutters to the windows, and a bulletproof steel lining to the insides of each door concealed under a coat of paint. It was strange how everything they needed was already waiting in Koukounaries or obtained from the mainland in only a few days. Even the radio sets and radar units were in crates, marked fragile, waiting in a warehouse near Skiathos harbour ready for use. With a wave of Fergus's magic wand, two RAF electronics engineers suddenly arrived in Skiathos on 'holiday' who volunteered to install the units. By then absolutely nothing surprised Jim, as Fergus appeared to have all the contacts needed to equip and maintain an entire regiment.

Within a month, a local gardener planted olive trees down to the sea, and a central lawn with concealed movement sensitive lights added the final touches. Then the outside walls received the traditional coat of white paint with blue highlights. All they needed was an aircraft that probably Carl or Klaus could get if they wanted. Fergus arranged all the supplies and munitions they would need for many months, if not years. Their hidden armoury contained portable weapons ranging from 2-inch mortars and Bren guns to small Italian Beretta automatic pistols. They also had some hand grenades and limpet mines along with six of the latest French designed sub-aqua diving suits and an air compressor to refill the cylinders. Jim used the sub-aqua to teach the others to work underwater, starting by teaching them to hold their breath for at least three minutes. In days, they could use their snorkels to swim near the surface as well as be comfortable breathing compressed air from a cylinder. One by one, they mastered the breathing apparatus well enough to dive in teams to the seabed and signal safely to each other while underwater. They always surfaced with a speared fish or an octopus to give any observers the impression of tourists exploring the pristine marine environment. The only danger they confronted was a curious shark that swam away when it saw Jim. Mario said the shark realised that the animal in front of him was uneatable. Everybody laughed at his joke, including the highly amused Jim. It soon was time for Fergus to return to Malta knowing the Painters were operational and ready for action when required. Indeed, it was time for him to consult with Winston about the latest developments within the region and their role in a politically changing scene.

One Sunday in Skiathos after church, Jim and Mario while walking with Maria and her grandmother, met a priest with long hair and smiling eyes.

'Jim, do you recognise me? I am Father Mathias. I come a long way to ask for your help.'

Jim on seeing his confessor hugged the priest closely and kissed him on the cheek, as is the custom. Only then did he introduce Father Mathias to Maria, her grandmother, and Mario before taking him with them back to Koukounaries. Throughout the journey, Father Mathias said nothing but sat still as if meditating or in prayer.

At the house, Mathias had a glass of water.

'Jim, I reluctantly left the safety of my monastery of Varlaam in Metéora to request your help as I can think of no one else to turn to. One of our holiest icons of the Blessed Mary is missing, and we believe is in the Villa Verde near Tríkala pending sale to an American with Mafioso connections. We fear that within a week this precious icon will go to Bari and flown to America. The icon is not only large and very beautiful, but it is above all an important spiritual link with the past that unites all Greek Orthodox Christians,' Father Mathias informed them.

'Father it is not the work of the Mafioso because they never steal from the church or deal in religious artifacts. It is part of their ancient creed whose breach has been always punishable by death,' Mario responded.

'What you say is true, but alas even in the most religious families one finds a Judas. It is our fault for taking her from the safety of our monastery to show the faithful in our church in Kalabaka. It was after the night service that six armed men overpowered the guard to steal our holy icon from the altar. We believe an art collector commissioned the theft, or they may melt down the gold and take the rubies and diamonds adorning her. Whatever happens, we must recover her, and see her defilers punished as an example to all that God's treasure is not for sale. I beg you to help us if you can.'

'Well Father Mathias because you are Jim's friend and have helped everyone in need, it is our duty to do what we can. First, we must buy a reliable vehicle in Skiathos to take us to the mainland and on to Tríkala,' Carl answered before turning to Klaus. 'Klaus can buy a small bus preferably with comfortable seats for the journey?'

'I will try to buy one of the Mercedes Benz buses the Germans left behind. With luck, I should be back by evening with a suitable vehicle,' Klaus said and left for Skiathos town.

While they prepared for the task ahead, Carl looked over a map to find the quickest way to get to Tríkala unnoticed. If the thieves got wind of their intervention, they would either disappear or destroy the icon. Both would be disastrous. According to the map, the journey looked simple, first going by car ferry to the mainland, before driving inland to Vólvos through Lárisa to Tríkala. It was over 150 kms without allowing for diversions common in post war Greece. The route crossed many bridges that they hoped would be undamaged and not guarded by local partisans. The trouble with partisans is you do not know on what side they were. The communist probably would not like them travelling with a priest while the nationalists would ask why they were mostly foreigners. Worst still were the bandits who thrived by robbing travellers along lonely stretches of the road often leaving them dead or wounded by the side of the road.

Karl returned in time for dinner, driving a white Mercedes-Benz bus he purchased cheaply as no one in Skiathos wanted to drive a German bus, however, luxurious. Before buying it Klaus had examined the brakes to check they worked, made sure the engine ran smoothly and that everything was in good order. Once in Koukounaries, Mario painted on both sides of the bus, a large white dove holding an olive branch to indicate the vehicle was on a peaceful mission. It was a good idea, if it worked.

Early next morning they went on the ferry to the mainland then drove to Lárisa over a road marked with large potholes and sharp corners. When they came to a damaged bridge, they crossed it slowly. Often Jim walked ahead while Klaus gently edged the bus forward as the bridge rocked and groaned beneath the weight. It was a slow process, but the bus passed to the other side. Then, without warning, at a narrow bridge, armed men looking like partisans stopped the bus. They looked like pirates, especially when pointing their guns in everyone's face accusing them of being communist agents. Only the sight of Father Mathias sitting in the back saved the day as his presence transformed these unshaven thugs into devout Christians. Then they left, as suddenly as they had appeared, wishing everyone a safe and holy pilgrimage to the monasteries at Metéora.

It was 5pm when they stopped at a taverna in Tríkala. Here they asked the way to the Villa Verde. The innkeeper said it was three kilometres ahead, but they should be careful, as the occupants were unwelcoming, even to priests. So they sat down to what could be their last supper with Father Mathias blessing the food, knowing within the next few hours they would either retrieve the icon or die trying. Klaus ate a hearty meal, as though he had no care in the world while the others picked at the food. Eventually, they ate every scrap even complimenting the chef on his fine skewered lamb and feta cheese salad. Then they left. At 10 pm, they stopped a kilometre from the villa to put on black sweaters and trousers. When ready they left the bus at the side of the road to advance, each carrying a Sten gun and revolver while Jim followed holding the heavy Bren gun and plastic explosive. They were prepared to fight an army, but as it turned out, they did not need so many weapons to deal with a poorly organised group of greedy thieves.

An easily accessible old six-foot wall surrounded Villa Verde. Once inside the grounds, there was only a guard sleeping on the ground by the main gate. It all looked much too relaxed, but it was not all it seemed. Suddenly, out of the darkness came two large German Shepherd dogs running across the lawn straight towards them. Jim did not know what to do, so he held a knife in his hand ready to cut their throats if they jumped. It proved unnecessary as Carl walked towards the dogs with open arms gently whistling a low pitch tune. It calmed the dogs, so they slowly came up to Carl's feet and waited for his command. Yet again Carl produced the magic rabbit out of his hat full of tricks to pacify his canine friends and make everyone feel safe. In fact, the dogs lay on the ground to sleep. So the Painters moved to the villa under the cover of loud music and laughter as the people inside held a party without a care in the world. Indeed, they were much too busy having fun to notice anything unusual. Klaus peered through the window to count six men. He then climbed through a half-opened window into the empty kitchen to let the others in through the door. With shoes removed for quietness, they moved towards the noise to overcome the drunken partygoers. They searched the room but found no sign of the icon or any other loot.

Therefore, they had little choice but to search the house looking in every cupboard and under every chair. Then in the dining room, Mario and Klaus surprised an armed man guarding the icon and other treasures. When he saw them, he raised his arm to shoot, but he was too late. He died with Mario's stiletto dagger deeply embedded in his heart. When Father Mathias saw his icon, he held it up high, thanked God for his mercy, and with tears running down his face kissed the frame. His sacred duty completed; he wrapped the precious relic in a sheet to hide her from suspicious eyes.

Carl was in a rush, as he did not know if any more robbers would arrive or the sleeping guard at the gate awake. Therefore, they cleaned the crime scene leaving no evidence of their visit, but undressed the unconscious thieves leaving them tied up for the cleaner or the next visitor to find. Only after they cleaned everywhere did they leave through the kitchen door and over the wall without waking the guard or the guard dogs. Once aboard the bus, they drove to Tríkala leaving the other stolen goods in a bag outside the town hall before going on to Metéora. Here they entered a landscape dominated by sandstone pillars emerging from the ground like fabricated skyscrapers rising towards the sky. Most were just barren rock but on top of some of the pillars or on ledges were half-hidden monasteries. Father Mathias said there were twenty-four monasteries where monks lived to pray for all humanity as it was quiet, isolated, and close to God. As far as he remembered, the first monk was the hermit Barnabas in AD 985. In 1382, Athanásios came from Mount Athos to build the monastery of Megálo Metéoro. When viewed from below each monastery blended in with the sandstone rocks only identifiable by their red-tiled roofs. The access to some was very difficult. Often one could enter from a basket lowered from above, so isolating the community totally from the outside world. Others like the large monastery at Varlaam had steep paths leading to a gated entrance.

Father Mathias and Jim left the bus at the foot of the monastery of Varlaam while the others went off to the nearest hotel promising to collect Jim in the morning. The two men climbed the long stairs to the gate where Father Mathias rang the bell to tell the monks they had visitors. Once inside, the monks surrounded them to adore the icon and thank God for her return. Immediately, the head monk and Father Mathias led a procession to take the holy icon back to her rightful place on the altar. Once there the light from the windows illuminated the jewels on the icon, to make the Holy Mother come alive, appearing to smile upon them all. The monks showed Jim the frescoes painted around 1560 depicting scenes from the life of Christ and his disciples. Next morning an hour after sunrise, Jim left saying goodbye to the monks and Father Mathias. Before he left, Father Mathias gave Jim a package saying it was a token of their gratitude. At the bottom of the steps, Jim boarded the waiting bus to drive south. From a distance, they heard the monks singing in celebration for the safe return of their icon. Then Jim opened the package to find miniatures of the icon of the Holy Mother for each of the team. It was a fine gift from a valued friend who they were happy to see any time he visited. Meeting Father Mathias changed Jim forever, for the first time in his life he understood what real dedication to God meant and how Mathias served Our Lord at all times in every place even in prison.

18. The Ceasefire Ends

'Lord God!' the shepherds said, 'they come;
And see what hounds he has:
All dripping bluish fire, and dumb,
And nosing to the grass,
And trotting scathless through the gorse,
And bristling in the fell.
Lord, it is Death upon the horse,
And they're the hounds of hell!'

The Hounds of Hell in *The Collected Poems of John Masefield* (1923). Heinemann, London

After months of peace, the situation in Greece deteriorated as violence returned to the mountains. For reasons, no one has ever explained, the extreme Neo-Nazi combatants working with EDES, returned even after their defeat. It was not long before their bestial actions again drove many royalists to endorse communism causing the Orthodox Church to worry about its very existence. This time the terror was even worse. Now reports of burnt-out villages and a countryside strewn with the mutilated bodies of men, women and children lying next to their livestock was reported in most newspapers. Even the heavily censored pictures of the carnage polarised the fragile situation. Many Greeks could not understand what was going on, as the communists circulated the pictures saying fascism was back! Luckily, no fascists were in Skiathos and the neighbouring islands, but confined to the remote villages in the central and western regions. Sometimes they ventured east but did not attack the communists in the north, preferring to weaken the moderate royalist forces run by Janus. Therefore, an uneasy peace again erupted into a blood bath financed and led by the Americans as fighters for democracy. Now more people died than during the years of German and Italian occupation. No one knows exactly how many died, but their descendants still are the core of the modern socialist and communist parties in Greece. They are the same people who in the future would stand alone against the fascist rule of the American supported Greek generals from 1967-74.

On discovering that the fascists were back in Greece; Fergus flew to Koukounaries in a floatplane to tell them the alarming news. Within minutes of arriving, he gave them this warning. 'Everything has again changed because of our financial difficulties; the British government is withdrawing her troops from Greece even though worried about the unstable situation. They have agreed that the Americans take over to support the Greek military in their fight against communism. These new developments are dangerous. We believe the Americans OSS has a top-secret Department Department 6, also called Gladio, which uses hard-line fascists to assassinate or prevent socialists in France, Italy, and Greece from forming a government. We know that at the end of the war many Nazi war criminals were provided with new identities and recruited to work for Department 6 or allowed to escape to South America.'

'Fergus what you say is very disturbing. Sadly, many of the people who can expose me have escaped trial for their crimes against humanity. Do we know who these ex-Nazis are and where they may be?' Carl asked Fergus, worried about these changes.

'Dear Carl this is proving difficult. We know some of the Gestapo we were investigating suddenly disappeared to reappear in US uniform under new names. One was *Oberführer* Hans Kruger wanted for torturing resistance workers in France and executing Germans, including Admiral Canaris who we have identified from the photographs Janus sent us. If we are right, his new name is Helmut Kratz, who works with Captain Petros of EDES in central Greece with *Sturmbannführer* Franz Leitz now called Albert Mann. Both have American passports and military identity disks allowing them free entry into Greek bases as employees of the OSS Department 6. We have refused them access to all British facilities until they have been vetted by our people, not unsurprisingly the US has politely refused our request to interview them.'

'Are they responsible for the massacres of villagers in the central region?' Maria asked.

'Sadly we think they are directly or indirectly involved in these atrocities. We know from Janus that none of his people were at the destroyed villages, and he is losing control to this new force. Neither the Greek Government nor Britain feels powerful enough to accuse the USA of causing atrocities in their fight against communism. When asked about the rumours of fascist groups funded by America, their diplomats get angry and uncooperative saying 'you cannot make an omelette without breaking eggs, whatever that means! So we reluctantly believe they will do anything to defeat communism even using and encouraging fascism.'

'That is what we used to call the schoolboy syndrome. When guilty without an excuse for unacceptable behaviour, always look like having been insulted. Therefore, they are behind it. There is, and will always be, in all great nations an extremist element that believes in absolute rule. It is amazing how forcefully America expresses rightful concern over the evil German elimination of the Jews while supporting the Ku Klux Klan that kills and enslaves their own non-white minorities. Sadly, they have no history to be proud of and lack culture. Historically, they annihilated the Red Indians armed with bows and arrows while suppressing all minorities. The American Constitution is excellent but only protects the wealthy and powerful but not the poor and weak. It is why Klaus, and I work with Britain and not with the US,' Carl intervened vehemently.

'As far as the USA is concerned you do not exist, and if you are discovered we will say you work for EDES. I have invited Janus to join us to discuss how we can stop this reign of terror sweeping across Greece without letting the communists win. It is a tricky problem made worse because we are dealing with very skilled and evil men supported by our so-called ally, the USA,' Fergus said sinking into an armchair looking extremely haggard. The new political reality was beginning to strain even his strong constitution.

'Fergus, it appears to me Hitler's idea that fascism would succeed well after his death may be coming true. Only God and a few brave men stand in the way of the German fascists funded by the US and Nazi funds deposited in Switzerland. They always planned how, if Germany was defeated, they would go to the Americas where friends would hide them to await the day when the Swastika would again fly over Europe as it does over some remote villages in Paraguay and Argentina,' Carl noted as he shook his head slowly at the awful news.

'Carl can you remember either *Oberführer* Hans Kruger or his friend *Sturmbannführer* Franz Leitz and more importantly can they identify you?' Fergus asked worriedly.

'Sadly I remember both, especially *Oberführer* Hans Kruger, who is a weasel-faced man with an ability to lie to your face. Whenever we questioned his motives for interrogating our staff, he did not reply hiding behind his Gestapo uniform. He was afraid of tackling Admiral Canaris in person so he harassed our staff and intercepted our correspondence. Luckily, he was always one-step behind, often killing those people who given half a chance would have acted for him purely out of fear. I would recognise him anywhere with those deep-set black eyes, pale skin, and his short blond hair. During the war, he wore steel reading glasses perched on the end of his nose to look quite comical. I believe he murdered my wife as well as my friend Admiral Canaris. When the Russians entered Berlin, he probably discarded his Gestapo uniform to dress as a common soldier before leaving by air with Martin Bormann. The aircraft landed in southern Germany to drop off Kruger while Bormann flew on to Spain, the Azores, and Argentina. Kruger using the identity of a dead soldier tried to escape prosecution by hiding among thousands of other interned Germans. I know he will try to kill me as he is afraid I would tell the Americans that Kruger knows how they can find Martin Bormann,' Carl answered looking out of the window at the calm sea while nonchalantly smoking his Sobraine cigarette. Now Carl lost his smile as a deep sadness descended upon him that revealed how bad things were in Berlin and how much he missed his dearest Helga.

'Well I think that settles it. Friends, we must capture *Oberführer* Kruger and *Sturmbannführer* Leitz alive, if possible. For the quicker they are dead, the better for all concerned. We can only prevent Greece falling to communism by winning the confidence of the people and by stopping the terrorism in the mountains. Luckily, we have the support of Janus as well as copies of all the commands sent from the OSS in Washington to their man in Greece regarding Department 6,' Fergus remarked, proud of breaking the US secret codes. It provided an advantage in a deadly game of cat and mouse.

During the rest of the day, Carl and Klaus talked earnestly about their past and that, they would soon have to face their former enemies.

'We must destroy Kruger and Leitz, or Kratz and Mann as they are now known, even if it means getting Churchill angry,' Klaus stated vehemently not caring who heard.

'Don't worry friend, I feel both Churchill and Fergus will be quite pleased if these Nazi War Criminals' bodies were found outside the US delegation in Athens, with a note saying who they really are,' Carl commented. 'What does not make any sense to me is why they returned to Greece after being defeated and nearly captured by Janus?'

'They were probably ordered back by their controllers to continue the reign of terror, in order to remove all socialist forces and allow fascism to rule. Many capitalists still believe that fascism is the only way to fight and contain communism,' Klaus added.

'Well the re-emergence of the Nazis in our backyard must be dealt with decisively. They are a reminder that Hitler's doctrines are alive and not easily destroyed. What the West does not understand is that twenty years of Nazi indoctrination does not disappear overnight. Instead, it festers like a diseased wound waiting to burst out, infecting everyone within its reach. Now we must fight the communists while keeping the fascists at bay. It will be difficult but the consequences of losing are unthinkable.'

By dinner, everyone was back to the normal feeling safe in each other's company while waiting to travel to the mainland to settle old scores. Carl broke the ice by saying how much he liked the floatplane. It reminded him of the floatplanes used during the final days for flying senior Nazis and their friends from Berlin to freedom. Fergus explained it was a bit cramped inside and how bumpy the landing was. Adding it was the worse landing he had experienced even with Klaus. Everyone laughed at his joke knowing Klaus was an excellent pilot.

Janus and Christos arrived on a sunny morning unannounced. After the usual hugs and kisses, they ate a full breakfast with relish as if they had not eaten for a week. This was because they were in such a hurry to reach Skiathos they only had a few olives, washed down with a cup of coffee before the journey. Janus described the attack on Andreas's men by the fascist group he called the Jackals. Everyone thought the name was appropriate and agreed to use it when talking about the fascists. Janus omitted the more grisly details before asking Fergus to help him hunt them down.

Fergus replied, 'It would be a pleasure to give such sons of Satan a quick passage to Hell.'

Both men were satisfied, and after further discussion, agreed to warn all of Janus' units about Captain Petros and his two Germans. The only question was how much to tell them. Eventually, they warned the field commanders that Petros' men might have murdered loyal villagers and even EDES soldiers. Carl added that the commanders should be told that the Jackals were furthering the communist cause, while pretending to be democrats or fascists. Janus liked the idea, as it would prepare his people for the impending violence.

Next morning Fergus and Janus departed in the floatplane leaving Christos to guide the rest of the team to the battleground. They knew that destroying one arm of the American octopus of the OSS or Department 6 would not stop it, but were aware the adverse publicity was something

America did not want. They hoped that by wiping out Captain Petros and his men, America would think twice about employing fascist assassins. It would also inform them the rabbit, or was it the Jackal, was well and truly out of the hat for all to see.

19. Shadows from the Past

All of the time somewhere in the world evil men flourish by destroying the sanity and the lives of the innocent for cash or to promote their own religious or political beliefs.

It was in early May when Kratz and Mann returned to join Petros and his Jackals to continue their anti-communist activities. Their timing could not have been worse, for the Painters and Janus were expecting them from radio messages intercepted in Athens and the growing violence in the mountains. With the melting of the winter snows, Janus' men moved into the higher places reoccupying some of the territory held by the communists. They did not advance towards the borders but instead, reinforced their positions to form a defensive line to stop communist infiltrators without provoking a border incident. Then they waited for reliable news about where the Jackals were and what they were up to. When Janus heard the Jackals were in the north-east, he informed Carl and his group on Skiathos. Immediately, the Painters drove their bus to the mainland with Klaus at the wheel to take Carl, Mario, and Christos north. At the same time, Maria and Jim sailed Snow Goose II to the harbour in Thessaloniki to be their base. This was an area controlled by Janus with a mountainous terrain making it easy to set up an ambush.

While waiting in Thessaloniki, Maria and Jim walked around the town eating in tavernas and sleeping in Snow Goose II. They thought Thessaloniki was a beautiful town founded by King Kassandros in 315 BC; it was then known as Salonika whose fortunes changed as empires came and went. The initial Greek rule ended when the Romans captured the town in 146 BC making it the capital of Macedonia Prim. It later became part of the Byzantine Empire. As the Roman power declined, the Turks arrived in 1430 to rule until 1912, when it again became part of a free Greece. Foreigners had ruled the people for nearly two thousand years and yet their culture survived. The town was a mixture of ancient Greek, Roman and Turkish architecture, interwoven with modern buildings. Small shops lined the long straight streets selling everything from food and furniture to fine art. Looming over the town was the Turkish White Tower built in 1430 as part of now dismantled city defences. Maria thought the city was simply magical, a delightful cultural melting pot.

After the bus arrived in Thessaloniki, the Painters planned their next move involving setting a trap to catch or at least try to eliminate some of the Jackals. When ready, they drove west to Edessa where according to Janus was an ideal base hidden among a forest of large Greek fir trees, near magnificent waterfalls forming easily defended natural barriers. It was a perfect site for an ambush if only they could attract Captain Petros and his Jackals to visit. At Káranos, they established a well-concealed camp above the waterfalls hidden among the trees that they reinforced with tree trunks and rocks. It took hours to cut down a few trees and move some rocks to establish a viable barrier against a much larger enemy. They took care to make it look as natural as possible, so not to alert the most skilled observer. Once ready, they informed Janus and waited for him to lure the Jackals into the killing field. For days, nothing happened until the Jackals arrived in Siátista and started asking about Janus. They learnt that Janus was meeting his commanders near Thessaloníki. The Jackals then left in two vehicles for Vergina. This meant the Jackals had heard the rumour of the secret meeting at the famous Káranos waterfalls not far from Edessa that, Janus told the loyal villagers to tell any visitor who asked. By now, Janus established a defence line running from Pélla to the foothills of Mount Olympus, to prevent the Jackals attacking the EDES forces fighting the communists to the east. Then Janus arrived at the Káranos waterfalls with Andreas and ten men they hid their lorry near Carl's bus. At the foot of the waterfall were three large partially camouflaged tents, with a highly visible trail of broken grass leading to the caves hidden behind the waterfall. Around the tents were strewn empty cans of meat, a map of the area, a portable cooking stove, and a number of cigarette butts. They hoped this would convince the Jackals it was where EDES would return after their meeting. Then they all settled above the waterfalls to rest and wait to see if their bait would attract the bloodthirsty Jackals out for revenge.

All that Jim saw while on duty during the first night was a large brown bear moving nearby among the trees who seemed only interested in gathering food. Then he heard the scuffling of little feet coming closer until through the darkness, there were many eyes staring at him. In the torchlight, he found a pack of five fierce looking grey wolves with mouths wide open scavenging for food. He did not know what to do as he had never faced hungry wolves before and was certain they would try to attack him.

'Shoo, shoo, silly dogs,' shouted Andreas appearing from nowhere to make the wolves vanish into the darkness.

'Thanks Andreas. Are the wolves dangerous?' Jim asked.

'Some grey wolves are dangerous, especially in winter when food is scarce. The wolves were curious and not hunting for food. If you look on the ground, you will see the rabbit droppings indicating there are many living here. The only really dangerous animal is the large brown bear which usually leaves people alone, but when angered, is capable with a swipe of his large claws of cutting a man to pieces.'

'Oh I saw a brownish bear about an hour ago. I thought he looked harmless more interested in sniffing the ground than attacking me,' Jim remarked a bit frightened and aware he did not know much about Greek wildlife.

'Jim you have all the luck. While on watch, I only saw a solitary owl that did not even bother to hoot or move. He could have been dead except his eyelids were half-open and now and then he twitched. Later, the owl broke his silent vigil to swoop down and catch a rat. I am certain when he flew off to take his prey to his nest, he gave me a wink,' Andreas commented as always making a joke of everything.

Andreas is a remarkable man Jim thought. He was joking even when his torturers could appear at any moment!

That night the Jackals slept soundly at a small hotel outside Vergina. After breakfast, they enquired about Janus to learn the meeting of Janus's commanders was in the caves behind the Káranos waterfalls. Captain Petros thanked the hoteliers as he paid their bill and left to join his fifteen men wearing camouflage suits. They drove off in a lorry and a small jeep towards Lefkádia to survey the vineyards, stopping only to ask the local people about the whereabouts of the communists and EDES. Everyone gave the same reply that the communists were to the north of Thessaloníki, and Janus was meeting his officers at the Káranos waterfalls.

'Tell me the truth old man. Are you sure Janus' meeting is at Káranos?' Petros threatened a fragile looking man.

'Sir I am too old to fight and only know what others tell me. I am told that tomorrow around noon, Janus will meet his commanders to discuss operations against the communists. We hope Janus will attack those red devils threatening Thessaloníki to drive them out of Greece,' the old man answered as honestly as he knew how.

Petros was still not convinced that it would be so simple to catch Janus and his leaders in one place at the same time. Therefore to confirm this information, they travelled another ten minutes before asking some men sitting outside a taverna enjoying their beer about the meeting.

'Good morning gentlemen I wonder if you can help me as we are lost. I have to meet Janus near Edessa. Do you know how we can get there?' asked Captain Petros looking very much the Greek officer and using his best manners.

For a while, the men chatted with each other trying to remember where in Edessa Janus was to meet his men. Eventually, they agreed the meeting will be tomorrow at noon, but they could not agree exactly on the site. Then an old woman appeared who was much more forthright.

'Why do you want to find Captain Janus?' she sternly inquired.

'Because we're to meet him tomorrow in Edessa but can't remember exactly where. I am getting frustrated because no one can tell us how to get there and most are proving difficult even deliberately unhelpful. What chance do we Greeks have of being free from the communists if you people are so uncooperative?' Petros answered angrily.

'Don't you get bossy with me? How do I know you are with us and not a communist or even a fascist?' she pointedly asked staring Captain Petros directly in the eyes.

'As you know, we've fought the communists since the Germans, and Italians left. If you do not want to help we will ask around, but I hope for all our sakes, we are not late for the meeting. Janus hates people being tardy in anything,' Petros commented starting to walk away.

'Sounds like you know our Janus. Therefore, I can tell you behind the waterfall at Káranos are a large cave where the EDES holds their meetings. It is ideal because they cannot be seen from the air, and their voices are hidden by the noise from the waterfalls,' the good woman added.

'Thank you very much for your honesty and information. Nowadays, none of us can be too careful. May God keep you and your family safe,' Petros said with his usual disarming smile. Then he walked slowly to the car satisfied he knew where to find Janus without raising any suspicion and returned to the hotel.

'After we've destroyed Janus, we will return to the taverna to punish them for not trusting us and so no one can identify us. I'm certain when the bodies of Janus and his men are discovered; Athens will send men to search for their murderers and must find nothing,' Helmut stated.

'Will we have time to question a few prisoners and search for vital information,' Albert Mann added eager to have another victim on which to practice his sadistic ways.

'I promise you can have Janus and any foreigner to investigate to your heart's content. As far as I am concerned, all I want to do is to weaken the group and find out if the rumour they work with foreigners, especially two Germans, is true,' Helmut Kratz replied.

'I don't understand why you always mutilate your prisoners,' Captain Petros added.

'It is simply because the sight of mutilated bodies sends waves of horror that deter most people from being involved with EDES. I doubt if during any interrogation, we discover anything useful but always hope it may lead us to their paymasters. If we can find the source of their money and supplies, we can stop it,' Helmut replied sitting back to light a cigar. Now he wanted to kill off the brains behind EDES while blaming their deaths on the communists. Then his people would run a new fascist EDES tough enough to defeat the communist forces, driving them back across the borders.

Next morning the Jackals left the hotel to drive to the waterfalls at Káranos that according to Helmut's map were south of Edessa. They stopped at Lefkádia for coffee and cake before driving to within 800 yards from the waterfalls. After hiding their vehicles, they walked cautiously towards the noise of the waterfalls until they saw it ahead sparkling in the sunlight. They found a good place to see everything, so settled down to wait for people coming to or leaving the cave. By noon, nothing had happened, so Helmut decided it was a trap, or they had the wrong information. Either way he would punish all involved. He was not a patient man, which had caused him many problems in the past. Therefore, he handed the field glasses to Albert Mann before going to hide behind some rocks to smoke another cigar. Cuban cigars were his latest vice giving him pleasure while waiting for something, anything, to happen. Helmut considered punctuality very important, so he was always early for any appointment and did not know what it was like to run to catch a train. Albert used to joke that Helmut was more reliable than the best Swiss watch.

At noon, Andreas, Klaus, and Jim walked out into the open from the trees carrying boxes to go behind the waterfall. At the time, Jim felt like a sitting duck parading directly into the enemy's line of fire, but someone had to set the bait. They were relieved to be unharmed and safe in the cave. Maybe no one saw them or the Jackals were not coming. Still they carried out their orders by making a lot of noise, as though they were greeting old friends hoping the Jackals would hear. It was unnecessary as the Jackals saw them entering the cave. It made Helmut smile at Captain Petros as both agreed the meeting was in the cave before dividing their forces. Petros' group would attack the cave behind the waterfall while Helmut would take his men to clear the area above the waterfalls. The plan would have worked if Carl had not prepared an effective defence above the falls that could stop an army in their tracks. For whoever attacked, the Painters had to climb up through a forest full of concealed firing positions where Christos and Janus lay hidden. A few yards away behind a large fallen tree trunk were Carl, Mario, and Maria, who waited guns at the ready to repel all comers.

Inside the cave, the trio aimed their Sten guns to cover the entrance while hidden behind the rocks either side of the cave. Andreas made the sign of the cross while Jim and Klaus simply waited for the enemy to make the first move. Then a hand grenade came through the curtain of water, caught and thrown back by Klaus. Two seconds later there was an explosion followed by screams from outside as some of the attackers were injured. This indicated that there were a few less Jackals. There was a brief lull before six Jackals rushed into the cave firing blindly into the darkness with little effect only to die in a deadly crossfire. They checked that the attackers were dead and then rushed out of the cave to shoot killing two others and wounding in the leg Captain Petros as he was running away. When the area was clear, they moved into the forest to help Carl waiting for the other Jackals. He did not have long to wait as Kratz led his team up the wooded slope thinking victory would be as simple as attacking unarmed villages, so he threw all caution to the wind. Even when he came across a recently felled tree, he was not worried but ordered his men to take cover before advancing more cautiously. The order came too late as they came under fire from the hidden Painters, who eliminated the exposed Jackals one at a time killing six as the others hid or ran away. Klaus arrived just in time to recognise *Sturmbannführer* Franz Leitz (Albert Mann) trying to escape through the trees and after slowly taking carefully aim shot him in the chest. Realizing they faced defeat or capture Helmut Kratz ran away with another Jackal as if the hounds of hell were after them. In many ways they were, so they ran for their lives.

'Jim, catch the men running towards you. Be careful because one is *Oberführer* Kruger, who is deadlier than any poisonous snake and as slippery as an eel,' Carl shouted.

'*Oberführer* Kruger you can't escape me. I am Klaus Weiss, who worked for Admiral Canaris. Do you remember I am the man you denounced as *Juden* to die in a concentration camp? You can run as fast as you want, I will follow to hunt you down and destroy you and your world of flesh eating worms,' Klaus yelled out into the distance.

Klaus' message from the past disturbed Helmut Kratz because he had too many powerful enemies among Admiral Canaris' staff. Was he the same Weiss, who disappeared before Helmut could arrest him for being a Jew? A cold shiver went down his spine knowing he could not expect any mercy and must escape as fast as he could knew the positions had reversed, and now he was the hunted. He did not care whether the enemy captured or killed Petros or Mann, as he never liked them. Petros was just another arrogant Greek while Albert enjoyed his work too much to be a survivor. As he ran over the ground covered with loose leaves, he fell over. In seconds shaken and very frightened, he was up rushing madly until reaching his car to drive away as fast as he could.

The manhunt was on as Carl, Klaus, Mario, Maria, and Jim followed in the bus, in an attempt to catch Kratz and if possibly find his safe house. They did. It was a villa in a large wooded garden called Ancient Pella. Then they waited outside for Janus to arrive.

In Káranos, they searched the bodies of Jackals before removing their weapons. Then the hurt Albert Mann and Captain Petros received medical attention while carefully guarded by Andreas. He was delighted to have the wounded Mann to consider whether to torture him or not, but decided he would not descend to such bestiality. Albert Mann recognised Andreas to make him shake with fear at the thought of what

Andreas would do as revenge for being tortured. The fear of just retribution turned Mann from an arrogant cynic into a pathetic lump of crying humanity hoping for mercy while deserving none. He need not have worried as Andreas always forgave those who hurt him. It was just his manner.

'Come closer please,' begged Albert Mann speaking in a whisper. 'What I am going to say is very important. Please tell Admiral Carl von Graf, I did not arrest or torture his wife Helga. It was Helmut. Indeed, I was sorry to hear she died. It was not long after her death that we first heard of Admiral Canaris' dossiers hidden in the House of Mirrors, but we never had the opportunity to retrieve them. I believe they are in a concealed chamber behind the bathroom mirror if no one has since removed them. I tell you as payment for my sins. I hope you will pray for my evil soul. Beware, though I am a sadist, Helmut is much worse. I beg you to pray for me...' With those words Albert Mann formerly *Sturmbannführer* Franz Leitz took his last breath and died with his eyes staring vacantly into space.

Andreas was shocked but did what he always did; he prayed to God for Mann's soul. Then he turned his attention to Captain Petros who was still bleeding through his bandages. Though he tried, he could not stop the bleeding. It was a pity, as they wanted Petros alive to learn about Dept 6. Nearby, Janus' men cleared the site removing every little cigarette and cigar butt even the empty cartridge cases to leave the area spotless. Only when there was no evidence of a battle did they load the equipment and bodies into a lorry along with the wounded Petros. They drove to a quiet place where they threw the bodies into the ebbing tide to be washed out to sea. Next, they took Captain Petros to a hospital outside Thessaloniki where a doctor did his best but said his patient would not survive the night. Janus stayed with the wounded Captain Petros until he died and then wrapped his body in a canvas shroud to travel in the lorry to the villa Ancient Pella.

Hours later Janus found the Painters outside a very quiet villa having decided it was safer to wait for the fugitives to break cover rather than try an assault. Jim thought the villa was beautiful with shuttered windows and ivy climbing up the walls. The front door was made of thick hardwood styled in the Arabic tradition with large brass studs making it nearly unbreakable! With its ancient walls of stone and small windows, it made an ideal defensive position, so all they could do was wait for someone to leave or open the door. If they attacked, they would suffer many casualties.

At sunset, the two fugitives left to drive away towards Thessaloniki closely followed by The Painters. In Thessaloniki harbour, the fugitives boarded a blue yacht flying the US flag, which immediately left to sail south. Minutes later Snow Goose II followed until both were off the vast wetlands formed by the Delta of the River Axiós, famous for its diverse birds and wild flowers. At night, few people came to this remote area making it the perfect spot for what Carl had to do. Very gently, Snow Goose II came alongside the blue yacht so Mario could throw his knife to kill the helmsman. Then he jumped on board, recovered his knife, and made sure there was no one else on deck before Klaus and Carl followed to take up positions around the stairs to the cabin door. Very carefully, Carl opened the wooden door with a pistol in his hand and Klaus by his side. The door made a slight squeaking noise that hardly anyone heard except those watching from inside, who fired blindly into the dark from the well-lit cabin missing Carl by inches. Klaus and Carl fired back hitting the American skipper, another Jackal and Helmut, apparently killing them. However, the always-resourceful Helmut survived to lie still on the ground and wait for Carl to come closer before spinning around to fire. He only had time for one shot; it hit Carl in the left arm before Klaus shot him in the chest. Even then, Helmut stirred to lift his pistol to fire, but it was too late; he died with a bullet in the head.

When the shooting was over, Mario helped Klaus carry the wounded Carl and Helmut's body onto Snow Goose II. Inside the cabin, Maria examined Carl's wound finding it was not life threatening before bandaging it. Meanwhile, Mario doused the blue yacht in diesel fuel then left as the Snow Goose II moved away. At a safe distance, Mario fired a flare from the Very pistol at the yacht to set it on fire. As they sailed towards Thessaloniki, they watched the fire burn so intensely it turned everything into ashes until the remains of the blue yacht slowly disappeared beneath the waves. As soon as they had docked, Klaus took Carl to a hospital where a doctor stitched his wound and injected morphine to stop the pain.

Later, Janus drove the three bodies down to Athens arriving just before dawn. They were found on the doorstep of the US Military Attaché Paul Muller's office, by a cleaner. Around their necks were large labels written in Greek giving their real names, and that they were the war criminals who mutilated innocent villagers. Within minutes of the hideous discovery crowds gathered to look at and photograph the hated enemy. Soon all Athens reverberated from the shock of the bodies of two wanted German War Criminals, and a Greek officer found on the doorstep of the US Military Attaché's office. What did it mean? It begged the question as to how many more such monsters still hid in Greece waiting to rape and plunder the land. Not surprisingly, for weeks afterwards the photographs and commentary, concerning the Nazis were in the newspapers along with commentary from concerned journalists. They asked whether the dead men were responsible for the massacres of so many villagers and what connection they had with the US Attaché. The socialist and communist press wrote vitriolic articles about Nazis working for the Americans against the Greek peasants to enslave the people. However, most Greeks thought these comments were political propaganda. The pro-western press debated for weeks how it was possible for wanted Nazi criminals to be killed fighting in Greece. No one knew who killed them or who the three men worked for. The publicity and political reactions throughout Greece set Paul and his office back a few years, but it did not stop their activities. However, from then onwards Paul was very careful what he said, deciding to live a quiet life until all the commotion had died down. He was sad at losing Helmut Kratz/ *Oberführer* Hans Kruger, as he was brilliant and totally without mercy. Indeed, he was the ideal assassin Department 6 desperately needed but luckily, easily replaced. Paul hoped, no; he prayed; the British did not know his role in this affair. If they did, maybe they would send someone to assassinate him. This nightmare was to cause him many sleepless nights, especially as his murderer could be Greek or indeed of any nationality!

He decided that attack was the best defence. Within days, he sent agents around Greece looking for whoever killed his men vowing to kill or remove every one of them. He had one great advantage in so much that, he had access to large unaccountable funds and an army of men desperate to work for him. It appeared to him that everywhere he turned, there were fascists seeking revenge or needing protection. This time he would learn everything he could about his enemies before lifting a finger so he could destroy them. Maybe death was too good! Perhaps they should be humiliated! He liked the idea of his enemies ending up in some terrible South American prison to rot, with their presence only indicated by a number.

20. Admiral Canaris' Secret Dossiers

*By telling the truth, the words of the dead have
a habit of returning to haunt the living.*

After their victory near Thessaloniki, the Painters returned to
Koukounaries to rest and wait for orders. Most were happy in
each other's company enjoying the fine scenery but Carl was
impatient. Every day, he sent messages to Fergus requesting
action, any action, as long as he felt useful while blaming
Klaus for not capturing the two Germans alive. Their presence
in Greece opened deep wounds Carl found hard, if not
impossible, to heal. Unusually, he had nightmares and troubled
by bad memories flooding back into his mind. This made him
appear distant, very unhappy, and often bloody irritable.

'Carl, why are you so angry. The two men who could have
identified you are dead, and we should thank God for that
small mercy. What else did you need to know that only they
could tell you?' Jim asked being worried about Carl's sudden
unreasonable behaviour.

'Jim my friend you don't understand. It is not your fault
because you were not in Berlin when everything was
collapsing and the only man I trusted was awaiting arrest. You
should have known Admiral Canaris; he was a man in a
million. His curiosity and attention to the minutest detail made
him the master spy. Canaris understood our mistakes, along
with those who openly condemned Hitler while secretly
financing him. Late at night when everyone had gone home, I
would find him writing a dossier on what he liked to call the
secrets needed to save Germany after the war. He wrote
everything in green ink, using old German script and initialled
the bottom of each page with a C. When disturbed, he tried to

hide what he was doing until the day he ordered me to leave Berlin. Then he told me of the accumulated dossiers on important people who not only traded with Nazi Germany but who were setting up escape routes and homelands for many important engineers, bankers, and party officials. Indeed, the Third Reich was preparing for a more powerful Fourth Reich to rise like the Phoenix from the fire, and rule the world,' Carl said quietly. It reflected how much he missed Admiral Canaris.

'Did you or anyone find the dossiers?' Jim inquired ignorant of the hurt he was causing.

'Why did you have to ask that question? If I asked Canaris when I was leaving, he may have told me where he hid them. All I know is they must be in Berlin, but I have no idea in which zone or in what building. Just think the good we could do by exposing the Nazi networks and their friends. We could start to cleanse the world of all traces of fascism together with those who benefitted from their actions,' Carl answered before offering Jim a cigarette as they sat down to drink another glass of Ouzo.

They did not notice Andreas entering the room, or that he overheard their conversation. So not wanting to cause offence Andreas made a loud coughing noise before speaking. 'Carl, I must apologise for overhearing what you said. I'm not sure it will make any sense but in my bones I have something important to tell you.'

'You never need to apologise to any of us dear Andreas. We are one large family that licks its wounds publicly with no grace or manners. You can tell me anything, and I will not criticise you, for there have been many times when I was not a good person,' Carl commented, his mind still miles away in Berlin.

'I should have told you earlier, but everything happened too quickly. I was with Albert Mann when he was dying, he asked for my forgiveness for what he did to me. I could not forget the terror but, of course, I knew I must forgive him,' Andreas said.

'Just what I would expect from the good man you are. Pity he did not live long enough to tell me about the death of my friend Admiral Canaris,' Carl mentioned with a smile as he acknowledged Andreas's humanity.

'Herr Mann said something you should know so you can tell Admiral Carl von Graf, if you know him,' Andreas stated not sure how important the message was.

'I knew Admiral Carl von Graf so please tell me the message,' Carl pleaded anxious to know Mann's secrets.

'What he said was something like this. Please tell Admiral Carl von Graf, I did not torture or kill his wife Helga. It was Helmut. I was sorry she died. It was about this time; we found out about Admiral Canaris' dossiers hidden in the House of Mirrors, but we never located them. They are in a concealed chamber behind the bathroom mirror. I tell you this in payment for my sins and in the hope, you will pray for my evil soul. I am sure that is what he said. I hope it helps,' Andreas explained with great relief.

In seconds, Carl was hugging a startled Andreas with tears streaming down his normally impassive face. It proved the little bird was right when she whispered in his ear long ago in Berlin that Helga was murdered and now, purely by accident, he had avenged her death. At last, she could rest in peace. The time for mourning was over, and he could live again. He was now like Sherlock Holmes excited about going to solve a new mystery and expose the villains. There the similarities ended; as Carl was much too wise to take cocaine, instead, for the first time for many years, he sat down to play the piano with the touch of a maestro. He was happily lost in his own world playing a short piece by Wagner, followed by Tchaikovsky's beautiful Piano Concerto Number 1 in B-flat minor, as Klaus hummed along with the tune. Now Jim saw the real man behind the dignified mask, the Carl he met before the war when painting with Churchill and Fergus. The music coupled with the images of times gone by, with his long departed parents and Wendy in Poole brought a lump in his throat. Jim smiled feeling privileged to be alive in such wonderful company as the villa reverberated to the beautiful piano concerto played with passion.

During all the noise Maria and grandmother were in the kitchen preparing a surprise feast to celebrate their victory over the Jackals and above all their safe return. Even Carl's bullet wound proved minor, healing quickly helped by an injection of some magical potion Fergus supplied called penicillin. Jim and Mario went swimming, catching fish, or just helping everyone. While Carl and Klaus were visibly relieved some of the dark shadows from their past had been permanently removed. Janus, Christos, and Andreas were also writing reports on the activities of rotten elements in EDES suggesting how they came to Greece and who employed them. When their reports reached the government in Athens, after reading every word, they ignored the reports for complex political reasons. It was when friendship with powerful America was much more important than revealing the truth. Many nations feared that if their people realised just how much influence America had on their governance it would ignite a bloody revolution. Sadly, copies of the reports reached Paul Muller to inform him where to find his enemies.

When everything was ready, grandmother called them to the feast. To their astonishment, the large dining table was resplendent in a lace tablecloth with napkins, the best glasses and cutlery and even a splendid display of flowers in the fine vases. By each seating was a menu listing the meal consisting of the finest food anyone could find in all Koukounaries and probably in all of Greece. It made everyone feel very special, indeed honoured at being guests at such a fantastic banquet.

The menu was:
Mezédes (Aperitif) Olives
Taramosaláta (salted mullet roe puree with breadcrumbs)
Psária (Fish)
Psária plakí (baked fish with leeks, potatoes, and fennel)
Kréas (Meat)
Choirinó souvláki (kebabs of grilled pork)
Choriátiki saláta (Lettuce, onions, tomatoes, and feta cheese)
Glyká (Desserts)

Giaoúrti kai méli (yoghurt with honey)
Tsouréki (A loaf of bread made for festivals)

For the next two hours, they enjoyed each mouthful of food, washed down with large amounts of the tasty wine called *Tsípouro*. Afterwards, they relaxed listening to Carl playing the piano and drinking brandy with cups of thick Greek coffee. As the sun set over the bay, they felt content to wait to see what tomorrow would bring.

Carl contacted Fergus requesting the latest street map of Berlin. Carl made the excuse that someone had found some of his papers, so he must find the rest before the Russians or the Americans read them. He did not say what were in the files, but Jim suspected some were personal details he did not want even Fergus to know about, such as the death of his wife. There are always some secrets so precious no one except God should ever share, such as things that make us laugh or cry and those leaving a hole in our hearts that no one can fill nor time erase. A week later Carl received the maps together with identity disks and papers for himself, Klaus and Jim to enter the British zone of Berlin. When Carl showed them their new papers, Jim saw a deep sadness in Carl's eyes at the prospect of re-visiting his past even if it meant risking his life. Carl once said about death. 'Death comes to all of us sooner or later. It is only an idiot who fears its inevitability and a fool who does not pray for a painless end and the hope of salvation.'

During the following days Carl and Klaus, spent hours carefully looking for long gone roads while locating famous houses that were still standing. Surprisingly, many of their old haunts existed though many were now hotels or accommodation for the occupying forces. Jim could not see on the map any reference to a House of Mirrors but Carl appeared to have located it but did not say where. Even now, the knowledge in those dossiers could lead to their torture and death by those who would stop at nothing to keep their support for the Nazis hidden from their closest friends. Fortunately, the position of Berlin as an enclave inside Russian occupied East Germany was a subject of intense debate. The Red Army disliked having so many American, British, and French soldiers facing them across a divided city. They felt that because they captured the city, and it was inside the Soviet administered East German State, nobody else had any right to be in Berlin. They did what Russian bears do when perplexed – they made life in Berlin difficult by sabotaging allied convoys bringing food, fuel, and ammunition to their garrisons in Berlin. It was the start of the Berlin blockade, though no one at the time knew it.

The Red Army Generals did not want a direct confrontation with the West but wanted to drive them out of Berlin. All sides distrusted each other as well as the German people they governed. This situation worsened the life of the people living in Berlin where everything was hard to find. Most homes had broken roofs and windows that let in the rain, wind, and snow. Fuel was so expensive and hard to get that people scavenged through bombsites for wood to use, for cooking or burn to keep warm. The authorities rationed everything, forcing people to wait in long queues whatever the weather for even a loaf of bread. Some fuel and food were distributed by the occupying forces, but it was only enough to keep people alive not satisfy even the smallest appetites. Most lived from hand to mouth in the hope of help and the chance of finding work or discovering the occasional piece of wood or coal. The spectre of death and disease hovered over this ruined city destroying the old, the very young, the weak, and the poor. To survive, Berliners tried anything to keep themselves and their loved ones alive. Crime thrived throughout the city under pitifully ineffective military administrations while some sort of policing was established. It was a repetition of the deprivation and the horrors of 1919 that fuelled the rise of fascism, but now the victors tried to alleviate the worst shortages. Sadly, it was often a case of too little, too late.

21. The House of Mirrors

One name often has many meanings to different people.

In September 1947, Jim, Carl, and Klaus returned to Black Island where they were met by an anxious Fergus and an excited Winston. Life in Britain was rife with rumours concerning Russian spies and American agents undermining Britain's security. The tragic death of John Maynard Keynes in the USA from the stress of negotiating a billion-dollar loan and debt repayment shocked all British politicians. Nothing was said in public to upset the Americans whose demands for repayment of war loans from a bankrupt Britain for saving the free world, as they called it, was causing bitterness throughout the land. No longer were meetings between the former Allies jovial affairs but serious negotiations behind firmly closed doors. President Truman like his predecessor President Roosevelt was on the surface friendly towards Russian President Joseph Stalin while publicly criticizing the British and French Empires. Much to the disgust of both nations, the US showed no intention of leaving their bases in either country now the war was over. Instead, they moved more long-range bombers to Europe on the fact that their presence provided a real protection against Russia. The result was the US and Russia instead of reducing their forces in Germany, increased them to face each other across a fragile and volatile border. For every US bomber arriving in Germany or Europe a similar Russian aircraft flew to East Germany and other border countries. It was an infantile dangerous game where at any moment a small incident could be the match to ignite the flames of a Third World War!

While Carl, Fergus, and Winston spent hours in deep discussion, Jim walked around his estate. He found everything flourishing. There were more sheep than he remembered and a yard full of chickens. The caretakers were a nice family who lived well from the land with a salary from MI 6. Everyday Jim talked on the radio with Maria to learn that everything in Greece was calm, though there were still fascist groups causing trouble, but none murdering villagers. Jim missed Maria, feeling if anything happened to her, he would go mad or die of grief. When Jim arrived back in the house, he could have cut the tension in the air with a sword. Everyone looked angry and ill at ease.

'Young Jim, can you believe that this stubborn Carl wants to go to Berlin. Whatever happens, he must not, I repeat must not, be discovered for who he really is. I have told him it is too risky, but he insists if he does not go we will all live to regret it. He is aware Berlin is a dangerous city where former Nazis and gangsters walk the streets. Even so, he stubbornly insists on going whether I damn well like it or not,' Winston said gruffly never liking anyone who ignores his advice.

'Sir I promise we're not going to Berlin to cause trouble but to find Canaris' papers before others get them. Their existence endangers all of us if they fall into the wrong hands, so they must be recovered or destroyed,' Jim answered as clearly and decisively as possible hoping he had said enough.

'You have always appeared to me an honest man, and therefore, I must reluctantly trust you. Just remember, if anyone recognises you, there is nothing I can do to help. God speed and I trust that you find what you are looking for. The quicker you go there the sooner you will return. So go to Berlin and let Fergus arrange the details,' Winston commented boarding the Norseman to fly to Prestwick. They watched the aircraft disappear, hoping they would soon meet again and still be in one piece.

Jim had no idea why Klaus and Carl insisted on him going with them to Berlin. Firstly, he could not speak German, and secondly; he was not good at visiting new places without a guide. Carl said Jim had one important advantage in that, he was an Englishman and would give their mission an aura of truth. Jim was still apprehensive when they flew to Blackbushe airport to board an RAF cargo plane flying supplies to the British garrison in Berlin. The journey was uncomfortable as there were no seats, so they sat wedged between the boxes filling the fuselage. Luckily, a regular supply of sandwiches and hot coffee kept their spirits up during the journey. When the pilot announced they were soon to land in Berlin, Carl and Klaus became restless about returning to where they nearly died. The fear was infectious as Jim wondered if they would come across former Nazis, who would kill them without blinking an eye. Then when the plane descended to land, Jim noticed both Klaus and Carl were silent as if in prayer.

The arrival at RAF Gatow was easy; no one examined their papers as they had the highest military clearance and the power to commandeer any transport or equipment deemed necessary. They carried their British issued revolvers on their hips and at RAF Gatow collected extra ammunition. Officially, they were in Berlin to assess the needs of the population in case the Russians prevented or seriously interrupted the overland supply of essential goods. It was an ideal cover as it gave them access to all of West Berlin and a jeep with a driver. From the airport, they drove to an official safe hotel where they checked into their large room before sitting down for lunch. It was a plain meal but enough considering most people in Berlin had nothing or little to eat. On the way, they passed many ruined buildings with doors and windows boarded up. The few shops open for business had long queues of people desperately waiting for a delivery of freshly baked bread or horse-meat. What they saw was just like in Britain having numerous large bomb craters and damaged buildings, except in Berlin where the devastation was much greater. Occasionally, there was Nazi graffiti still on walls that no one bothered to remove.

Jim's heart went out to the men and women wearing what appeared to be rags trying to survive among the ruins of a once magnificent city. He felt no bitterness because their poverty and hardship were more than enough payment for their years of benefiting and enjoying from Nazi plundered wealth. They could see the effects caused by the bombing, and the excesses of the conquering armies from the poor state of the buildings. Berlin had suffered grievously from looting, rape and murder, as the victorious warriors took what they considered their rightful rewards. It must have been terrible being German, trying to get enough to eat and shelter their families from the bedlam raging in the streets. Most of the surviving shops had no glass and showed signs of having been plundered. One antiques shop displayed a few damaged clocks and tables on sale for fuel; people needed wood to burn to heat their homes, especially during the cold winter nights. In many ways, Berlin was a ghost town where millions struggled to live having nowhere else to go. Nobody, but especially the Germans, could escape from the enclave without risking capture by the Russians. Some tried to stow away in aircraft or on freight trains, but the Soviets interned everyone they caught. Therefore, the people lived in an enclave inside the Soviet East Germany worked hard and scavenged to survive. Some remained honest finding work while others joined criminal gangs stealing from everybody, including the allied soldiers, especially when drunk. No one was safe at night when only a few street lamps lit the darkness.

After a good night's sleep, they started their quest by walking towards the ruined Reichstag passing people scurrying about, picking things off from the streets. On every corner, there were armed British soldiers who appeared confused as exactly what their duties were. Occasionally, officials trying to find known criminals, Russian agents, and former Nazis war criminals asked them for their papers. Then Jim did all the talking, so when the officials saw the senior authority in their papers they saluted and tried to be helpful. Clearly, the concept of being on an investigative mission assessing Berlin's problems was effective. Sometimes the security men would give their opinion on the situation, some good some bad. Some asked why Britain sent supplies to Berlin when times were so hard at home. Their comments shocked Carl and Klaus more than Jim. It was absurd that the buses and the *Untergrundbahn* or *U-Bahn* trains ran on time while nearby posters announced the performances of the Berlin Philharmonic playing

Mendelssohn next to those warning people to obey the directives of the occupation forces and to rebuild their city. The question was how they could rebuild their homes when building materials were scarce and too expensive for ordinary people to afford. Most windows were covered with cardboard to replace the broken glass while became doors were often just old curtains. During the day, life was simple, while at night, criminals roamed the streets. The street people were a mixture of refugees from East Germany and all over Europe looking for food, shelter, and work. They sold everything from matches to people. Life was cheap – too cheap.

Some fifteen minutes from the *Reichstag*, a British patrol with a German police officer stopped them. The German was too arrogant and inquisitive for Jim's liking. First, he looked at Jim to examine his papers before asking. 'Captain Brown RN why are you in Berlin?'

'We're on a mission to study the needs of the British Garrison and the German people. You have no right to question anything we do or say. Have I made myself quite clear?' Jim firmly answered.

'Sir, there is no need to get angry,' he replied sullenly. 'I am only doing my duty.'

'Then I suggest you do it. This is a difficult enough mission without you questioning us when you should be keeping the streets safe and free of criminals. Did you know there is a Nazi motif painted on a house only a street away? London will not be pleased to hear Nazis roam the streets leaving their propaganda on the walls for all to see. Show me your papers and state your name?' Jim demanded now enjoying his new role.

'I am Corporal Hans Wits, sir. Please do not cause me any trouble. If I lose this job, it will be very hard to find another,' he pleaded offering his papers but Jim handed them back unread.

'This once I'll forget your impudence, but remember visiting delegations must be helped and protected at all times. If not, heads will roll,' Jim promised while ending the conversation.

The patrol all saluted as Jim walked away. They were probably relieved he was not going to put them on a charge of insubordination. They did not look back fearing someone would follow them, but nothing happened.

Carl led them around in a circle stopping at intervals outside a shop or a bomb site to be seen writing notes. He recorded everything to show any curious person his notebook with comments written in immaculate English. They lunched at a restaurant that only served allied personnel that paid in pounds or HM occupation currency. Here they ate sausages and mashed potato with strong cups of tea among British soldiers who talked about the football starting in England. Even in Berlin, there was a football match every Saturday between the British and French watched by a large number of Germans. After leaving the restaurant, they walked in a straight line, as Carl knew exactly where he was going and intended to get there fast. Soon they were near the Gatow Airport on the north side of a lake where there stood a large derelict house. There was no name or even a number to indicate its address, but both Carl and Klaus knew the large garden with the waters of the lake lapping gently at its edge. A remarkable house, it must have looked fantastic when its gardens were full of flowers.

'This run-down mansion was once a famous venue for musicians where the best classical music could be heard. Admiral Canaris called it his House of Mirrors as music portrayed every emotion exposing our deepest feelings. He said a good overture told the skilled listener about the composer and the theme while the audience's responses exposed their concealed, often closely guarded, sensitivities. It was our secret. I think some people thought the House of Mirrors was a nightclub, museum, or ancient building,' Carl told Jim.

'That is a clever idea. I would never have thought it was a musical auditorium,' Jim commented.

'Not an auditorium, more a place where musicians could perform together and where we learnt to professionally play the piano. In fact, it was more like a conservatoire,' replied Klaus.

'Now we are here we must be more cunning than the fox and cautious like a cat as this is where danger may lurk behind every corner. Remember we do not know if anyone has found Admiral Canaris' dossiers or knows why we came. Therefore, Klaus and I will enter first while you keep watch from inside the front door. Do not worry about killing anybody, as no one will notice another body in a city where there are five murders and two hundred and fifty robberies reported every day. I expect there are many more undiscovered. Sadly, this is a place where organised crime melds well with espionage and with the ghosts of fascism rising from the grave,' Carl said adding a serious tone to the occasion.

Inside the building, everything was derelict with boarded windows and parts of the ceiling hanging down under a damaged roof. In places, sunlight came in from the roof to reveal a floor covered with layers of leaves mixed with dust and rubble, but importantly, no footprints. It looked like they were the first people to come inside the ruins for a long time. As requested, Jim hid behind a pillar near the closed front door and loosened a board over a window to have a clear view of anyone approaching the old house. While waiting for the others to return, he noticed the finely fashioned but dirty plaster friezes adorning the walls and ceilings with a golden chandelier that rocked gently in the breeze. The walls were covered with faded and in places torn luxurious textured wallpaper with the classic blue and white Wedgwood pattern. The remains of the staircases of the finest mahogany still shone through a layer of dust as if just polished. Clearly, this was once a spectacular magical place when vibrating to the sounds of music and people laughing. Indeed, a place one always remembered.

Carl led the way down a staircase at the back of the auditorium to the women's cloakroom. It was mostly unchanged, not large, but beautifully decorated with three mirrors and four wash basins. A small door led to a toilet with a little mirror above it that Carl removed from its hidden spring setting to reveal a layer of plaster behind which was a little wooden door opening into a chamber with the documents. Carl carefully put ten bundles of neatly wrapped documents into a bag before replacing the mirror. Expertly they covered every footprint, so they left everything as they had found it, that is, minus the dossiers. On getting back to the front door, they fell silent as a dark haired sixty-year-old man approached the building, lit a cigarette before walking around the house. He tried with all his might to open the front door but could not because Jim was holding it fast. After a while, the man gave up to walk to a car and drive off. Klaus looked shaken holding his pistol ready to fire.

'Easy Klaus, it's probably just a coincidence that Herr Diedrich Hoffmann came here. If he found us, he dare not say anything because we know he was one of the businessmen who funded the escape of many Nazis and still does,' Carl calmly said.

'Of all the turncoats we should run across, it had to be that rat Diedrich and wearing a US uniform. I wonder what he is doing in the British zone. If he isn't careful, someone may recognise him to settle old scores in a permanent way,' Klaus remarked with an evil grin.

'Let the disgusting dog run away to hide among his new masters. We must not draw attention to ourselves and imperil the mission. Now we should return to our hotel,' Carl commented.

Back in the safety of their hotel room Carl read the documents one by one setting four to one side. Canaris numbered every page so anyone finding one missing would know it, but they would not know who had taken it. However, Carl was not going to take any risks and sent Klaus out to find an old friend. It was risky but less dangerous than letting Winston destroy any evidence against some of his fascist friends. Carl laid each dossier on the table to photograph. Some dossiers were only a page while others up to ten pages. The meticulously Carl photographed every word and diagram on each document twice on two separate films using a Minox miniature camera he took from his pocket.

'Jim I must ask you to forget I photographed the dossiers. I am only doing this as a form of insurance in case Winston decides one day to play the politician and abandon us. It probably will not happen but all politicians are experts at playing to the gallery; they only differ in what they say and do. Sadly, few understand loyalty like you and I, for most politicians and diplomats change their allegiance as often as we change our underclothes. You must tell no one about the copies, not even Klaus,' Carl solemnly demanded and seeing Jim's nod offered him a Sobraine cigarette.

'Carl you know I owe you my life, especially after Albania, I will not say a word because I believe our survival is so interwoven that betraying you would be like committing suicide,' Jim answered with a laugh, making Carl thankful for having such a good friend. Then Carl spent the next two hours pacing up and down the room chain smoking and looking agitated. By the time, Klaus returned the cigarette trays overflowed with butts, and the air was disgustingly heavy with cigarette smoke. With Klaus was an old grey haired man who was clutching a leather briefcase.

'Greeting dear friend, I never thought I would see you again Gunter Kohl. Can you still make accurate copies of documents like you used to?' Carl asked.

'Carl it is good to see you looking so well though like all of us not young anymore. I still secretly make my living forging handwritten papers even Russian IDs, but I am very careful not to produce false identities. I keep clear of the many Gestapo rats still in Berlin reportedly working with criminals of all nationalities. Please be careful as I often see Diedrich Hoffmann in a US uniform, who would kill you if he could. He visits my shop to look at the old books trying to remember who I was, but so far, he does not see in this old broken body the man he left for dead, and you kept alive. My life is your life. So what can I do for you?' Gunter said.

'If I asked you to copy four pages of old German script on textured paper in green ink, could you do it?'

'Of course, it's very easy.'

'Could you do it tonight in this room?'

'Yes I can because Klaus told me that you may need me to copy letters written in green ink on old parchment. Therefore, I have brought all I need including the old-fashioned pens and parchment that are in great demand by those wanting forged birth certificates looking like the originals to replace those they say they lost. Their necessity pays for most of my meagre needs. Please pardon an old man rambling on and let me start?' Gunter remarked sitting down by the table to set out his pens, paper and ink neatly in front of him on a drawing board.

'Gunter I want you to copy these four sheets with exactly the same words but just changing the names to common ones such as Brown, Jones, Black, Smith, etc.,' Carl answered.

'I will start straight away, but it would be better if no one smoked as it can interfere with my work. The smoke gets in my old eyes and affects the time the ink takes to dry. Then if you would be so kind, I would like a cup of real coffee, something I have not tasted for years, and maybe a very large ham sandwich,' Gunter requested.

'Of course you can. What a rascal you are eating ham and coming from a once famous Jewish family,' Carl commented with a laugh.

'Since you saved my life by making me a Christian, I have followed their ways even attending Mass on holy days. No more idle talk as I must start copying good Admiral Canaris' beautiful script. I must take my time to give his work the justice it deserves. I always admired his beautiful handwriting that I would recognise anywhere,' Gunter replied as he started writing.

It was two in the morning before all four pages were finished; the green ink carefully blotted and dried. The copies were exact even to the extent of having Canaris' initial C placed on the bottom right hand corner of each sheet exactly as in the others. The copies were so good that the best handwriting expert could not distinguish them from the originals. Then everyone sat around drinking Schnapps, smoking Carl's cigars and chatting. Gunter spoke excellent English as Carl refused to speak German in case the walls had ears. During the night, Gunter referred to Carl's family; whose graves were in East Berlin, killed during the Nazi regime, but nobody said how. However, they did emotionally toast to fallen comrades and departed loved ones.

At first light, they went to an excellent restaurant for breakfast before Gunter left to go home. Gunter was pleased with his night's work and felt more hopeful for the future, especially with twenty fresh British five-pound notes in his wallet. It was worth a fortune as the *Reichsmark* was nearly worthless. He hoped no one would bother him and luckily; no one did. He was glad to know some of Admiral Canaris' staff survived but hoped he would not meet them again in this life. That night in bed, he prayed for them and all friends past and present, the living and the dead. He remembered the good times before the war when he saw Carl laughing with Helga by his side at a grand music recital. Maybe Carl would marry again, but like him, he may be content to live with the memories of those he lost. Why did so many innocent people have to die and for what? He felt there was no German alive who had not lost a loved one in that theatrical farce known as the Third Reich. Then he wiped the tears from his eyes to sleep with his Luger pistol under his pillow. Old habits are hard to stop.

Carl, Klaus, and Jim arrived at RAF Gatow in the middle of an emergency as someone reported a nearby murder of a man who from the photographs was Diedrich Hoffmann. Someone cut the poor man's throat then tore his clothes as if searching for secret papers or money. Clearly, it was time to leave before they ended up murdered. Jim shuddered at the thought that only yesterday they worried if Hoffman would recognise Carl or Klaus, and today he was dead. Violence was getting too close for comfort, and with Hoffman's death, could come many questions they did not want to answer. The Americans would be angry that their man was dead, and if they recognised Carl or Klaus, they could arrest them as murderers.

'Who would do such a foul deed?' Carl asked the Duty Officer.

'Probably, it was the *Lehrter Banhof* gang. It consists of deserters from the Red Army and refugees from all over

Europe. In May about a hundred men attacked a train at Anhalter Banhof and shot it out with the Military Police until they were either dead or captured,' the Duty Officer replied as if violence was normal. Sadly, it was.

With some relief, but also a great deal of regret, they left RAF Gatow. As the aircraft took off, they saw through the window the heavy rain battering the isolated city. Each drop felt like the skies opened to cry for the suffering of the people. It was a sobering thought that the average German was as human as their British cousins were. The only difference was the language, and a twist of fate.

Throughout their journey back to Black Island, Carl said nothing important but held on to his bag as if his life depended upon it, as Klaus passed the time talking and joking with Jim. It was the first time Klaus was relaxed since arriving in Berlin. His good mood was infectious so soon Jim was smiling, and Carl looked calm as he tried to sleep.

22. Dark Secrets

History is written by the victors often hiding unpleasant truths.

Two days after returning from Berlin an unusually agitated Fergus arrived on Black Island. He hardly said a word to anyone until he met Carl to ask. 'Did you find Canaris' dossiers?'

For a moment, Carl said nothing but just sat smoking a cigar, as though he had all the time in the world. He knew he held the winning hand knowing it was Fergus and Winston, who worried what the dossiers contained. For Carl knew he had secrets that were better hidden behind closed doors, suspecting both Fergus and Winston of being no purer than he is. It is strange that the company one keeps even when they do things we abhor may judge us. If a friend spies for the enemy, whomever that may be, how can we know, especially if he or she is good at their job?

Fergus wisely decided to change his approach when he saw his initial bullying manner was not getting him anywhere.

'I am very glad to see that you all returned unharmed. Was the mission successful or must I wait to read the latest revelations in the gutter press?' he asked with his old usual smile.

'We were in luck as we were not recognised by anyone and recovered the documents. I cannot tell you whether they are originals or copies as anyone could have been there before us and changed them. It would have to be someone who understood Admiral Canaris' code, which means Klaus and me. All the others died long ago. As agreed, I have them all in this bag for you to do with as you please. However, I must recommend you read them carefully as they provide information about neo-Nazis and communists, who at this moment may be walking the corridors of Whitehall,' Carl said as he handed over the dossiers.

'Have you read them?' Fergus demanded.

'Of course I've looked over them to think they will be useful. Though I doubt if you will dare punish the people concerned, but knowledge of their treachery may help in the future. Think of the dossiers as a warning from the grave about those who pretended to be loyal while betraying their families.'

'Will Winston be upset by what is written in the dossiers?'

'Well he won't like the fact that Hitler offered your exiled former King Edward VIII now the Duke of Windsor, the British Crown when Germany occupied England, and that he accepted the offer. Then there is the list of aristocrats who would support Hitler's invasion of Britain and those who sold military secrets to Japan,' Carl commented as if it was not important.

'My God if this was published it would rock the country, even endanger the monarchy! Is there any more information that will cause Winston more sleepless nights?'

'It is hard for me to tell because I do not know how much, he is already aware of. I can say I was surprised to read Admiral Canaris' list of eight British men in public life that spied for the Soviet Union. The one man who interests Jim is Kim Philby, who runs the Balkans Office of the Foreign Office, who Canaris says has been a communist since university. You may find the writing hard to read as it is in the classical German script where the letter P appears to look like an F or vice versa. He implies two of Philby's friends, a Burgess and a Maclean also spy for Russia. He thought this was out of a belief in communism rather than for the money - so they are very dangerous people.'

Each word hit Fergus like a bullet forcing him to sit down looking ashen. Could it be true the Russians had penetrated the Foreign Office and MI 6 even before the war was over? It was much worse than he expected and confused he sat with mouth wide open.

'I think it would be wise if you make copies of the dossiers in case Winston decides to patriotically destroy them,' Carl advised before continuing. 'I have done my part and given you Admiral Canaris' dossiers. You will like the description of Winston as a born leader whose stubbornness could be his downfall. Canaris comments that if they had met during peaceful times, they would have enjoyed each other's company and become friends. One of the last dossiers tells how the Nazis planned to hide their gold for use if defeated, using ODESSA to smuggle their supporters to Spain, then on to Paraguay and Argentina.'

'This ODESSA link may explain why so many high-ranking Nazis have disappeared. They must have settled around the world like the Kraken awaiting the call to bring forth a Fourth Reich,' Fergus subconsciously said aloud. Then scratching his head added. 'We know many are in Russia and America, but how many are hiding in Britain and her colonies?'

Next day, Fergus slowly read the dossiers page by page sometimes stopping to make notes and at other times saying comments like 'Oh God, he surely can't be another traitor!' While all this was going on Jim and Klaus disappeared into the outhouse to a small dark room. Very carefully, they developed the films from the Minox to give the finest grain and best contrast. Only when the negatives were dry did they make prints of each document using the enlarger. They emerged from the darkroom five hours later with two fine copies of the dossiers they placed into an envelope and handed it to Carl.

At dinner, Fergus was very quiet and yet surprisingly happy. What he read shocked him, but it was what he expected. From his experience of the shady world of espionage things changed rapidly as yesterday's friends became today's enemies. Winston would not like the list of Americans who helped the Nazis but could not change the fact that in all wars the unscrupulous make money out of other's misery. In fact, many of Britain's biggest companies made armaments or financed dictators around the world.

'Carl, do you think the USA before Pearl Harbor would let the Germans or the Russians destroy Britain?'

'Fergus you ask difficult questions. I am certain America would never have attacked Germany until Hitler declared war on them. So the answer to your question is no, they would have happily let Britain stand on her own against Germany and Italy.'

'But why would they just sit back and watch Britain being destroyed?'

'I believe America fears socialism more than fascism; and out of jealousy wants to destroy Britain and her Empire. Remember they never backed the fledgling League of Nations when it condemned Italy for conquering Abyssinia or Germany for annexing Alsace Lorraine. In fact, when France and Britain demanded that Germany does not invade Poland, America was as quiet as the proverbial grave. The average American politician is a rich man who believes in capitalism even if it enslaves their own people. President Roosevelt cunningly played lip service when he supported Britain through Lend-Lease to supply essential equipment, including some new liberty boats to carry American exports across the Atlantic. It was what the Americans call a 'you lose; we win situation'. By arming Britain and Russia in their fight against fascism, America could delay or even avoid getting directly involved in the fighting and if Britain survived, she would have to repay the cost of all the exports. I know Britain needed more ships than she could build but one day someone will question the nature of the deal. However we must be grateful for their considerable help in fighting Germany and keeping the Russian bear out of Western Europe. Many of the American generals recognise the danger that the Soviets pose to the free world and by standing firm have stopped the Russians from taking over all of Germany and most of Europe. We may not always agree with their methods, but they are good strategists and their presence gives peace a chance. I sometimes wonder whether the President knows what his secret services are up to especially regarding using fascists to keep communists at bay.'

'Your problem Carl is you think too much about matters few, if any, of us can control. Only history will tell whether we stopped the spread of communism without letting the fascists take over. It is a very difficult balancing act. Now we have a chance of winning with the information you, and Admiral Canaris have given us. I am familiar with some of the names of Hitler's friends such as the committed fascists Sir Oswald Mosley and Unity Mitford, but some of the others are worrying. Did Paul Getty really purchase stolen artwork from the Nazis via his hotel in Paris? Did some American millionaires fund the Nazis right up until, and maybe after, Pearl Harbor? Does the CIA even today help Nazi war criminals escape to Argentina and Paraguay or ignore ODESSA? I expect the dossiers will cause Winston many sleepless nights as he decides what to do with this information. Still I must say, well done as you have prevented the dossiers from getting into the enemy's hands and made us better prepared for the future,' Fergus said with a childish grin.

'Gentlemen, I propose a toast! To Admiral Canaris, long lost friends and for a world worth living in,' announced Carl with a glass in hand and standing to attention.

'To Admiral Canaris and long lost friends,' everyone shouted sincerely. They all hoped that because of him, the world would keep tyranny at bay.

There followed a long discussion concerning the dangers that were all around like sharks circling this island nation. Fergus expressed his anger at the American refusal to share the secrets of the atom bomb which British scientists helped develop. He was angry at how much help America gave Japan and Germany, some said much more than Britain. It did not bode well for the future of a secure Europe or even a peaceful world when the most powerful nations selfishly took all the winning for themselves leaving their allies bankrupt.

'We understand hundreds of gold bars disappeared from German banks and from depositories hidden deep in abandoned mines. While in the Far East no one knows what happened to the Japanese gold and the treasures taken from China, only that they vanished without trace. These included large objects too big to hide such as the famous prehistoric skull known as Peking Man (*Sinanthropus pekinensis*) and the Imperial Chinese jade statues. It appears that the thieves roam the world stealing as much as they can before we can keep them safe or return them to their rightful owners,' Fergus said.

'In my opinion, nothing disappears without a trace unless someone silences all those involved, usually by killing them. Small items such as precious jewellery and gemstones, which can be put in the pocket, can disappear. However, governments or groups of people could only steal large items such as bullion and paintings. They're either sold to unscrupulous collectors or hidden and later retrieved,' Carl responded, as it was common knowledge.

'I think it is best that you remain here because the Americans are angry about the loss of their fascist supporters in Greece, at least until things calm down. There is no emergency because the OSS is being careful that no one asks too many questions about the fascists found in Greece. We have made it quite clear to them that if they interfere with our people, we will publish what we know about Captain Petros and his Nazis. This appears to have made a small, but I hope, significant dent in their confidence. So for now, you will no longer be combatants but research anything and everything you can find about the missing gold and hopefully how we can get hold of some of it,' Fergus informed his attentive audience.

Fergus made it clear that should they find anything they were to tell only him, adding there were too many people who worked for the side paying the most, and that was not Britain.

In the following months, they turned the study into a sorting office where all the information to be collated was put together like a giant jigsaw puzzle with many of the crucial bits missing. Carl suggested they could start with the ex-Nazi SS commander and war hero *SS-Obersturmbannführer* Otto Skorzeny then living in Spain. Reports indicated that he was the head of ODESSA short for *Organisation der ehemaligen SS-Angehöngen* meaning the organization of former SS-Members. Some believed Skorzeny was the brains behind the disappearance of many Nazis and their relocation under new identities in the Americas. Others suggested Skorzeny also ran *Kameradenwerk (*Comrade Work) which found jobs for Germans around the world often with Spanish or South American companies. The most difficult person to trace was the evil genius *Reichskanzler* Martin Bormann, who distributed millions of dollars of Nazi funds through his *Aktion Feuerland* project. Reports said that Bormann died in Berlin but his body not found. Where he lived and what he did was one mystery, Carl wanted to expose. Jim was shocked when he read Herman Schmitz's statement to the Nuremberg War Crimes Tribunal that Martin Bormann was safe with his millions because he had loyal friends in Washington.

Hidden among the files was the case of Heinrich Mueller, who died in 1945 or was he arrested fleeing from Berlin and interned. The final was marked terminated under US National Security. Another report suggested he joined a US Intelligence agency while yet another said he worked for the Russians. It did not matter what was true because neither side would give Britain access to their files. As Churchill bravely stated - a cold wind was blowing across Europe bringing a new Cold War based on fear and subversion.

Meanwhile, Carl was shocked to learn that *Generalmajor* Reinhard Gehlen, who commanded German military intelligence regarding the Soviet Union, now worked for America. This Nazi had replaced Admiral Canaris before escaping to surrender to the US Army Counter Intelligence unit in Bavaria. Then he went to Camp King near Oberursel and interrogated by Captain Bokor where he offered the Americans all his files on Russia and their contacts around the world. He had prepared for defeat by copying on microfilm all the records of the Foreign Forces – East Unit or *Fremde Heere Oest* before burying them in sealed containers in Austria. Gehlen shocked the Americans by telling them the names of their staff who were members of the US Communist Party. Nobody knows if this information was true, hearsay, or just made up, ruffled feathers in high places when his work came to their attention. On hearing of Gehlen's offer General Bedell Smith checked with Washington before accepting it. Within days, American operatives recovered the buried microfilms and released Gehlen to run the South German Industrial Development Organization based in Munich. Actually, this spy network had over three hundred and fifty former Nazi agents operating throughout Europe. They avoided prosecution by changing uniforms to serve new masters, mainly the OSS.

Eventually, Britain decided she could do nothing about the former Nazis working for the USA and the USSR, but knowing who they were might prove useful when dealing with them. This information was sufficient to arrest or scare them when cornered. However, their presence was a constant reminder to Britain that the Soviet Union and America were prepared to fight a dirty war to get what they wanted. Both had secret organizations employing assassins and covert operatives to penetrate most organizations. The OSS and Department 6 mirrored the Soviet SMERSH or *Smert Shpionam* (Death to Spies). Both recruited agents from all occupations to undermine, disgrace, or kill eminent people who opposed their activities or were uncooperative. They selected agents from their past records such as military successes, intelligence, ability to operate on their own for years and a total lack of morals. The agents must be able to eliminate any target, whether men, women, or children without feeling, while remaining undiscovered.

Carl became increasingly intrigued concerning the disappearance of some of the latest submarines such as the type XB and XXI U-boats capable of transferring people and bullion over long distances underwater such as across the Atlantic. From Carl's work during the war, he knew that Germany built submarines to use for secret long-distance operations. These special ships did not appear on the inventory of U-boats. Then to confuse observers they had the number of an older sunken vessel painted on the conning tower. This meant that they could operate away from the eyes of the navy to drop agents, equipment and transfer technical staff between Germany and Japan. He felt that such phantom ships took many Nazis secretly to South America. They probably included the later versions of the older large type XIV 'Milk

Cows' once used to supply U-boats at sea. Whenever he was about to trace a vessel, the German records reported her sunk, but often this did not agree with allied reports. This could be because after completing the mission, they scuttled the U-boats, and their crew transferred to ordinary vessels. Maybe they renamed some and moved them elsewhere. If they had sunk, it would certainly hide all evidence of their presence. For instance, one more wreck on the seabed will go unnoticed, as will a submarine hidden in a shelter on the banks of a larger South American river.

If Carl wanted to prove his theory, he would have to come up with enough evidence for Churchill to agree to fund a treasure hunt. In time, he could find allies among the Jews who wanted the Nazi war criminals executed and their goods returned. However, for the moment, he had other urgent matters to deal with.

23. Muller Strikes Back

US Military Attaché Paul Muller discovered that the anti-fascist group he was after had a base on Skiathos. Therefore, he recruited the pro-German Greek Grivas who was serving in EDES with ten extreme right wing fighters for a special mission. This was because they had all had taken part in the massacres carried out in the mountain villages by Captain Petros and would do anything for money. Then Paul had them vigorously trained to attack a villa from the sea, using a modified motorised metal-hulled yacht armed with four Yugoslav, heavy machine guns and a forward 4-inch gun. He reckoned this should prove to be more than enough to destroy any building his enemy, The Painters, used as a base. Using all his resources, Paul secretly obtained a captured Yugoslav vessel that he painted navy gray and fitted with a 4-inch forward gun. Then she was sailed to a remote island twenty miles from Skiathos. On the island, he established a camp a long way from prying eyes to get everything ready for the operation that he hoped would eliminate all the British funded anti-fascists. Then for the next few weeks, Captain Grivas and his men practised attacking an old stone barn until they could reduce it to rubble in less than fifteen minutes. This pleased Paul as he waited for the enemy to return, and to gather more information on where the base was, when they would all be there and most importantly when the Greek navy was not operating within the region. Of course, this took time and a lot of money but the only thing that mattered was to destroy the Painter's base, kill them so that all of the blame was placed firmly on the communists. Paul decided to give Captain Grivas a free hand as when to attack and how much damage he caused to the surrounding area. So Paul ordered that his men kill all witnesses; however innocent, without hesitation, but later when questioned he denied it. It was important that no one traced the attack back to his office or to Department 6 to exasperate an already deteriorating situation. He knew the British and French governments were angry about American activities against their forces abroad, in their own countries, and in some colonies where they instigated revolution or trained indigenous people to lead and fight for their independence. The great American ambition of dominating all nations was no longer a secret except among the uneducated and the blind. For the US plans to succeed, they must be seen as liberators who equally fought colonialism, communism and fascism. Indeed, they would become the acceptable face of capitalism that would fund economic and political development. The Americans never told of the poverty and near slavery under which their indigenous red Indians and former black slaves lived. Instead, they preached that in the USA, everyone was equal in a democracy based on one-man one vote. They also demanded that all people should determine their own future, especially in their allies' colonies. However, this did not apply to any of the many American occupied territories because they supplied cheap labour and materials.

When ready, they waited for the Painters to return to their large villa in Koukounaries that was situated in an exposed position at the end of the southern arm of the bay. Paul felt its location would make it ideal for a naval assault. Though he would like to use a few rocket firing aircraft, but that would tell everyone who did it. Anyhow, his orders were to be nice to the British while undermining them at all times. He certainly charmed enough local politicians to make the US presence in Greece popular and financially rewarding. Paul found many of the senior Greek army officers were right wing with political ambitions that he could foster. Meanwhile, he continued his charm campaign to infiltrate the British Embassy by having a number of affairs with the wives of the diplomats. Often he only discovered that the women were eager for some extra-marital experience. At other times, after an evening or afternoon in his bed, others told him nearly everything he wanted to know. Usually it was silly, unimportant rumours until one afternoon an insatiable woman told him the Painters were returning to Skiathos to help in the fight against the communists. Therefore, after a few more drinks, he asked her when they would return and the woman told him the date. He could hardly suppress his excitement but continued satisfying her appetites until she happily left for home. Then he sprang into action leaving Athens for his new island base to meet with Captain Grivas to discuss the coming attack. It must be secret, swift and completely eradicate the base preferably with no survivors or witnesses. This was his chance to hit back at socialist Britain, who Washington distrusted more than the communism. To make the scheme plausible he supplied Captain Grivas with a Yugoslav flag to fly from the boat both during the attack and when leaving. Of course, they would scuttle the boat after the attack so no one could find out where it was and who was involved. It would be a perfect operation to revenge the loss of his men!

The Painters returned to Skiathos on Snow Goose II to resume operations in cooperation with Janus and EDES. On arriving, they set up communications with Fergus in Malta and Janus near Thessaloniki. Then Maria and Jim sailed to the mainland to buy all the consumables they needed for a month, while they planned a surprise wedding party for the couple. Keeping the celebration a secret was nearly impossible, but with grandmother's help, they contacted their friends giving them the time and place. Next, they arranged adequate security so that no violent act could spoil the happy day before sitting back to relax. Carl played the piano with Christos by his side while the others kept a look out for unwelcome visitors. Mario watched the south with a loaded Bren gun by his side while Klaus scanned the sea to the north. They did not know why, but something said that life would never be the same again as they were now an increasingly violent war. Mario was the most apprehensive having recently heard that right wing assassins had seriously wounded his father in Bari. For once Carl's sixth sense abandoned him but luckily, Mario's awareness had not. Maybe Carl's little bird had now befriended Mario to whisper in his ear that the Jackals were coming, whatever the case Mario was ready for them.

Meanwhile, Christos had arrived with a new recruit, Takis, who came to prepare the 2-inch mortars for use in a firework display for the wedding, using star burst rounds and homemade explosives. Takis was an expert in using mortars as well as enjoyed making fireworks of every type and had recently made a spectacular display in Athens.

Long before sunrise, Grivas' team sailed for Koukounaries to attack the villa just as the sun rose making their boat hard to see. It was a perfect plan that should have taken thirty minutes to execute relying on the ship's 4-inch gun to destroy the building while eight men attacked from the beach. Such a well-practised bombardment would destroy all but the strongest fortification as well as killing all inside. Each of his men carried a Russian PPSh41 Shpagin machine gun holding 65 rounds that should be enough to fight most skirmishes without reloading. Normally more than sufficient to destroy the target, but they did not know it was not a normal building but had reinforced walls. Once off Koukounaries Grivas landed eight men in two rubber boats on the beach to move undetected before taking up their allotted positions and await the naval bombardment. The first shell flew over the villa to land harmlessly in the sea before exploding, but the noise awoke the Painters. Christos and Takis raised the alarm after seeing the gunfire from a vessel some four hundred yards offshore.

'Klaus go to the radio and call for help. Mario get ready to fire your Bren guns as I'm sure after the bombardment, we will be attacked from the land,' Carl ordered handing out metal helmets. Then Christos arrived carrying a 2-inch mortar followed by Mario and Takis each with four mortar shells. In seconds, Takis set up the mortar to fire back on the vessel as Christos loaded each round. The first mortar shell exploded ten feet from the attacking vessel sending water up into the air but causing no damage and the second rocked the vessel but did not hit her.

'Takis and Christos get under cover,' Carl yelled, but they did not listen as they concentrated on trying to hit the boat.

Then a shell from the boat hit the building.

'Mario and Klaus shoot at the attackers on the ground while I help with the mortar.'

Another shell hit the house breaking a wall. One piece of shrapnel struck the back of Takis as he watched a mortar shell hit the bridge of the attacking vessel silencing the deadly 4-inch gun. Takis said nothing but stood bleeding while Christos fired another round into the enemy craft before turning the mortar to fire on the attackers on the ground. Carl found the mortally wounded Takis collapsing and tried to stop the bleeding, but it was too late. Unaware of the tragedy, Christos continued firing the mortar until the surviving attackers and Captain Grivas retreated in a dinghy. Then he turned to see his friend bleeding on the ground and held him tight.

'Carl we sank her, thank you,' Takis said as he quietly died while Christos held his friend's hand. With tears streaming down his face, Christos prayed for the brave Takis.

'After losing Takis, we must postpone the wedding,' Carl said feeling very sad that he failed to protect their newest member. Takis was their first fatality and a reminder; they were only human.

'Don't you dare,' Christos angrily yelled back. 'It would tell the enemy that they won and mean Takis' died in vain. No, you will not. You must not tell anyone except Janus and Fergus what happened. I am sure we can clear up this mess before anyone finds out.'

'Maybe we can but what about all the noise?' Carl questioned.

'We tell everyone that our preparations for a firework display at the wedding went wrong, and now we must clear up the mess,' Christos replied daring anyone to answer back.

Carl smiled, and Mario added. 'I think that is what we will do.'

Therefore, in the next two days they cleared up the mess, made running repairs to the house, and told everyone in the bay that they were sorry for the noise promising not to repeat it. Because they were well loved and supported by grandmother, no one questioned the apology though some of the older men knew the difference between fireworks exploding and a 4-inch gun. Christos quietly buried Takis in the local cemetery before preparing for the coming wedding. He was not disloyal but was used to burying his friends and then returning to fight the enemy. For he knew that the Jackals were reeling from the defeat, and their American controller would be disillusioned even shocked that he had again failed. The following Sunday before Jim returned Carl, Christos, and Klaus went with grandmother and Mario to the Church in Skiathos town to attend mass and thank God for the life of the brave Takis, who gave his life to save them.

24. A Greek Wedding

After commuting between Skiathos and Scotland, Jim convinced Maria to be his wife saying it was preferable to fighting communists in the hills. She agreed on the condition that Father Mathias married them in Skiathos and her grandmother made all the arrangements. Jim found that acceptable as a few day's festivities were a small price to pay for a life of happiness with the woman he loved, no, he simply adored. There were people to invite, food purchased, clothes made or borrowed so that it would be the best wedding Skiathos had seen for years. Then Father Mathias arrived to officiate at the ceremony with the local priest according to the ordinances and customs of the Greek Orthodox Church.

On the eve of the wedding at Janus' request, a Royal Hellenic Navy frigate docked in Skiathos to help celebrate the wedding of a Greek hero and prevent anyone disturbing the special occasion. The sailors together with Janus' men searched every person and vehicle even examining every basket brought into town as well as stopping fishing boats at sea. No one complained, wanting to have a festival without fear of attack by the few remaining bandits. After the wedding was announced, distant relatives and friends of the couple travelled for days from the other islands and down from the mountains to attend. Others sailed in from the mainland aboard the overcrowded car ferry and in small boats. So many came that soon there was not an empty room in Skiathos with most places accommodating more people than usual. No one cared about sharing a small room as they came to attend the wedding and enjoy life as it was in the past.

Jim stayed in Koukounaries with Carl, Klaus, and Janus, trying to forget that tomorrow he would marry his beloved Maria. As was the custom, she stayed with her grandmother and women friends, banning all men from visiting their house or seeing her. They honoured the old Greek traditions down to the smallest detail. Only Father Mathias could enter but could not see the bride's gown. However, he did, as was his duty, bless her and give her the advice priests give most young women about love, family, and charity. In the Orthodox Church, divorce was unknown. Couples must stay together through thick, thin, through the good times, and even terrible ones until death did them part. For Father Mathias, love involved many things such as caring about each other before anyone else and the genuine forgiveness of each other's human failures and indiscretions. So even in unhappy marriages couples stayed together for the family's honour and the sake of the children. Often as they grew older, they understood each other better as they mellowed like a good wine with age. In marriage, the couple must share everything and accept whatever fate bestowed upon them. They also must teach their children to be grateful for all they had, never to be greedy, and always be loyal to their parents and mother church. By tradition, no friend or even family may expect too much from them as they made a home for themselves. Indeed, family and friends must help while expecting nothing in return. This tradition kept the island community strong and united.

Jim was embarrassed when Father Mathias said God considered both partners to a marriage as having a sacred duty to work hard at making it a success. He wanted to tell him that he was only marrying her out of love and not for any other reason, but wisely said nothing. While Carl added, everyone should be married once to give every part of themselves into the lifelong task of keeping their partner happy. He added a heartfelt personal message that whatever happened, they would always have glorious memories and their love to cherish which nobody can ever destroy!

That night Carl and Klaus took turns in playing on the grand piano Tchaikovsky or some Scott Joplin jazz they had just discovered. As Jim watched the sunset over Koukounaries Bay, he was aware this was his last day as a bachelor. He had no regrets at the thought of being married as up until he met Maria his life had been hard indeed often cruel. For the first time he had money, a woman who loved him and very good, loyal friends. What more could a man ask for? It was just after midnight when he went to bed feeling privileged to have his German friends by his side and hoping Mario or Fergus would turn up for the ceremony. They were not only his friends but also more importantly his only family. He was proud of every one of them.

Jim was up at sunrise to hear the cock crow and see the sun's rays reflecting on the sea make it glisten with a myriad of tiny lights. The house was quiet, as everyone, including Carl decided to get some sleep. Therefore, he walked alone down to the beach to swim while watching the locals collect shellfish from the rocks for breakfast, lunch, or dinner. He found the water refreshing but a bit cold. Then when he had ceremoniously washed away all his sins in preparation for his wedding, he returned to the house. On returning, he saw no one and convinced himself that his friends had forgotten what day it was. Just as he started to worry, Carl and Klaus appeared immaculately dressed in morning suits to tell Jim to hurry up and get dressed. After he dressed in a morning suit with top hat, they took him to the car waiting outside the front door. Then Christos in military uniform drove them carefully into town. Jim noticed for the first time that both Carl and Klaus wore their old wedding rings in support of him or in memory of departed loved ones. Whatever the reason it brought a lump to Jim's throat and a deep feeling of gratitude.

As soon as the car arrived at the church Maria's grandmother took Jim by the arm like a naughty boy to rush him inside a chapel where Father Mathias was standing. A few minutes later Carl, Klaus, and Christos joined them to kneel in silent prayer before Father Mathias led the men up to the altar steps to stand waiting for the arrival of the bride. It was a long wait as the congregation gathered to fill the church until there were so many that they had to stand outside occupying all the available space. Meanwhile, they loudly sang Greek hymns raising their voices in praise of God until without any warning the singing stopped. Everyone looked at the church door in anticipation of being the first to see the bride. Maria entered on the arm of Janus in his brand new Major's uniform followed by a kilted Fergus and Mario. However, Jim only saw his Maria dressed in a white lace dress with a simple tiara on her head and a thin veil covering her face. It appeared that her smiling eyes shone through the veil dispelling all Jim's fears while making him feel like a child opening his best Christmas presents. For a moment, the sunlight coming through the stained-glass windows illuminating the bride with a multitude of colours to produce an image of perfection. Then Jim knew God and all his angels were around to bless their marriage.

Of the rest of the service, well that is history. Alas Jim remembered very little about the service other than when Father Mathias announced them man and wife. Then two choirboys held crowns over their heads while Father Mathias enjoyed anointing them with liberal amounts of holy water before leading them out of the front door of the church to present them to the waiting crowd. He yelled out 'Jim and Maria Hands, may everyone present salute them and help them live a happy life together.' The crowd responded yelling their names while the couple stood trembling holding hands and feeling the new wedding rings on their fingers.

Father Mathias stood aside to allow the newlyweds to walk down the steps while people showered them with flowers and rice. For a moment, Jim was suddenly afraid someone would appear from the crowd to shoot his Maria. It happened in Lorna Doone, but God was with them and the bad men stayed away. He need not have worried as Janus' men and a strong contingent from the Greek navy carefully guarded them. This was one occasion Greece, and the people of Skiathos did not want sullied by violence and sacrilege. Today was the first of many happy festivals the island of Skiathos would enjoy without any fear of reprisal or even any bad behaviour.

They had transformed the waterfront taverna into a large tent with every space adorned with bouquets of colourful fresh flowers, and tables laid for the wedding party with spare food for everyone. Nearby in the open air, a bevy of chefs roasted on huge metal spits over roaring fires an enormous Ox, three lambs and two pigs. On tables spread around the taverna were dozens of bowls of olives, lettuce, fennel, and feta cheese for all to enjoy. Of course, there were baskets of freshly baked festive loaves, the famous *Tsouréki*, near *Pitta* unleavened bread, *Eliopsomo* olive rolls with herbs, and the crescent-shaped biscuits called *Gouraiethos*. Then, there was a choice of Greek cheeses cut up into small portions with cakes and a multitude of dipping sauces. Indeed, there was enough for everyone whatever their taste.

Jim and Maria sat at the head table next to grandmother, Father Mathias, Carl and Claus, and Mario and Fergus, Janus and Christos all proud to be alive in such a glorious place. Maria's grandmother was in command so no one could eat until after the speeches, which luckily were few and short. Jim responded simply by saying *Efcharisto* that he hoped meant thank you as he lifted his arms towards his precious Maria. The crowd roared approval with clapping and yells of encouragement only falling silent when Father Mathias stood up to bless the food. Afterwards, the feast started as everyone enjoyed the fine food to relish in such grand company. The many chefs toiled under the sun to cut slices of meat from the roasted animals on a spit that gradually became smaller. A continuous stream of waiters served the guests and cleared away after each course while keeping their glasses full of the finest wine and the traditional carafes of water. There was enough food and drink for everyone, including all the late comers such as Demokritos, Tomas, and Andreas, who had travelled for days to be with their friends.

After everyone finished eating, the musicians started to play classical Greek folk songs while men danced a very rhythmic dance the simple *Chios*, followed by the slow *Hassapiko* and finally, the fast *Hassaposerviko*. Next was the solemn traditional *Karsilina*, which Maria and Jim had to dance on their own until gradually joined by other couples. Afterwards, everyone had to dance whatever their age or status, including Carl and Klaus but especially Maria and her Jim. So for all that day until well into the night the sound of music and laughter echoed around the magical island. Jim felt like an observer at a beautiful ancient ritual. He did not understand many of the comments but felt all the love given. He did notice on a large table inside the tent a pile of parcels growing larger. When Jim asked about them, Maria kissed him, saying they were wedding presents that by tradition they must not notice or open until the next day. In this way, no one present was bigger or better than others were so even the smallest crumb was a blessing. This still did not stop people running up to Maria to pin money onto her dress, encouraged by the applause from the crowd so that soon Maria looked a bit like a money tree!

Jim asked Maria what happened to all the leftovers. She laughed saying it was for the musicians, chefs and the waiters. They were not allowed to eat until the taverna was clean and all the rubbish neatly taken away to be burned. Anything remaining after they had eaten went to the church for the sick and the poor. In this way, everybody in the community shared the feast and in so doing was a part of the celebrations.

People of all ages danced until they were exhausted, including the Royal Hellenic Navy. One of the first to dance a solo was Fergus, who executed an energetic highland sword dance with arms held high and his Royal Stuart Tartan kilt swinging in the breeze. It was so much fun that the people urged him to continue. He gave one encore before sitting down exhausted amidst loud applause. Next Carl and Klaus led by some of the Greek men took part in a slow, rhythmic, sensational traditional dance the *Hassapiko*. Gradually, Mario, Christos, and Janus joined in. Surprisingly, the navy provided a dance group complete with musicians, who dressed in white with red belts and hats, showed everyone how a real Greek performed. Afterwards, as though the navy had thrown out a challenge, more and more men demonstrated their agility or, in some cases, lack of it. Therefore, it was around two in the morning before Janus, and Christos drove the couple back to Koukounaries the house. The others spent the rest of the night in Skiathos town. As the couple drove off women ran up to Maria with tears in their eyes while men clapped or sang Greek songs.

Next morning the newlyweds lay in bed thinking just how lucky they were to have each other and such friends. While Maria was still sleeping, Jim got up to go out on the balcony and look at the calm sea. From there he saw Janus's car, with Christos asleep on the back seat and Janus shaking himself awake. Nearby against an olive tree another of Janus's men yawned with his rifle cradled in his arms after a night's vigil. Jim realised that all through the night, they were safe in each other's arms, while their Greek friends protected their love nest. Then Jim put on his swimming trunks, kissed his sleeping beauty, and went down to the sea with Janus. Suddenly, the water felt warmer and the morning sun brighter as a cool light breeze blew between the olive trees to sweep across the sand. The two men pranced around in the sea like a couple of silly schoolchildren feeling happy to be alive in such a wonderful place. Eventually wet and in need of a shower they returned to the house to find Maria busy setting a large table for some thirty people.

'Do we expect visitors?' Jim asked Maria hoping she would say no.

'Jim, don't sulk like a spoilt child! Of course, I expect our friends who travelled from the mainland to stay as our guests as well as those returning from their night in Skiathos. It is our duty to look after them before they start their journey home. Remember this house is not ours but shared with Carl, Klaus, Mario and Fergus,' Maria said with a smile meant to dispel any jealousy.

'It must have taken Fergus days to get here and collect Mario on the way. Then many of Janus's men, including Demokritos, Tomas, and Andreas came together with Father Mathias from the mainland. Now let us start by opening the presents to see what we have. Traditionally, they could be anything from a beautiful seashell to bed linen and even money,' Maria commented laying out bread and cheese next to the cups and plates.

'Yes, I've forgotten our house mates in the joy of living with you. Forgive my loss of memory and let me help get things ready.'

Maria said nothing except give him a long kiss and a big smile. Therefore, he accepted his new role as husband in supporting his wife in her duties. It was a strange way of starting a married life with not even a day alone as Maria taught Jim never to take anything for granted. Everything was peaceful as they walked down to invite Janus and Christos back to the house for a meal. They asked the guard to join them, but he politely refused to say he must remain alert but would not mind a piece of bread and maybe a cup of coffee. Just after Jim took the guard his breakfast, a large van arrived bringing the captain of the Greek frigate with the frogmen Dorus, Georgias, and Jonas. The white bus with the dove on its side closely followed them driven by Klaus and filled with old friends. The first to descend were Maria's grandmother, Demokritos, Andreas, and Tomas followed by Father Mathias. Last, to come were very tired but happy Fergus, Carl, and Mario. Soon the house resounded to the noise of people chatting about the previous day and what they did last night. They looked as if they had attended an all night rave, well in some ways they had. Though they were tired, they had not lost their appetites and soon Maria, helped by Mario and grandmother, were busy cooking eggs and bacon to satisfy everyone. Mario and Demokritos brought enough baskets of freshly baked bread and cheese for everyone.

It was sunset when the last visitor left.

'I was just thinking; Jim and Maria should have a romantic holiday away from us old folk,' Carl announced at dinner.

'That's a good idea,' Klaus said.

'So I have taken the liberty of renting a beautiful house on a nearby small peaceful island for the next two weeks. I hope that the newlyweds like my suggestion to sail there tomorrow in Snow Goose II and enjoy themselves while we slave away looking at more files. Is it agreed?' Carl asked looking Jim straight in the eye daring him to refuse his generous offer.

'Well, yes we accept your offer with thanks. That's if Maria wants to,' Jim replied realizing for the first time the decision was not his alone. This married life could prove both exciting and very difficult.

Maria snuggled up to Jim to add. 'Thank you Carl, I will obey my husband in everything he wants and says.'

There was a roar of approval.

'Maria you say the nicest things at the right time, but being a woman you will often disagree with my friend Jim,' Mario said.

'No, she will probably agree with all his suggestions then do the opposite,' Fergus suggested.

Everyone laughed.

Therefore, they spent their honeymoon alone on a neighbouring island. They didn't do much except swim or lie in the sun and make passionate love while surrounded by sea, white sand and flowers, which appeared to blossom just for them. It was so peaceful, so perfect, and so relaxing. They listened to the wind blowing through the olive trees and the sounds of birds celebrating life. For the first time in his life, Jim felt he had everything he dreamt of, and for those mercies, he thanked God before exhausted, falling asleep as the waves broke gently on the rocks below the house. Unknown to the lovers even in this paradise they were discretely protected by Christos and Andreas with rifles at the ready to repel any unwanted visitors. For after the attack on the house no one felt safe.

25. Goodbye Koukounaries

After their two week honeymoon, Jim and Maria returned to Koukounaries Bay, happy to be home. They were worried that there was no one waiting to greet them, in fact, it was very quiet – much too quiet. Being cautious, Jim went ahead with his Beretta in hand through the olive grove up to the house expecting at any moment for something nasty to jump out. Of course, nothing did. Instead, he found Mario asleep in a hammock, as happy as anyone can be in the glorious sunshine when a gentle breeze just brushes one's face. Maria gently approached the sleeping beauty to give him a kiss on the cheek to waken him. It worked, for in seconds Mario was up kissing Maria and hugging Jim as if they had come back from the dead rather than returning from a short honeymoon. His yelling brought Klaus to see what all the noise was about closely followed by Carl. In minutes, they were sitting around the kitchen table, all trying to talk at the same time while eating bread and cheese with cups of coffee.

After breakfast, Maria went off to visit her grandmother while Carl and Jim discussed the latest developments in Greece and the region. The war between the communists, the socialists and the fascists still continued as each side waged assaults on the other's bases. Carl offered to help the government forces, but Janus insisted it was the wrong time for them to reappear. Janus thought that the fledgling government in Athens did not want to do anything that might upset the Americans, who were replacing the British in Greece and re-arming the National Army. The older, wiser heads in Athens were not sure whether the American involvement was a good thing or a dangerous move towards fascism. They knew they needed the US funding for reconstruction as the British could not afford to continue keeping their troops in Greece. One socialist Member of Parliament requested the Americans to remove their Military Attaché Paul Muller because he had employed former Nazis as mercenaries. He received a polite reply saying America never employed fascists knowing how evil they could be. No one believed the reply, but they all hoped they would survive the communist threats from the north while suppressing any fascist tendencies within the army. They were starting to feel more confident when a socialist politician was mysteriously killed by bandits in a previously peaceful part of central Greece. The murder sent shock waves through Greece and Italy where both governments were confronted with political assassinations and the growth of a new fascist secret order called *Gladio*. This right-wing organization was run by the OSS with the motto *Silendo Liberatem Serva*, or 'Silently; I Serve Freedom'. The term *Gladio* was coined from the Italian for *Gladius*, the Roman fighting sword, to identify them with the military and ancient Rome. The symbol was similar to the Roman devices used by Benito Mussolini's Fascisti and so a blatant link between the Americans and the defeated fascists. Their creation as a force to assassinate all socialist or anti-American politicians showed how little the OSS understood Europe or her people. It resulted in many politicians publicly supporting the USA, while in private wishing they had gone home or stopped the communists.

In counties like Britain, France, Greece and Italy, many politicians united to create a fairer, more modern Europe from the ruins of war. In meetings held secretly, they tried to forge new alliances to protect them from the feeling that America was occupying Western Europe like the Russians had in the East. Their large military power was necessary to save Europe from Russia, but at what price? The American use of Nazis was to cause severe embarrassment when nationalist General Charles De Gaulle later came to power, resulting in France leaving NATO to distance herself from America and develop her own national defence. Many Europeans who suffered under the Nazis and other fascists, were appalled at how many war criminals escaped arrest for their murderous activities. Some people believed they were being colonised by America, made worse by clandestine meetings of American bankers and politicians to decide how to cash in on rebuilding Europe. Some of those covert organizations, still operate today to include most of the influential politicians and power brokers in the US and friendly nations.

The Painters remained on Skiathos waiting developments and feeling they were not as welcome as before. Carl started to think that many politicians considered them to be an embarrassment that was best forgotten even though still needed. Things suddenly became clearer when a messenger delivered a letter from the American Military Attaché in Athens addressed to Jim. It simply read:

Dear Mr. James Hands,   **Dated as postmark.**

I regret to inform you it has come to our attention that you work for a clandestine organization which in our opinion endangers the very essence of Greek democracy. Therefore, it is my sad duty to say that from the above date, you and your colleagues are hereby prohibited from entering any US base and the USA itself. You are all considered as dangerous enemies of America, who must be stopped before you can colonise the world for your imperialistic masters.

This decision has not been easy as we do not wish to antagonise either the Greek people or the British Government. I, therefore, strongly advise you to leave Greece together with your wife and your colleagues at the earliest opportunity. Failure to do so can result in you being hurt by those who do not want your sort destroying the fragile democracy that is now Greece. Your past murderous behaviour must be stopped before you let the forces of communism, and socialism rules this nation.

This decree applies to the following:

Lt James Hands, Carl van Stoff, Klaus Weiss and Mario Carlini.

Signed

Captain Paul Muller, US Military Attaché Athens.

Copied to the British Ambassador to Greece.

When Jim showed his friends the letter, Carl gave a cynical smile while Mario and Klaus were angry at the American threat.

'Sorry Jim but it is not unexpected as while you were away we helped Janus destroy another Jackal group in Thessaloniki who were undermining the fight against the communists. It was well equipped with the latest American weaponry and vehicles. Afterwards, against my wishes, a very angry Janus took the men we caught, to Athens in an attempt to show his commander what was happening. Instead of being congratulated Janus was severely reprimanded and ordered to have no more dealings with any of us,' Carl informed Jim looking very sad.

'Then we have little choice but to sail Snow Goose II to Malta and leave,' Maria decided for the rest of them. She did not hesitate for one moment knowing they would leave her grandmother, her island, and her people for the sake of survival.

'I don't think we have to act immediately but must inform Fergus of the latest developments. I can assure you he will be very angry, but I expect unable to interfere,' Carl added.

Jim felt devastated that their life in Skiathos was over for the foreseeable future but hopefully not forever. Maria's grandmother was very angry saying what the Germans failed to do, America and her allies in the Greek military were succeeding by sending her Maria into exile or face death. This attitude grew stronger as more and more local people visited the villa, promising their support even offering to form a militia and declare the islands independent. Christos and Andreas arrived with three others to guard the house. They were followed by two old soldiers ready to die fighting for their friends; their weapons cleaned and prepared for war or an invasion that never came. The disillusioned locals trusted no strangers even those from respected Greek families. One visitor from Athens who asked about buying land in Koukounaries was harassed, especially after remarking how nice it was to see so the Americans in Greece. Some said that socialism was the only way forward and following America was like being colonised, something all Greeks had experienced, dividing the nation into communists, fascists and socialists. The war continued as the fire of wrath seethed below the surface waiting to explode whenever someone went too far. Some say it has never gone away.

When Fergus arrived with Janus on a float plane, the noise of the aircraft's engines was just less intense than that of the brigadier exploding with anger at what he deemed betrayal.

'Jim what's all this nonsense about you working against the interests of the Greek people. What a way to treat newlyweds and their friends who have risked everything to keep this troubled nation free. I wonder if it would not have been better if America had never joined in the bloody war. It appears Pearl Harbor was not a big enough disaster for them to realise how evil fascists are,' Fergus yelled as he entered the house.

'I suppose the Americans are more afraid of us British than of fascists and communists,' Jim remarked hoping to turn the matter into a sick joke.

'It's no joking matter! I have just come from a long discussion with Janus and his more liberal superiors. They are, like us, worried about how quickly the Americans and the hard-line fascists have jumped into bed together. One of Janus's superiors suggested we sell the house in Koukounaries or convert it into a hotel for Maria's grandmother to run and move our operations to Thessaloniki,' Fergus said while pacing the floor with his hands behind his back like the famous Felix the Cat cartoon.

Unfortunately, the situation was far from humorous.

'I think we should convert the villa into a hotel for Maria's grandmother while we move to Thessaloniki. From there we can help Janus to keep the fascists out of eastern Greece,' Carl commented looking around the house.

'I have a better idea. Why don't we do as Carl says but instead of going to northern Greece where the Americans expect us to go, return to Black Island where they have no influence,' Jim said trying to find a way of keeping them together and safe.

'I think that's an excellent idea. So let's leave in style so the world knows we have left Greece with our heads held high not running away like criminals. We'll have a large party here in Koukounaries for members of the Greek Army and Government plus certain important diplomats. They will include the British Military Attaché and the American Military Attaché Captain Paul Muller. During the party, we will announce that the network we established for the Greek Army is no longer necessary because of the timely arrival of our brave American allies. We will leave the maps we captured together with notes on how fascism and communism endanger democracy in the Free World. When the party is in full swing, we will quietly slip away leaving Fergus, Janus and a few others to entertain the guests. Hopefully, we will be at sea before our enemies know we have gone,' Carl stated.

That's an excellent idea. Perhaps you would consider one more mission this time in Italy to destroy the fascists working in the Adriatic port of Bari. It would send a warning to Paul Muller and the OSS, that though we have left Greece, we are not finished fighting fascism. It could help Mario's family who are important democrats and protect them from the fascists in their home town,' Fergus requested.

'It is *magnifico mio* Fergus, *mille gracie*,' Mario exclaimed jumping with joy at the chance of helping save his family and beloved Italy from fascism and communism in one stroke.

'I think a trip to Bari would send the right message to the American colonialist and their Nazis friends,' Maria commented as tears filled her eyes before she kissed Fergus on the cheek.

The Brigadier unashamedly blushed.

It only took a few weeks to organise the party. Meanwhile, they moved Snow Goose II to a hidden mooring and packed their personal effects in crates to be shipped to Fergus in Malta and forwarded to Scotland.

At the farewell Party, Jim was surprised to discover that Paul Muller was a short man with cropped hair he called a crew cut, looking like an SS officer. For such a powerful man, he looked insignificant. However, he proved tactless by asking the guests what they knew about Carl and where he came from. He only stopped when Carl stood up to make a speech.

'Ladies and gentlemen, I am pleased to say our mission to support the National Army ended when I handed over our final report to the honourable Minister of Defence. Let me say the Greek people have been both brave and constant in their fight for an independent, democratic Greece, free from outside interference. We thank them for their kindness and hope your new friends the Americans will prove to be as loyal to your cause as we have been. Now we're no longer on active service we intend to enjoy the night getting well and truly drunk. Thank you friends and farewell foes,' Carl announced drinking a glass of watered down white wine.

Paul Muller sent his associate Conrad Hoffman to find out who Carl really was. However, Klaus recognised him as a Nazi and shocked all present by lifting Hoffman's arm high up in the air and shouting. 'Everyone come and see that I have found a wanted Nazi war criminal that should be in prison for what he did to my people. Instead, he serves his new masters the US of A and is a reminder that all fascists are not dead or imprisoned as many wear American uniforms.'

The room went silent followed by quiet discussion as the guests expressed their discontent at the presence of Captain Paul Muller and Herr Hoffman. It was when you could have cut the atmosphere with a knife that Jim walked over to a very confused Paul Muller. The Attaché had no clue what Jim looked like and was shocked when Jim introduced himself before telling Muller very politely what he thought of fascists like him. Muller just made an uncomfortable laugh half expecting Jim to hit him. In fact, he was disappointed when Jim did not, but from then onwards he avoided Klaus and Jim while trying to enjoy the evening knowing everybody was watching his every move. Paul wondered what would happen now some of his operatives were exposed for what they were – former Nazis. Still he had the money and men to make or break any Greek democracy, so he expected nothing to be said or done in public and the comments forgotten. Indeed, they were. When everyone was busy eating and drinking Janus's men disconnected the telephone lines before Carl led the Painters silently to Snow Goose II. Nothing was said as they sailed away, except Maria cried goodbye to her island as Jim held her tight.

The first night at sea they dined on the excellent food Janus had supplied. Before they started to eat they prayed. 'Dear Father God and the Blessed Holy Mother we ask you to look down on us miserable sinners and give us peace. Bless our ship, her company and the food we are about to eat.

'Above all we request you to look after my people on Skiathos and in Greece,' Maria said. 'Gentlemen please join me in toasting Greece and Skiathos.'

Needless to say they all joined in enthusiastically with the prayers and the toast as she had expressed exactly how they felt, alone on that large sea. Being the skipper, Jim stayed on deck while the others enjoyed their meal. It was not that Jim had to be at the helm as the *Snow Goose II* had autopilot, but because he needed to feel the fresh sea wind in his face and thank God for blessing him with good friends, and a lovely wife.

26. Bari, Italy

The voyage to Bari proved uneventful as they sailed through calm seas with strong winds pushing them onwards. They arrived before dusk to anchor at the jetty beneath Mario's family home, the Villa Carlini. Just for secrecy, Jim re-painted the yacht's name to Odysseus XII confirmed by new ship's papers Fergus supplied. The name reflected Fergus's Classical Ancient Greek education and the region in which they sailed. According to the charts, Bari was the capital of the Bari province in the Puglia (Apulia) region and situated on the Adriatic Sea, north of the heel of Southern Italy. The old part of Bari consisted of a network of closely built buildings dominated by the grand Cathedral of San Sabino and Frederick II's Castello Svevo. On either side of the peninsula were two harbours being repaired after being bombed by the Germans.

Carl's orders warned of clouds of dangerous smoke coming from the wreck of the merchant ship USS John Harvey. The vessel was sunk by the Luftwaffe in December 1943 releasing mustard gas from containers on her deck. Unfortunately, the American in command kept this secret so even the doctors treating the affected people did not know what to do. In the end, the official death toll was sixty-nine though others quoted two thousand allied troops and Italians dying or seriously injured. America was more afraid of being seen to break the Geneva Convention on the use of poisonous gases than concerned for the safety of civilians and allied personnel.

Jim tied the Odysseus XII to the jetty. Then Mario ran up the fifty steps to greet his family, followed by the others carrying their luggage. From the top of the steps, they had a magnificent view of the Adriatic Sea and the Italian coast. It looked so peaceful and yet the city while recovering from the ravages of war was reluctantly being embroiled in the Cold

War. Senor Carlini was a politician, highly respected for his wartime activities against Mussolini and his *Fascisti*. Now he helped forge a democratic nation to re-establish her manufacturing industries. The war damage was extensive even after Italy had surrendered as Germany fought the allies all the way to the northern borders. Many Italian soldiers fought alongside the allies after their surrender at Anzio to be treated as heroes. No one wanted to talk about fascists. However, they joked that the only good thing about Mussolini was he made the trains run on time. Being a politician in post-war Italy was very dangerous as militants supported the two opposing factions. The largest was the communists supported by peasant farmers and the factory workers from Trieste in the north down the Po valley to Bari. While the right wing political parties, funded by the Americans were divided between the neo-fascists who supported industry and foreign investment, and the groups wanting a nation where everyone benefited.

Professor Carlini was a senior member of the central coalition that believed in helping the poor while developing industry and repairing the war damage. Factories like Fiat were kept running and promised that the Government in Rome would only purchase their vehicles. This did not please the extreme right who believed all the industries should be handed over to the Americans, while Italy imported foreign goods as war reparations. Like so much in post war Italy the differences were publicly aired by loud arguments in parliament, over the radio and in the press. Often the moderates were subjected to verbal and physical abuse from their rivals, especially the ex-fascists that formed the US backed right wing. The very religious socialists found themselves uneasily dealing with hardline fascists. It was a time when no one could tell how long a government would last as ministers tried to keep everyone happy while trying to rebuild Italy. No one party had an overall majority in parliament having to form uncomfortable coalitions. It resulted in very long sessions in which little was achieved.

A month before The Painters arrived in Bari; two moderate politicians were assassinated by gunmen while walking outside their homes. The right wing claimed it was the work of the communists who angrily denied the accusations by replying that it was the work of fascists. The situation deteriorated further with the arrival in Bari of Italian former *Fascisti* with their German advisors. This sent warning bells ringing throughout the region reopening old wounds. Professor Carlini asked the commander of the *Polizia Municipale* (town police) to keep an eye on them. His request was refused because they were part of an American group who came to help keep the communists from subverting their new democracy. Nothing more happened until on his way home for holiday Professor Carlini's car was sprayed with bullets. His driver died instantly at the wheel while the Professor survived only because a passing *Arma dei Carabinieri* car (military police) raced to his rescue. The *Carabinieri* opened fire on the attackers killing some while others escaped. Then the *Carabinieri* raced Professor Carlini to a hospital where he spent the next two weeks. Of course, the police investigations found that the dead assassins were foreigners, probably German refugees carrying no documents. In private, the Carlini family was told that since the end of the war, the Mafia was again exerting their power with financial support from America. However, some *Carabinieri* were assigned to protect the Professor and keep an eye on the local *Fascisti*.

During the first few days in the Villa Carlini, Mario showed the Painters around his city. They saw all the historical sites and important features even roaming the old streets. One evening after dinner Professor Carlini explained the situation, 'A mile away is the beautiful Villa Franco that used to be the headquarters of Mussolini's *Fascisti* party. It has a splendid garden consisting of hundreds of different trees from all over the world. Sadly, it has been neglected so now the vegetation reaches right up to the house. The villa is surrounded by a six-foot tall stone wall broken only by large iron gates that lead via a gravel drive to the front door.' He then added. 'I've had the house watched by friends from the old days who inform me that at any one time, there are at least twenty Italians and four Germans living there. However, unknown to the occupants both the resident Italian caretaker and cook work for me. They tell me that the newcomers you call the Jackals practise unarmed combat and shooting in an underground firing range. Recently, I've observed them taking frogmen out to sea in a motor launch to dive on the wrecks. The group includes two German war criminals, and I think others that I am trying to identify.'

'Stop prevaricating Papa! Tell us who they are,' Mario asked.

'Why are you always in such a hurry my dear son?' the Professor asked knowing Mario was too embarrassed to reply.

Still Professor Carlini did not reply but gave each of them a folder containing the pictures of the villa's occupants. He wrote against each picture their name, political affiliations and personal details such as height, weight, age and hobbies.

'Here are my files on your Jackals in the Villa Franco. The top file is on the Italian fascist who is in command. He rarely leaves the house except to visit his mistress and play tennis at the sports club. He is Giovanni Lucia, who in the war helped the Gestapo in the north, especially around Milan. Before then he was an officer in the army in Abyssinia where they used mustard gas against people armed with only spears and a few rifles. He is cruel, ruthless, but faced with danger is a coward. I've made it my business to get to know him by playing tennis with him when the opportunity arises. Of course, he knows who I am but thinks I'm more pro-American than socialist. I have taken care to make sure he doesn't realise I know his war record. Indeed, he is very relaxed in my company. We often talk about the Yugoslavian threat to our northern port of Trieste and how important it is that it stays in Italy. It is probably the only thing we agree upon,' Professor Carlini continued.

'I can identify a few of the people in the photographs,' Carl intervened. 'The first is *Oberführer* Walter Schmidt of the *Waffen-SS*, who helped liberate Mussolini and organised the German resistance against the allies advance into Italy around Monte Cassino. If my memory serves me well he was an expert in the use of explosives. I would consider him to be a tough soldier but not necessarily an evil man.

'The second photograph is of the elusive and cruel Doctor Aribert Helm. It is reported he performed experiments on prisoners in Auschwitz and is more evil than all the rest put together. He believes the way to understand our physiology is by experimenting on human Guinea pigs with and without anaesthesia. I know few details about his work except it was so terrible that he is one of the most-wanted war criminals. It is difficult to believe he is living freely in Italy. However, mark my words, he is a dangerous man who will do anything to get what he wants,' Klaus said in a voice full of emotion, even hatred.

'Sorry, but I don't recognise the others. They may be ex-soldiers or villains I've not heard about,' Carl said as a way of an apology.

'Well I can tell you that one of them is a war criminal called Johannes Albers, who as a chemist developed poison gases and their antidotes. He is suspected of testing his formulations on prisoners held in concentration camps and watching them die painfully,' Professor Carlini said before adding. 'I believe they're in Bari to recover the unexploded mustard gas bombs aboard the sunken USS John Harvey. Then they could release it anywhere to cause massive death and terrorise the people.'

'That's not a happy prospect, especially when the Jackals have no morals,' Carl commented.

'I'm told they've brought back at least one container that they transferred to their underground laboratory in the Villa Franco,' the Professor informed them to emphasise the urgency of the situation.

'So we must act before they take the gas away,' Klaus decided.

Everyone nodded.

'Papa, when is the best time to attack?' Mario asked his father.

'I suggest the best time to attack the villa is tomorrow night after the launch takes the divers to the wreck. Then, if my information is correct, there will only be three Germans and twelve Italians left in the building. So if you are swift, the villa can be in your hands before the launch returns. Then, with luck, you can capture the others from the launch when they return,' Professor Carlini suggested.

So they waited until the next night before acting, while Professor Carlini arranged with the *Arma dei Carabinieri* for six experts from their Special Forces to join the attack on the Villa Franco. When everyone was ready and the launch well out to sea, the small army approached the Villa Franco. The Professor watched the launch to keep them informed when it returned. Somehow they must kill or capture the occupants before the others returned. While trying to decide how to capture the villa without warning the occupants, Maria came up with the solution. She would simply knock on the front door!

Maria dressed as a nun carrying a collection box, simply opened the gate and walked to the villa. She firmly knocked on the door while the rest took up positions near the front of the house. The caretaker answered and seeing Maria let her and the others in while whispering that the occupants were downstairs in the laboratory. Maria told him to leave, but he insisted on staying to do what he could to defeat the hated *Fascisti*. Once inside they put on gas masks, rubber suits and gloves for protection if any of the mustard gas escaped. Then they moved quietly down the stone stairs to enter the laboratory. The Jackals did not see them coming as they were too busy trying to move an old gas cylinder into a sealed chamber. The cylinder probably contained *senfgas*, sometimes referred to as mustard gas. It was a slow process where one mistake could be fatal and the transfer of the toxic substance into smaller cylinders impeded. The Jackals wanted the gas in use small canisters that could be hidden in a car or van to be easily transported to wherever they wanted.

The Jackals did not see Klaus creep towards them as they were too busy connecting the cylinder to valves through which the gas flowed into the new containers. It was a masterpiece of improvisation. Only when the old cylinder was sealed inside the isolation chamber, and the Jackals were removing their protective suits did Klaus and Jim attack. In seconds, the pair disabled four Jackals while Carl, Mario and the *Arma dei Carabinieri* Special Forces dealt with the others. All the prisoners were tied up and placed in a large disused storage room. Only the Nazi chemist Johannes Albers tried to escape and was shot in the head. He died on the spot so avoiding trial and the hangman's noose.

The *Arma dei Carabinieri* set explosive charges strategically around the isolation chamber and the laboratory. When ready, the captives were taken one at a time out of the villa to be driven away in a large unmarked police van to a high-security prison. Meanwhile, the caretaker and the cook were sent home so the house was empty except for Carl's team waiting for the other Jackals to return. They did not have more than ten minutes to wait before Professor Carlini phoned to say the Jackals were returning carrying another canister. Somehow they must have sensed something was wrong because they entered the house with guns at the ready. Probably, it was because everything was too quiet. The *Arma dei Carabinieri* attacked the Jackals entering the villa while the Painters shot those escaping through the gardens, including Giovanni Lucia and Dr Aribert Helm. Within minutes, the Jackals were all dead or prisoners with only two of the *Arma dei Carabinieri* slightly injured. The bodies were placed in the building with the new gas canister before the incendiary devices were set off. From a safe distance, they watched the fires consume the old villa and the strange yellowish smoke spiralling skywards to disperse into the night air. Again, they prevented the neo-Nazis and their American masters from totally running post-war Europe. Nothing more was heard until weeks later when a US Navy diving team came to remove the remaining mustard gas from the USS John Harvey at the urgent behest of the Italian government.

A week later the Painters were in Valetta where they left the Snow Goose II with the Royal Navy to be sold. Mario stayed in Bari with his family, while the others flew from

Malta to Prestwick and in their Noorduym Norseman for the journey to Black Island.

27. A New Beginning

The Painters settled down to a new life on Black Island to relax and try to behave as if retired and no longer a threat to anyone. Every month, Fergus MacNeil visited to keep them informed of the latest news. Day by day, the rift between the USA and Britain grew more serious. The British asked for the plans of the V2 rocket and German jet engines. When the US refused to comply with the requests, the British dismantled captured V2 rockets and jet engines to make working drawings. By now, the political temperature was so high between Britain and the USA that one cartoonist drew a picture of a boiling North Atlantic. Of course, it was censored ending up framed on Fergus's desk.

Politically, America changed. In America, anyone who was not an ally was declared an enemy as even war heroes were investigated and questioned about their so-called socialist tendencies. It was the beginning of the anti-communist witch hunt run by the narrow minded people who enjoyed destroying the advances made by President Roosevelt. Many critics said that having won the war the US wanted to control a new world order. Others said the Irish American caucus under the Bostonian Senator Joseph P. Kennedy wanted to destroy what was left of Britain's power and influence. Within a few years, the welcome to Americans as liberators of the Free World turned to anger at their presence and influence on world politics. Even in tolerant Britain on the walls of American bases were painted with 'Go Home Yanks'. Inevitably, all America became paranoiac, looking for communists under the bed to form the infamous House Committee on Un-American Activities chaired by the ruthless Senator Joseph McCarthy. For the next ten years everyone from politicians, soldiers, film directors and people from all walks of life were subjected to a witch hunt that some considered comparable to Stalin's secret police. A few Soviet spies were discovered, but thousands of innocent citizens were publicly humiliated or had their lives destroyed. Sadly, action against the Ku Klux Klan and other fascist organizations did not happen, even though the House Committee was set up to investigate them. Instead, they hunted down communists who were said to be about to storm the White House. To escape the humiliation of being insulted by the committee, some excellent film makers and writers went into exile in Canada or Britain. Their presence in Britain helped develop an innovative and adventurous cultural movement. They influenced the British film industry to make better films with more creative photography.

Back on Black Island the Painters scrutinised all the numerous files they could obtain about the missing German gold bullion and reports of senior Nazis seen in South America. One evening Carl summed up their situation. 'Our days in Greece are over, but our work has only just begun. We must find the missing U-boats and more importantly what happened to the gold bullion? It is not easy to hide heavy gold bars, unless they are being slowly melted down to be sold in small amounts.'

They decided to try to find enough evidence of the whereabouts of the missing Nazi gold to be funded by Fergus and his bosses. Carl knew that the cash starved government would only fund their work if there was a chance of success. In time, they started the search, but that is another story.

Historical Notes

At the height of the Second World War, many different political groups united in their fight against Fascism to harass the enemy wherever they were found. In the mountains of Greece, Italy and Yugoslavia, they effectively restricted the enemy's movements and hastened the end of the official war. Sadly, after the German surrender the same people were again forced to take up arms to fight former allies as a new conflict between the USSR and the West started. Both groups wanted to control or at least influence as many of the liberated countries as they could. In an attempt to resolve these differences, the leaders of Britain, Russia and the USA met at Yalta in February 1945 where their differences became apparent. Churchill representing Britain wanted a free democratic Poland while President Roosevelt was prepared to agree with President Stalin that the USSR would control of Poland in exchange for the Soviets declaring war on Japan. In the end, the only winner was Stalin, who controlled all of Eastern Europe. They agreed that Greece would come under British influence.

However, this did not stop Stalin from clandestinely using force to take over Greece. The result was the bloody Greek Civil war that in many ways has not been resolved. The assassination cadre known as *Gladio* sadly existed and some say still does. This was the right-wing organization whose motto was *Silendo Liberatem Serva*, or 'Silently; I Serve Freedom' and officially did not come into existence until the 1950s. It was formed from other 1940's covert groups operated by the CIA. The term *Gladio* was coined from the modern Italian word for *Gladius*, the Roman fighting sword, and was selected to identifying *Gladio* with both the military and the ancient Roman Empire. The symbol was similar to other

Roman devices used by Benito Mussolini, and his *Fascisti*. It was a blatant link between the victorious forces of America and the defeated fascists. The creation of such secret armies set out to assassinate all socialist or anti-American politicians was a sign of how little the CIA understood Europe or her people. It resulted in many politicians publicly supporting the USA, while in private wishing they had gone home, or worked in NATO to keep communists out of post war Europe. *Gladio* was incriminated in the forcing of many socialist ministers in Italy to resign from government in 1964 and the assassination of former Prime Minister Aldo Moro in 1978. Initially, his death was blamed on the Red Brigades but later confirmed to be the work of *Gladio*. It is a chapter in American and NATO history that few can be proud of. During the economic turmoil of post war Europe, many clandestine meetings occurred as a rich minority attempted to rule the world. One such meeting was held in May 1954 at the Hotel de Bilderberg in Arnheim in the Netherlands Of the one hundred and twenty people invited, most were bankers, industrialists or politicians from America and Western Europe. Since then the first meeting, the Bilderberg group has met annually to discuss how to run the world however no third world politician or business leaders have ever been invited. If the group is so innocent, the question remains why are all the meetings held behind closed doors and all the media barred from the meeting place by very visible security guards?

There are many books about the Greek resistance to the German and Italian occupation and the subsequent Civil War. Some are:

Edgar O'balance. Greek Civil War 1941-1949. (1966) Faber and Faber, London. ASIN: B0000CMZK6.

C M Woodhouse. The Struggle for Greece. (1976). Hurst and company, London. ISBN-10: 1850654872.

Nicholas Cage. Eleni. (1997). Vintage Books, London. ISBN 10:1860463464.

There are only a few books written about *Gladio*. Some are:

Leopoldo Nuit. (2007). The Italian 'Stay-Behind' Network - The origins of Operation '*Gladio*'. Journal of Strategic Studies 30 (6): 955-980.

Daniele Ganser. (2005). NATO's Secret Armies: Operation Gladio and Terrorism in Western Europe. Routledge, New York. ISBN-10: 0714685007.